MW01673804

The Story of a Siberian Exile

SALZWASSER
VERLAG

M. Rufin Pietrowski

The Story of a Siberian Exile

Reprint of the original, first published in 1863.

1st Edition 2022 | ISBN: 978-3-37500-282-4

Verlag (Publisher): Salzwasser Verlag GmbH, Zeilweg 44, 60439 Frankfurt, Deutschland
Vertretungsberechtigt (Authorized to represent): E. Roepke, Zeilweg 44, 60439 Frankfurt, Deutschland
Druck (Print): Books on Demand GmbH, In de Tarpen 42, 22848 Norderstedt, Deutschland

RECOLLECTIONS OF SIBERIA.

THE STORY

OF

A SIBERIAN EXILE.

BY

M. RUFIN PIETROWSKI.

FOLLOWED BY

A NARRATIVE OF RECENT EVENTS IN POLAND.

TRANSLATED FROM THE FRENCH.

LONDON:

1863.

TRANSLATOR'S PREFACE.

IT has not been thought advisable to give these papers to the public without a few words of explanation to those readers who see them for the first time in an English dress. It may seem that the three parts of which the book is composed have little connection with each other, but this is not the case. Along with the story of a Polish Exile in Siberia will be found two chapters on the political aspects of Poland. The first of these contains an account of those measures and events by which the dismemberment of ancient Poland was effected. But the Poles contend that the wrong done to their country has not stopped there; and that she has been not only dismembered, but denationalised. On referring to the Treaty of Vienna they find that this loss of nationality was not contemplated by the European powers, and that it is contrary both to the letter and to the spirit of the Treaties of 1815. By degrees, however, whether rightly or wrongly, Russian supremacy has asserted itself, and the story of M. Rufin Pietrowski is intended to demonstrate what are the amenities of that régime. The Poles will not submit to a government in which they are not allowed to participate; and they are engaged in ceaseless attempts to elude its vigilance, and to defy its power. They wish to organise themselves; and the executive, obliged to act both on the defensive and the offensive towards them, has recourse to cruel and arbitrary methods of repression. The narrative of the Siberian Exile is a strange one, but there is no reason to believe that his tale is otherwise than authentic. The candour and moderation with which he speaks of the Russian officials is highly creditable, and it deserves to be noticed, that it is the system, rather than the men, which he attacks.

The last paper in this book will be found, without doubt, to be the most interesting. A moment's reflection will convince its readers that there is no European country in which so great a change is being effected, and of which they hear so little, as Russian Poland. Yet the events which have recently agitated Poland are events of historical interest, and they are not in themselves unimportant to Western Europe. An outline of their nature and extent is given here. This history of 'twelve months of agitation' makes us spectators of a struggle which the Poles have maintained against the Czar, and in which they have proved themselves to be still full of that high, haughty, and stubborn spirit of liberty which Edmund Burke discerned in them of yore. Their recent efforts towards civilization and self-improvement will not fail to ensure for them the sympathy of all who can discern in its energy and its self-control the true greatness of a nation. Sketches of some of the leading men of Poland will be found here: and, at this crisis, it has been thought that an account of the career of Count Andrew Zamoyski could hardly fail of being acceptable. If the destiny of Poland, as a nation, be eventful and yet obscure, the destiny of individuals has often proved under the Muscovite rule to be more tragic and even more obscure. The Polish party in emigration, who now welcome Count Zamoyski, have great cause to congratulate themselves that their 'civic hero'—the best and worthiest of their patriots—has not been sent to expiate a life devoted to his country's good in the fortress of Akatouïa, or in some of the desolate wastes of the Russian Empire in the East.

The translator is in no wise responsible for any of the sentiments to be found in this book. His task has been simply that of rendering into English the thoughts and words of other men. In the story of M. Rufin Pietrowski he has felt the disadvantages that attend upon the translation of a translation; but he has striven to preserve the integrity of the narrative, even in the smallest particulars. It is with a view to this end that he has adopted all those Russian and Polish phrases, idioms, and words which occur in the text of M. Klackso.

London:
November 1862.

CONTENTS.

INTRODUCTION.

CHAPTER I.

OF A MISSION INTO POLAND.

CHAPTER II.

OF MY ARREST AND IMPRISONMENT AT BRAÇLAW.

CHAPTER III.

OF MY IMPRISONMENT AT KIOW, AND MY DEPARTURE FOR SIBERIA.

CHAPTER IV.

OF DEPORTATION, AND THE LIFE OF AN EXILE IN SIBERIA.

CHAPTER V.

THE KATORGA.

CHAPTER VI.

SIBERIA.

CHAPTER VII.

THE FLIGHT.

CHAPTER VIII.

THE PILGRIM AND THE PILGRIMAGE.

CHAPTER IX.

THE WHITE SEA.

CHAPTER X.

THE RETURN TO PARIS.

POLAND

A CENTURY AFTER ITS DIVISION:

AND THE LATE AGITATION IN WARSAW.

A YEAR OF AGITATION IN POLAND.

THE

STORY OF A SIBERIAN EXILE.

INTRODUCTION.

SIBERIA — ADVENTURES OF BENIOWSKI — MADAME FELINSKA — M. RUFIN PIOTROWSKI.

THERE is an expression in use in Poland which surpasses all that human eloquence has ever employed to give intensity to despair; it consists of the words '*we never meet again*:' and thus it is that any political exile, when about to depart for Siberia, takes leave of his family and of his friends; '*we never meet again!*' for the only way in which an exile could find himself once more among those whom he loves would be for him to meet them in the same place of torment. The conviction is deep that they who are once transported to those regions of pain can quit them no more; that Siberia never relinquishes her prey. For nearly a century she has torn from Poland her most devoted women, her most generous sons. Back to those realms of snow and of blood fly the thoughts of every Pole who inquires into the past fortunes of his family; and when the poet dreams for his country a future which is all liberty and bliss, it is again Siberia which rears herself before his eyes, ready after victory itself still to demand her victims. It is a mysterious and dismal land! — a land 'from which one returns no more,' as the Polish peasants say, or, as Hamlet speaks of that other region which Siberia so fatally resembles, it is an 'undiscovered country from whose bourne no traveller returns.' And yet now and then some one does come back. Sometimes at the accession of a Czar to the throne, an amnesty (which, however incomplete it may be, receives no less the surname of general) sends back to heart-broken families some of those who have not wholly succumbed to pain. At least, this did happen twice in one century; at the accession of Paul I. and of Alexander II.: the Emperor Nicholas never felt a similar weakness. In other cases, very rare ones, and therefore not hard to enumerate, entreaties and prayers backed by some distinguished protection have, after years of persevering efforts, obtained the return of the condemned exile. Finally, we have even seen, reappearing in the light, and among the living, those who, neither waiting nor hoping for an amnesty, whether general or particular, have found, in their own courage and in their own despair, a way of extricating themselves from their horrible fate; but such a phenomenon as this is not to be met with twice in any hundred years. Several of those who have thus returned, like ghosts from the tomb, have afterwards written an account of their sojourn in these desolate places; others again left notes on the spot, which were afterwards to be piously collected; and thus it happens that the literature of Poland possesses a complete collection of the writings of Siberian exiles, a collection already sufficiently large, and which, in spite of the monotony of the subject, certainly is not lacking in interest.

Very strange in truth are the adventures of Beniowski, a soldier of Bar, deported to Kamtschatka, organising there among its indigenous savages a vast conspiracy, administering to them an oath of fidelity to the confederation of Bar, passing Behring's Straits, conquering Madagascar, and coming to offer the sovereignty of it to the French king. A very different fate awaited General Kopec, who was banished some years later to the same district. Submissive, patient, almost serene, during the time of his exile, his mind became clouded at the moment when he was told that the hour of his deliverance had come. Joy was too great for his soul, and he took back to his native country only the remnants of his reason. He had some sane and lucid intervals, and these he employed in dictating a few pages of a history of his past sufferings, in a style at once sweet and subdued. During thirty years did poor Adolphus Januszkiewicz, for the use of an aged mother, who still lived in Lithuania, note down day by day the events of a life which flowed away among the Kirghis of the Steppes; and a brother's hand has lately discovered to us how much filial piety and indomitable courage filled that exile's breast. We omit many other names; but how can we avoid recalling Madame Eva Felinska and her book — that noble lady and noble Christian, whom the severity of Nicholas sent to be a dweller in Bérézov, in the middle of the Yakoutes and the Ostiaks, and whose son has recently (April 1862) been promoted to the archbishopric of Warsaw? What constitutes the sensible charm of Madame Felinska's work is not only the absence of all recrimination (the annals of the Siberian exiles being in general free from all bitterness), but it is the feminine modesty with which she instinctively conceals her personal misfortunes. One might imagine while reading her pages that they were the remarks of some enquiring person, who sojourned among unreclaimed tribes out of pure eccentricity of mind, did not the cries of a mother who asks for her poor little children undeceive us, and make us only too often aware that the choice rested not in that mother's will. One day at Bérézov,* while digging a well, there was discovered a corpse, which (thanks to the

* We use here the Latin *v* as the best equivalent for the *b* (viedi) of the Russian alphabet, although the letters *f* and *w* in Russian have nearly the same sound. To be consistent, it is necessary to write not only Moskova, Iainbov, Bérézov, but Orlov, Menstchikov, etc.: as for the name of Kiow, we adopt the orthography of the inhabitants of this town (Little Ruthenes); the Russians alone write it Kiew, pronouncing it always as Kiow.

glacial nature of the soil) seemed by its preservation, and the state of the brilliant uniform and orders, to have been but a thing of yesterday. By dint of enquiries and recollections, they succeeded, however, in proving that it was the body of Prince Menstchikov, who more than a century ago had died an exile on this very spot, after having lived the minister and the favourite of Czars. Madame Felinska in recording the event contents herself with exclaiming, 'What a strange chance!' She leaves to the mind of the reader the task of filling in the outlines of this touching picture, where a Polish woman, in this same land of banishment, finds herself face to face with the man who first dared with impunity to trample on the Sarmatian soil.

One of the most recent and remarkable publications in this the literature of the deported (for so it is called in Poland to distinguish it from the literature of the emigrated) is that which has just been given to us by M. Rufin Piotrowski.* His book recommends itself not only by the richness of its detail and the breadth with which it is composed, but also, and chiefly, because the author of it is an escaped 'Siberian.' In him, since the case of Beniowski, we have the only example of a deported person who has attempted such an enterprise, and who has also succeeded in it. It is the more extraordinary because M. Piotrowski was also condemned

* Pamietniki Rufina Piotrowskiego, 3 vols. in 8vo. Posen 1861.

to hard labour in the public works. Beniowski, as we have seen, had much assistance and many accomplices. A comparatively narrow tract alone separated him from the land of freedom, whereas our cotemporary had no one to rely on but himself, and without map or succours, almost without money, he had to traverse Siberia in its entire length, and a great part of Russia in Europe in addition. On foot he made the long and perilous journey from beyond Omsk in Western Siberia, penetrating the Oural mountains to Archangel, Petersburg, Riga, even into Prussia, never imparting to a living soul his fatal secret, in order not to involve any one in his own probable and terrible fate. If the narrative of M. Piotrowski has not all that romantic brilliancy which the story of the confederate of Bar can afford, it reveals to us greater dangers and a perseverance of will far superior in every way. Nor is the marvellous element wanting to this strange Odyssey, albeit its hero is no mythological being; he exists, nay, he lives among us, and we rub shoulders with him every day. This escaped convict and exile from the banks of Irtiche, this former *unhappy one* (for thus do the natives of Siberia call the deported Poles), is now a modest professor in that excellent Polish school of the Batignolles, for which the emigrated sons of Poland are partly indebted to the generosity of France. M. Rufin Piotrowski was one of those heroic emissaries who, from the extreme limits of Polish emigration, sought to carry back and impart to an oppressed country the hopes, the ideas, and the dreams of exile; and his narrative begins precisely at the point when he started from Paris, on the journey which he undertook to Kaminiec in Podolia. These emissaries brought with them, generally speaking, impossible plans, and calls which could not be answered, because sufficient reflection had not been bestowed upon them. Sometimes, too, they imported ideas which were positively dangerous, and if they almost always half atoned for their errors by a constancy which braved both death and danger, they did not the less draw along with them in their own unhappy fate some generous and innocent victims. M. Piotrowski has at least this consolation, that he never made himself the apostle of perverse doctrines, and that he never sowed the seeds of hatred. His actions as an emissary were always enlightened by sentiments of that religious charity to which mob law in all its meanings is utterly repugnant. The same profoundly religious spirit characterises his book — a book which was written now many years ago, but which, for reasons obvious in a case of Polish publication, it was impracticable to publish before 1861. We have thought that the recollections of M. Piotrowski were likely to find favour with the French public. At a time when nothing else is heard of in Poland but sentences to Siberia pronounced upon the most respectable of her citizens, upon canons, rabbins, provosts, merchants, professors, students, and artisans, it surely cannot be useless or amiss to explain by one striking example all that is contained for Poland and the Poles in the single word '*deportation*.' Is it necessary now to add that what we are about to read in these pages is in every particular strict matter of fact? The narrative of M. Piotrowski bears the stamp of truth, and of a good faith which pleads for itself, and removes every suspicion of exaggeration. For the rest, as we shall see, the author hardly, if ever, blames persons; as often as not, he expresses himself with regard to them in words marked by a lively sense of gratitude. It is the *system* only which he accuses; and, shall we confess it, the countrymen of M. Piotrowski, and above all his companions in misfortune, while unanimous as to the perfect authenticity of his tale, have rather reproached him with an excessive indulgence in speaking of the Russian officials. How many Poles, for example, have been surprised to see the portraits which he has sketched of Prince Bibikov and of M. Pissarev, men whose names are so painfully distinguished in the annals of the Poland of to-day? As we do not think it necessary to anticipate or preach a conviction which will soon make itself felt, it remains for us only to point out the method which we have followed in borrowing here from the Polish original of the book. A mere analysis would have effaced its character of individuality, while it spoilt the originality of the book. What is presented here is a faithful abridgement of a more detailed and lengthy narrative — an abridgement of an abyss, if one may borrow Pascal's energetic phrase — for the 'Recollections of a Siberian Exile' reveal to us a perfect abyss of suffering and of misery.

CHAPTER I.

OF A MISSION INTO POLAND.

A PASSPORT—THE JOURNEY—THE RUSSIAN FRONTIER—KAMINIEÇ—A TEACHER OF LANGUAGES—ANNOYANCES OF DISGUISE—M. ABAZA—SUSPICIONS OF THE POLICE.

I HAD long decided to take my departure for my native land, and was only occupied by the necessary preparations for it, when I fell suddenly sick in Paris. It was in the year 1842. I was received into the hospital of *La Pitié*, then under the direction of Baron Lisfranc, who had formerly served with Polish troops during the wars of the Empire, and who still preserved towards them a friendly sentiment. A number of my compatriots and companions in exile found themselves along with me in the hospital, a prey to the two forms of disease so common among us emigrants — consumption and madness. More than one of them died in my ward, and at my side — a sight which was well calculated to sadden my spirit, for they died, though without uttering a single complaint, in utter prostration and gloom. One would almost have said that they had felt, in leaving this world, as if, even in the next, for them there might still be no country.

This sojourn in the hospital was nevertheless not without a good result on my projects. I had the fortune to make the acquaintance of another invalid, an American from the United States, who promised to get a passport for me, a thing which was indispensable for my undertaking, and which up to this time I had never been able to procure. Leaving, after a detention of about six weeks, the hospital from which the American had been discharged a few days earlier, I went at once to seek him at the address which he had given me. He then and there handed over to me an English passport, made out in the name of '*Joseph Catharo, native of La Valette* (*Malta*), *aged* 36.' The document was quite regular, delivered at the English embassy in Paris, and signed by the ambassador, Lord Cowley. I could desire nothing better. In my situation an English passport was preferable to any other. I spoke Italian perfectly, whereas I could only speak English very imperfectly; but then my supposed Maltese antecedents would make good any failings on that score. The different *visa* of Baden, Wurtemberg, Bavaria, Austria, and Turkey, were soon procured; but at the office of the Minister for Foreign Affairs there had been put alongside of the seals two printed lines containing these fatal words — 'Bound to present himself at the Prefecture of the Police.'

Now I had all sorts of reasons for not wishing to announce my departure at the Prefecture of Police, where they might very likely have had more inquisitiveness than I had found in my American friend. After casting about in my mind for a long time how best to dispose of this luckless clause, I selected the not very ingenious plan of spilling some ink over the two lines, thus counterfeiting a big blot, and leaving nothing visible but the seal of the Minister. The method was a rude enough one, but it was not the less serviceable, and at none of the numberless police stations at which the passport had afterwards to be presented was any exception taken to the blot which disfigured it.

Thus accommodated, and furnished with 150 francs, which were to suffice for the wants of a long journey, I left Paris on January 9, 1843. After having traversed without hindrance Strasburg, Stuttgart, Munich, Salzburg, and Vienna, I took the road from the last-named place to Pesth. In the interests of my mission I was to make a month's stay in the capital of Hungary; and I profited by this delay, for I addressed in the meantime to the English ambassador at Vienna the request that he would renew my passport, my intention being to go to Russia instead of to Constantinople, and to make a stay there of considerable length. An answer was soon returned. At the end of a few days I received from Vienna, in exchange for my old passport, a new one, of a recent date, happily free from any ominous blots of ink, and *visé* for Russia. On February 28th, I quitted Pesth, meaning to reach Kaminieç in Podolia, the term and goal of my voyage. I found that the small sum which I had brought with me from Paris had, in spite of the most frugal way of living, greatly diminished; and I resolved to make the rest of my journey from Hungary to Podolia on foot. The season was favourable, the scenery magnificent, the passage of the Karpathians so splendid as to make me forget any slight fatigue. It was a strange, sometimes almost a diverting, sensation for me thus to traverse Galicia, and to have to ask my way in execrable German of the few Austrian officials, while the peasants gave utterance to the most minute remarks upon me, all in that Polish speech which I declared I did not understand. The pleasantries of our peasants on the subject of 'the dumb man' did not, however, miss fire or fail to amuse me greatly. To these jokes there were often added on their part marks of respect to a stranger come from the ends of the earth. 'I am sure he comes a long way off,' they would say to each other; 'from very far, from where even the crow brings no bones.' At last, on one fine March morning, 1843, I found myself at the boundary which separates the Austrian and Russian territory, near the village of Bojany. The frontier was marked by two barriers, which were distant the one from the other by a few dozen paces. Upon showing my papers the Austrian barrier was opened for me without any difficulty; but when I arrived at the Russian side, it was in vain that I called and looked round in all directions — no one came. Tired of waiting I passed by, stooping under the beam, and directed my steps to a house at a little distance, which seemed to be the Custom House office. The astonishment there was great when I was seen to arrive thus unaccompanied by a soldier.

'How did you pass the frontier?'

'At the barrier, down there.'

'Who opened it for you?'

'Nobody. I called in vain, and at last determined to slip underneath it.'

'What! the guard was not there at his post?' cried the functionary, as much exasperated he rushed out to give orders, of which his menacing tones only too fully explained the nature. Having returned to his room, he emptied out upon me the remains of his ill humour; but the sight of the English passport had a sudden and pacifying effect on his wrath. While my papers were being examined, and they took down the answers which I made to sundry questions relating to my journey, I heard the distant cries of the poor soldier, who was expiating under the bastinado what had been either his negligence or perhaps indeed only my hastiness. At last I was free to leave the office, with a feeling of satisfaction which was not, however, wholly unalloyed. There was indeed something ominous in this incident attending my entrance into the territory of the Emperor Nicholas. From the first step I had defied Russian vigilance, but I had at the same time, albeit involuntarily, caused the punishment of an unhappy creature, and my heart was pained at it.

On March 22nd, I reached Kaminieç, at midday. I had my portmanteau in one hand, while with the other I opened the door of an inn that had been pointed out to me, and I found myself suddenly in the middle of a large assembly of people, and in a room where they were playing billiards. I had purposely kept my hat on my head, and by this sign, so contrary to our national habits, I was immediately recognised to be a stranger or a *Frenchman*, for the two words are among us considered to be synonymous. The sensation, which was evident in the room, was very curious. '*A Frenchman*, a *Frenchman*,' they murmured on all sides, speaking with interest and even with sympathy, but with a manifest fear of compromising themselves by an imprudent or even a friendly word. Two men only ventured to come forward frankly and converse with me — the one was a Pole from Cracow, only passing through Kaminieç, and therefore less obliged to be circumspect; the other was a Russian officer, who left the billiard-table when he heard me utter a few sentences in French, and who immediately showed the greatest readiness to make my acquaintance. 'You are, then, come to stay here for some time? Oh! pray remain, I beseech you. It is a fine country! beautiful women, too! But it is at Warsaw especially that one finds charming women. Ah! Warsaw! I have been garrisoned there: it is a famous place, and *there* really *are* pretty faces!' And the young man seemed not to be able to stop in pouring forth praises which could not but be disagreeable to me. Strange that this Poland, of which he trod the soil, and of which he had visited all the principal towns, should have given him nothing to see or to appreciate but the beauty of our women! Not one word to say of the government, of the fate of the inhabitants, of the misery of the people! His only subject of preoccupation, of praise, and of conversation, was the female population of Poland. One thing only turned him from this favourite topic. I happened to say something incidentally of Paris; then he began to ask questions about the Parisian womankind, and seemed at once pleased and excited at my replies. On the whole he was not a bad fellow, this officer Rogatchev; and he wound up by sharing with me the national dish of *pierogi*, laughing all the time at the strong foreign accent with which I pronounced the word: but he did me the justice to say soon after, that in the matter of *pierogi* my good appetite had made ample amends for my bad pronunciation.

While we walked up and down the room and talked

in a loud voice on trifling subjects, the other occupants of it, all Poles and young people, kept themselves apart and whispered together, directing towards me from time to time oblique and curious glances. What a striking contrast there was between their attitude of reserve and the full-blown confidence of the happy Rogatchev! While keeping up my conversation with the Russian officer, I endeavoured to catch the words which were passing among my countrymen. 'From France?' 'Does he know anything of our people?' 'Do the French care about us?' 'Perhaps something new is about to happen.' My emotion was great, but I had to redouble the animation with which I was describing to my new acquaintance the beauty and the glories of Paris.

While so discoursing I did not omit to inform M. Rogatchev as well as the other persons present that I had come to Kaminieç to push my fortune as a teacher of languages, and that I desired nothing better than to settle in the town, though, if my interests required it, I might penetrate even to the interior of Russia. This declaration I repeated next morning at the station of police, for I was anxious to lose no time in establishing my position. The permission to remain was accorded to me without hesitation. As regarded my intention of giving lessons in private houses, I was warned that some formalities must in the first place be attended to, and that I must formally ask and obtain the consent of the military governor, of the director of the Lyceum, &c. It was not long before I obtained the necessary authorisation, and thanks to the recommendations of my officer and of other persons whose acquaintance I made on the first day,—thanks, above all, to those obliging cares of which a stranger is always the object in our country, orders for lessons came to me from all sides, and from the very first. I preferred, I must say, the houses of the different Russian officials; it was the surest way to avoid suspicion for myself, and to prevent compromising my countrymen. The offers made to me by the Abaza family were really precious, and it may be supposed that I did not neglect such connections as these; for Colonel Abaza, President of the Chamber of Finance, was a Russian functionary at once highly placed and very influential. I did not, however, refuse to attend on Polish families; but I selected those which any discovery would have the least affected, such as the houses of widows and elderly gentlemen — those, in short, where there were no young people. After a few weeks I had made good my position, and my relations were well understood. I went into all circles, and all over the town I was well known as the M. Catharo whom they persisted in calling a Frenchman.

Thus it was that, after having been an emigrant for twelve years, I found myself again in my native land, not very far either from my own family (which dwelt in the Ukraine), and in the quality of a Maltese, a British subject, teaching foreign languages, and not understanding a word of either the Russian or the Polish tongues. This last circumstance was one which often put my caution and my *sang froid* both to some severe trials, trials which my professorial office only aggravated. How many times was I not tempted at some difficult idiom or expression to explain myself to my pupils in a speech quite as familiar to me as it was to themselves! One of my first pupils was a certain Dmitrenko, a clerk in the Chamber of Finance, a cheerful being, who was bitten all of a sudden with a fancy for learning French, of which he did not know a single word. At the end of the pantomime which was necessary to make us mutually understand each other during the lesson, he wound up by proposing to give me some notions about Russian, with which I was perfectly conversant; but he never managed to make me read fluently, and he could not conceal his astonishment at this want of intelligence in one of those Frenchmen whose wits he had heard so much vaunted.

Among my own people, the incognito which I preserved exposed me very often to scenes that made both my inward feelings and my sentiments as a man of probity suffer acutely. I was the involuntary and helpless confidant of the relations, even of the secrets, of families, who thought that they concealed them perfectly from my knowledge by speaking together in Polish. Nor in such conversations did I always hear remarks that were flattering to myself. One day, for example, a visitor who was unknown to me meeting me in a room for the first time, and hearing that I had recently come from Paris, wished to ask me if I knew anything of his brother, who lived in that capital, an emigrant, and a man whom in truth I knew perfectly well; but the master of the house dissuaded him warmly from it. 'You know very well how strictly we are forbidden to make any enquiries about our emigrated relations; take care what you are about; one is never sure of one's self with a foreigner.' I felt as if all the blood in my body were rushing to my head, and I bent down quickly over the book in which I was cutting some leaves.

I must be permitted one other recollection of this sort. I was giving lessons to the two daughters of the good and amiable Madame Piekutowska. One day, while conversing with them, I touched on the subject of Poland. The beautiful Matilda replied to my careless expression with one of those words which we sometimes utter before a stranger, not witting that we are making some deep wound bleed. The elder sister took her up sharply in Polish, 'How can you speak of sacred things before a hair-brained Frenchman?'

Such incidents happened nearly every day, and they caused me sometimes pleasure, sometimes annoyance; but that annoyance turned to a concentrated rage when in Russian houses I was obliged to swallow in silence, or discuss with the passionless calmness of a stranger, topics wounding to my country, and such discussions as her oppressors permitted themselves to indulge in. It was in the house of Monsieur Abaza above all that I suffered this torture most frequently; and I should try in vain were I to attempt to give any idea of it.

As my own safety, as well as that of others, would assuredly be compromised were I suspected of knowing the language of the country, I was obliged in this respect to keep a constant watch upon myself. If I may use such an expression, I was forced to watch myself even in sleep; and I always arranged (especially when I happened to be invited to any of the dwellings in the neighbourhood) so as to sleep alone, and in a separate room. I feared that during my slumbers I might chance to mutter some sentences in Polish. But no incident disturbed me in the part which I had assumed; and during nine months I was enabled either to remain in Kaminieç, or to make short excursions into the provinces, without awakening the suspicions of the police. In the eyes of Poles, as well as Russians, I passed always for M. Catharo, an inoffensive man, who liked society, and who was well received in it. As to the true object of my stay, and my real character, some of my countrymen alone became privy to it, and the secret was most rigorously kept. The alarm, as I afterwards learnt, came from St. Petersburg, and Kaminieç was convulsed with astonishment when it discovered all of a sudden that the French teacher of languages whom it had harboured so long within its walls, was a native, an emigrant, and an emissary of emigrants. . . .

They say that men are often warned by a strange inward feeling that danger is approaching. I had no need of such a supernatural gift to be made aware, during the first days of the month of December, that peril was imminent; I had only to keep my eyes about me. By the beginning of December, I perceived that I was watched and spied upon at every turn by emissaries of the police. The counsels which were given me from different quarters, as well as the manner half inquisitive and half constrained with which the Russian officials treated me, could not but confirm my apprehensions. I have since heard that the moment of my arrest was delayed not only from their wish to inform themselves perfectly of my conduct, but from the difficulty which they experienced in completely identifying my person; and their fear was lest, in case of any mistake, they should get themselves into trouble by interfering with a British subject; that is to say, with the subject of a power well known not to stand any practices of that sort, or any joking on such a matter. Very soon, however, I felt both that there was no doubt, but that my arrest was close at hand, and also that it was time for me to arrange my plans. Up to this moment flight had not been altogether impossible, but it was repugnant to me. Why should I shun the dangers to which my accomplices were exposed, who neither could nor ought to choose the path of exile? It was therefore a strict duty which I owed to them, and to hundreds of persons who had nothing whatever to do with me, not to be absent when the day of enquiry came. To tell the truth, the Russian plan, in any political search of the kind, is to arrest all those who, from far or near, intimately or casually, may have known the suspected person. Now, as I was acquainted with everybody, both in the town and in its environs, the disappearance of the guilty principal would only have served to aggravate the case of thousands of suspected persons. The inquiry would have dragged on for years; it would perhaps never have come to an ènd. My presence alone could prevent countless misfortunes, and, if the worst came to the worst, it could limit the number of the victims. I resolved therefore patiently to abide the fatal hour; and I spent the days of freedom which yet remained to me in concerting with my accomplices the plan of conduct which I ought to follow. The last interview which I had with one of them was in a church on the eve of my arrest. We agreed as much as possible upon all points, and then embraced one another with an emotion which may easily be understood. Remaining to the last, and alone in the church, I prayed with fervour that God would give me strength to come through the trials which might await me.

Like every Pole of my generation, I had imbibed from my mother's teaching a fervent attachment to the Catholic faith. But those convictions had had their times of eclipse, and I can still recall the moment at which they were for the first time absolutely shaken. It was in 1831, when, after our glorious campaign, I passed into Galicia with the corps under General Dwernicki. One day I was at confession, when the priest, a brother of the order of St. Bernard, among other exhortations full of charity and of the spirit of the Gospel, represented our revolution to me as a sin, and as a violation of the oath of fidelity to Nicholas. Respect for the sacred precincts prevented my replying to him, but, as I rose to go away, I said to myself that the priests did not always teach the truth, and that there were a good many tares among their wheat. Some time later, while living in France, I began to take up, like the rest of the world, new ideas in religion, as well as in politics. I neglected all religious exercises and practices, and had come to look on Jesus Christ as an excellent philosopher, or, at the best, as a democratic teacher. But the frivolous pleasures of unbelief are soon exhausted; and long before the period at which my narrative begins, and before my return to my native land, I had reverted to the feelings and the belief which had guided my youth, and in which I was to find the only true support throughout the sad destiny that was in store for me.

CHAPTER II.

OF MY ARREST AND IMPRISONMENT AT BRAÇLAW.

ARREST — EXAMINATION — MAJOR POLOUTKOVSKOÏ — JOURNEY TO BRAÇLAW—AN ACCIDENT—THE PRISON AT BRAÇLAW—A RUSSIAN SCENE—KIOW.

ON December 31st, 1843, and just at the late dawning of the day, I felt myself shaken by the arm, and I was addressed in a loud voice by my assumed name. Though awake, I was in no hurry to reply; I wished to gain time to compose myself for my part. When at last I opened my eyes, I beheld in my room the Director of Police, Colonel Grunfield; a Commissary; and Major Poloutkovskoï, of the Council of Prince Bibikov, Governor-General of Volhynia, Podolia, and the Ukraine; the Major having come from Kiow to take steps for my arrest. I expressed my surprise at so early a visit, and my astonishment was naturally redoubled at the intelligence that I must be taken, under escort, before the Governor. I did not, of course, fail to represent my rights as a British subject, or to remind them of the grave results that were likely to accrue to themselves for this inconceivable conduct towards me. After having thus gone through all the formalities necessary to keep up my character, I asked permission to go into the next room, to perform my toilet. While I was dressing, the Commissary took possession of my papers and effects, and we were soon on our way to the house of the Governor Radistchev, with whom I had been personally acquainted for some time.

This first interview was both short and indecisive. The Governor entered the room abruptly, and addressed me in Russian. I pretended not to understand what he said, and requested that I might be interrogated in French; above all I begged that he would explain the cause of my being arrested. 'You will learn that presently;' and, at a signal given by his hand, I was then hustled out of the room. I was conducted to the house of the Director of Police, and there installed in a room which opened into a saloon. The doors were locked, and the official in uniform left to keep me company strictly observed the rule that he was not to speak to me.

Up to this time I had preserved my presence of mind, and I had even been astonished at my own perfect calmness at the moment of my awakening; but now, when alone or nearly so, I suddenly felt a great sinking of my heart. The thought of the many sufferings in store for me, in store also for so many of my brothers, seemed to set my brain on fire, and tears forced themselves into my eyes. To hide this dangerous emotion, I turned to the wall, and leant my forehead against it; but through the walls I fancied that sighs and moans were audible, the voices of the companions of my unhappy fate. Determined to distract my thoughts as much as I could, I took up a pack of playing cards that lay on the round table. A child of the Ukraine, I was by nature a little superstitious; I began to draw the cards, and they promised . . . . my deliverance! Shall I say it? This fortunate augury only increased my irritation, and I was almost obliged to the head official who entered the room at this instant, and who, after enquiring into my wants, carried away with him the tempting game.

A few minutes later a distraction of a more important kind took the place of the childish consolation which I had found in the cards. Another officer had been sent to join the one already in charge of me, and between them a conversation soon began which certainly was not devoid of interest for me. I was so well known in Kaminieç, and everyone was so thoroughly convinced of my ignorance of the two languages used in the country, that even now these two officials still thought me a foreigner, and they put no restraint on the remarks which they made to each other in Russian and in a loud tone of voice. I need not say that I lost nothing from want of attention to such a colloquy.

'It is a serious matter,' said the one; 'a political

business. They have arrested twenty people in the town already this morning (he gave the names), and orders have been sent out to the country, and all on account of this foreigner, who, they say, is come here to intrigue against the Tzar, and who is accredited by some other power, England or France—the devil knows which! They do not speak very well either of President Abaza; if anything happens to him it will be a pity, for he is an honest man; but I must say that at *his* age it *was* an odd idea to wish to learn French! Much he is like to make by his French lessons!' . . . 'What a pity! what a pity to be sure!' answered the other one; 'when this gentleman came here nine months ago I was ordered to watch him, as we do every new comer. I dogged his steps, I compassed him about on every side; but his conduct was so very open, his relations with both Russians and Poles so frank, and he appeared to me to be so really inoffensive, that at last I lost sight of him; and it seems he was a very pretty fellow after all, and now another man has been down upon him, and will claim the reward! Now I call *that* having no luck! Scoundrel that he is! bah! what a pity, what a pity to be sure!' . . . . I could not help being amused at the strange way in which this poor wretch condoled with himself for having lost the opportunity of bringing about my ruin; but the rest of the information which I extracted from their talk gave, if possible, a graver turn to my thoughts. I could no longer doubt that many persons had been arrested on my account; but the names which I had just heard repeated belonged to such different classes of my acquaintances that I discerned in them at least one source of hope. They were evidently groping in the dark as yet, and arresting right and left, while suspicions reached as far, or rather were as far astray, as Monsieur Abaza! In another point of view I imitated the naive cynicism of my police official, and was quite ready to rejoice at the trouble in which I had landed the worthy President of the Chamber of Finance. If indeed the Russians whom I knew were to be implicated in the trial, the affair would get into a strange confusion, and who knows then whether my accomplices might not benefit by the perfect innocence of the others, which would certainly soon be made manifest?

At four o'clock in the afternoon I had a visit from the Governor, and from Major Poloutkovskoï. They represented to me that my position was an alarming one, and that it would be best for my own interest if I made the most complete confession. I persisted in my resolution. I declared I did not understand in the least what they wanted with me, and I spoke of writing to the English ambassador in St. Petersburgh, and of claiming his protection. 'You are then in a great hurry to leave Kaminieç?' replied the Governor, ironically; 'but keep yourself easy, I will furnish you with all the means for it.' The same questions were repeated on the following days, either in the house of the Director of Police, where I was still detained, or in that of the Governor, who had me brought to him under an escort; the same arguments were urged, on the one side, to make me confess my real character, and there was, on the other side, the same obstinacy in keeping up the part which I had assumed. The manners of the Governor were generally cold but polite, sometimes however they were ironical, and even vehement. 'It is in vain to say that you are a Maltese, and to play this comedy,' cried he, in one of his examinations; 'we know very well that you belong to the Ukraine, and so-and-so have already confessed that they have talked with you in Polish.' He named to me two of the co-accused, the least initiated into my sayings and doings, and also the least firm. Twice over I was confronted with them. These interviews were most painful, and in spite of the flat denials which I opposed to those who thus denounced me, I saw the impossibility of persisting any longer in the line which I had hitherto followed. Every day more abundant and more precise information arrived about me, and it became clear that in prolonging a useless game I ran the risk of aggravating the situation of my accomplices; but I determined to collect the greatest possible number of the accused, and to make them witnesses to my confession, so that they might know its limits and follow my suit. I waited to be confronted with them in a body. I had not long to wait, and one evening when summoned to the Governor's residence, I perceived in the hall a great number of my fellow-prisoners arranged along the two walls, and all standing up — they presented a moving spectacle, I might almost say a fantastic one. Many of them were persons with whom I had but a very slight acquaintance, others had been in my secret, all bore upon their faces the marks of suffering and fatigue. After a certain time spent as usual in pressing questions and in absolute denials, I exclaimed, as if out of patience, in a loud voice, and in my native tongue, 'Well then, yes, I am not a British subject, I am a Pole; I was born in the Ukraine, I emigrated after the revolution of 1831, and I came back here. I came back into this country because a life of exile was no longer endurable to me, and because I wished to revisit Poland. I came here under a feigned name, because I was perfectly aware that bearing my own name I should not be suffered to remain; I was ready at any price to be quiet and inoffensive, asking nothing but to breathe my native air. I have confided my secret to a few of my fellow-countrymen, I have asked their help and their advice, I have asked them for nothing else, and I have nothing else to say to them.' In spite of the certainty as to my identity which they must now have possessed for some time, the Governor and Major Poloutkovskoï could not suppress an exclamation of surprise at hearing me thus suddenly speak out in Polish; and while I was speaking I could see the Governor's face expand; he rubbed his hands, walked up and down the room with long steps, and when I ceased came up to me with a benevolent air, as if he felt obliged to me for having put an end to a situation which was really untenable. After a few insignificant questions, he gave orders to have me removed.

On my return to the house where I was detained, being still under the influence of the late excitement, I took every one strangely by surprise by suddenly beginning to talk in Polish. In this language I addressed the director, the officials, and my keepers. I took a childish and feverish pleasure in making use of a freedom which had been so long denied me; and I behaved in the same way on the following day, though, from an obstinacy which had its root in repugnance, rather than in any calculation whatever, I pretended, as before, that I did not understand Russian. As to my native speech I used it to my heart's content; it was as if I wished to make amends to myself by the liberty of a few hours for having had to abstain from it during an entire year.

Thus ended the preliminaries of my trial, and on the morrow Major Poloutkovskoï came to desire me to hold myself in readiness to depart on that very evening for Kiow.

It was on a fine but cold winter's night that I quitted Kaminieç. I took my seat in a roomy open carriage alongside of Major Poloutkovskoï. Opposite us sat two soldiers, with loaded muskets, and we were followed by a second carriage, in which were two officers of the secret Police. Owing to the season, and the lateness of the hour, which was midnight, the town was dark, and the streets were deserted; but as I passed before certain houses which I knew well, and of which the inhabitants were united in the same lot with myself, I looked up, and I saw lights still burning. Was it as a message of farewell? or did they bear witness to vigils full of anguish which were being held within? The plaintive tinkling of bells, fastened, after the Russian fashion, to the shafts of the vehicle, which was drawn by three horses, alone broke the mournful silence of the night, and I sank into a reverie of indulged sadness. I was obliged to my companion for not interrupting the current of my thoughts by words; he did not speak even when we stopped to change horses, and it was not till the day began to break that he commenced a conversation. It turned at first only on France; her administration, her commercial arrangements, her agriculture, her commerce, these were all subjects in which he seemed to take a great interest. By degrees we began to talk of politics, even of emigration, and I had the opportunity of convincing myself how perfect was the knowledge which my interlocutor had been able to collect of our means, our men, and even of our smallest publications. I expressed my astonishment at this to him; he smiled and replied, 'We are obliged to learn all these things, and the means of learning them are never wanting.' In general, the Major, whom I had had the opportunity of studying during the examination that had taken place at Kaminieç, and whom I was to meet again later in the Commission of Inquiry at Kiow, showed himself, though cold and almost indifferent, to be a well-educated man. He was polite and courteous in his demeanour to me, and in all my interviews with the Governor of Kaminieç he had never failed to call General Radistchev to reason, whenever he gave vent to any burst of violence. A spring of my *calèche* having given way on the evening of our arrival at Mohilow, I had to be put into a *kibitka* with the two soldiers, while the Major in another preceded us, along with the officers of the secret Police; and we were carried along with a rapidity of which no one who has not seen a Russian convoy of this kind can form any idea. There it was that I met with an accident the nature of which I am still far from understanding and which I despair of describing to my readers. At one of those jolts of which the *kibitka* at its furious pace bestows so many on the traveller, I felt something snap in the tendons which attach the head, and a sharp and terrible pain made me give vent to such a savage cry of distress that I was heard in the accompanying carriage. The Major called a halt, and asked what was the matter with me. I was not able to reply, I was simply sobbing; he ordered them to go at a walk to the post-house, which relieved me much, but at the least jar the same frightful suffering recurred, and I screamed while

I tried to steady my head between my hands. Arrived at the station I was not able to leave the carriage, and to my shame and distress I was crying like a child. Then the Major, who was obliged to press on in person to Braçlaw, left me in charge of one of the police officials and of the two soldiers, and desired them to go at a foot's pace. Thus we continued our journey, but, at the end of some hours, my companion, wearied by the slowness of our march, ordered them to go quicker. Hardly had the horses broken into a gallop when the pain became really insupportable. I felt I was becoming mad, and warned by my piercing cries, my guardian called to the driver to stop. 'You must go slowly; if you won't, blow my brains out at once; believe me, if you continue to gallop, I shall not be able to support it more than five minutes; I shall be dead, and what will be your position then?' I did not exaggerate in any way, and my words gaining force by my strong conviction, made an impression upon those who had the charge of me. We continued all that night walking slowly, and when at daybreak we reached a posting-house, they put me into a sledge, for the road, though not all covered with snow, was deep in mud. Finally, at one o'clock we reached Braçlaw, where Major Poloutkovskoï was in waiting for us. My deplorable condition touched him visibly; he put his hand on my arm, and looking at me with attention, he questioned me on the pain which I felt. It was the first and the only time that he showed me any true compassion. He told me that the wants of the service summoned him imperatively to Kiow, but that I should remain here until I had recovered my strength a little; he soon afterwards took leave of me, and after having pushed on a little longer, my sledge stopped in the town before a vast and sombre building. They bid me get out, the heavy gates grated on their hinges, and after having traversed several dim corridors, I found myself in the middle of a little room, which was tolerably clean, and of which the window was furnished with strong iron bars. I flung myself on the paillasse, which I saw in one corner, and covered myself with my cloak. A few moments afterwards I received a visit from the *sous prèfet*, and from the doctor, a Pole, who examined me with much interest, prescribed repose, and some medicines; and I was again left alone with the two soldiers. Repose was in truth the only remedy for my pain, of which I felt nothing as long as I remained quiet and lying down. Thus long hours passed away, when all of a sudden breaking through the deep silence I heard a strange clinking which I was not able to explain; but I soon distinguished the sound of chains, both behind the wall and in the corridors. I was then in one of those great prisons, called Krepost; but who might my companions be? Simple criminals perhaps; or, it may be political prisoners, countrymen of my own? My doubts were soon cleared up; I heard a song rise, sonorous, choral, and only broken by the sound of fetters; the words were Polish, the melody a familiar one: —

> In a cradle sleeping, the Babe Divine, . . .

It was then Christmas time, and these poor prisoners, my compatriots, were intoning at midnight, after our ancient custom, the venerable hymn which hails the Saviour's birth. Then followed other canticles in common use:—

> Thus to the shepherds did the angels say, . . .

and

> To Bethlehem running, &c. . . . .

Ah, those Christmas hymns! — songs which had rocked my childhood and pleased me in youth, and which I had not heard for the last twelve years — ever since I had emigrated to another land. How after twelve years was I to hear them again? Chanted by captives, and accompanied by the rattle of their chains!

On both the following days I was visited repeatedly by the *sous préfet*, and by the doctor. I felt very weak, but quite free from the pain in my head; and upon being asked by the official in charge whether I was ready to continue my journey, I replied in the affirmative, for I was anxious to reach Kiow. As we were stepping into our sledges, I noticed in the courtyard a regiment of soldiers, whose bearing was so fine and so soldierly that I made a remark upon it to the *sous préfet* as he stood beside me. 'They are,' he said, 'Polish soldiers of 1831, incorporated now into the army of the South.' Thus did I meet again after such a lapse of years my former companions in arms. I could not help uncovering my head to them, and calling out loudly in Polish, 'All hail, comrades!' 'Forward!' shouted the *sous préfet* immediately; and the horses went off like an arrow from a bow. We had hardly gone two or three leagues out of Braçlaw when we met a carriage driving at a fast and furious pace, and which pulled up alongside of us. An officer of the armed Police sprang out of it, who, after conversing for a few minutes with my companion, came up to me, and announced that for the future I should consider myself under his guardianship.

He seemed a young man of about twenty, or a little older; very tall, very slight, very tight in his uniform, with a waist like a wasp, and with a hard haughty manner. He was, as I afterwards learnt, a German by birth, and the sight of him gave me a curious sense of uneasiness, so that I began to regret Major Poloutkovskoï. At one place he made us drive off the high road, and we got out at a solitary house, a guard-house apparently, and there they fitted me with a pair of handcuffs. I was then led down to a hut, which was underground, and to a sort of forge, where a soldier farrier had with some difficulty lit the furnace fires. The officer produced some chains from some corner or another, and he now stood contemplating them with an expression of face which was both curious and fierce. These irons were the most detestable things that can be imagined; red with rust, they were composed of two long bars fastened in the middle by a bit of chain, and having a foot-ring at each end. Having finished all the preparations, the soldier tried the rings on me above each ankle, but they were so tight that I could not help shouting with the pain. The officer simply said, 'Come, come!' but when they were to be soldered up I pulled my feet out, and declared that I would lodge a complaint before the Governor-General if they did not let the rings out. This made the officer pause for a moment. He ordered them to attend to my demand, and bolts were at last let into them with hammers and punches; but I suffered a great deal from them still, and they remained always too tight, while the rusty bit of chain hindered the long bars from turning, and left me wholly unable to walk. They lifted me up, and hoisted me, thus trussed, into the carriage. Late in the night, and after we had left Bialocerkiew behind, the sleigh in which I was reached the top of an incline, and, coming upon some stumbling-block, it upset. The soldiers were thrown off, I don't know what became of the coachman; as for myself, pinioned and unable to move, I was flung out, but my fetters hooked on in some way to the vehicle, and I was dragged along through the snow and the mud by the horses, which continued their maddened course; my knees, elbows, and chest were bruised, and I finally lost consciousness. When I came to myself again, I found that I had been reinstalled into my sledge, and that all was restored to order. The young officer standing alongside of me asked if I was much hurt? I made no answer; and now began a scene which was truly Russian in its character. The officer struck with his fists at the two unhappy soldiers on account of an accident in which no one had had any part but himself, for he had been constantly calling out to go quicker. The soldiers, as soon as we were again under way, paid off on the driver the blows they had received from the officer; and he, in return, revenged himself on his horses by flogging them so brutally that we ran every risk of having a repetition of the adventure. More dead than alive, I saw all that was done; and, such is the weakness of our human nature, I had but one feeling, the fear of a second accident. At each pitch and at the least jolt I shut my eyes and nearly swooned; and yet I was not naturally timid, and my nerves were not precisely of the most delicate order. The following day I arrived before the fortress of Kiow.

CHAPTER III.

OF MY IMPRISONMENT AT KIOW, AND MY DEPARTURE FOR SIBERIA.

THE FORTRESS AT KIOW — PRINCE BIBIKOV — EXAMINATION — A COMMISSION OF INQUIRY — A BIBLE — FELLOW-PRISONERS — THE MANIAC — PREPARATIONS FOR 'DEPORTATION' — THE SENTENCE.

CARRIED in the arms of several soldiers, I was first deposited in the business room of the Commandant of the place. Here I was searched, registered, and inscribed on the books; while they plied me with questions, to which I know not what answers I made, for I had no knowledge either of what I was doing or of what I was saying. They set me upright at last, and I walked, supported by soldiers, through an endless number of rooms and corridors. A door was opened, I entered the cell, and I fell exhausted on a mattress. Two jailers and an aide-de-camp entered along with them, and the latter asked me if I wanted anything. I requested to have my fetters changed, or to have the foot-rings opened and made wider. He replied that he had no power to do so, but that he would report the request.

I was then left alone, and at the end of a very few minutes I fell asleep. I slept twenty-five hours without turning, and was only awakened at the end of that time by my keepers, whom this prolonged slumber had alarmed. Soon after, the colonel in command was ushered in. He was covered with orders, and addressing me in Polish, he asked how I was, and what might be the cause of my indisposition. I thanked him, but I said nothing of the accidents of my journey; for where was the use of making any complaints? He promised that some broth should be sent to me, and took leave of me with these words, 'Try to regain your strength, you are much weakened; and here, in our prisons, one has need of health to bear one's many sufferings.

I was indeed very weak, but I was no longer tormented by that terrible pain in my head, of which I was more afraid than of anything else. There remained the pains in my chest, elbows and knees, which were the consequences of the accident, and from which I was yet to suffer for several months to come. I looked round my cell; it was six feet by five, pretty high in the roof, in very bad repair, very dirty, and lit by a small window placed close to the ceiling, and grated with iron bars both within and without. Over my head I could read several names cut with some difficulty on the wall; among others that of Rabczynski, whom I was to meet hereafter in Siberia. The only furniture was a little table, a wooden chair, and a great stove in earthenware. Some broth and some bread were brought to me, but the difficulty of eating in handcuffs was so great and irritated me so much that I finished my meal before my appetite was appeased. Suddenly, the sight of the bread that remained suggested to me a providential idea. It certainly was not the first time that I had thought of Konarski, whose sufferings were fresh in every memory. I knew that hunger had been one of the engines of torture tried upon him, and I had no security that I might not have to pass through a similar ordeal. So I determined to lay up a fund against this extremity, and I hid the bread in a hole behind the stove, high up in the wall; and this I did on the following days with the bread that was supplied to me. I was quite pleased with the store of biscuit thus prepared against the time of famine.

Somewhat revived by the food and by sleep, I now became sensible of an annoyance which I could not at first account for. Presently I discovered that I was literally covered with vermin, the mattress, and the room were filthy with them, and the handcuffs prevented my even attempting to destroy them. I looked round and caught two eyes fixed upon me; it was the sentry on guard in the corridor, who had orders to watch all my movements through the aperture cut in my door; in vain, however, did I call to him, he paid me not the slightest attention; but happily for me on the following day the Commandant of the fortress caused me to be moved into the opposite cell, and had my room purified. He gave orders at the same time to have me shaved; an officer assisted at the operation, and when I requested that they would leave my whiskers, I received an answer which, all things considered, was rather out of place: 'No, no; we will leave you nothing but your moustaches, and that will be quite in the Polish fashion; the ancient Poles wore nothing but a moustache.' I soon returned to my cell, now a little cleaner than it had been; but what most moved my gratitude towards the Commandant was that he had my handcuffs taken off; and with the recovered liberty of my hands I recovered, strange to say, all the freedom and former energy of my mind. I kept constantly stretching out my arms, hardly daring to believe in my happiness, and I felt like a child escaped from its swaddling bands.

A week, or nearly a week, now elapsed without bringing any notable change in my position. My food was wholesome and plentiful, the room was cleansed every day, but the want of air and of exercise had completely enervated me. My chains prevented my walking, or even standing. I remained almost always lying on my paillasse, rising in general only in the morning to kneel and repeat the Lord's Prayer. The nights were long and without any light, and their quiet was only broken by the sound of the hammers, when they fitted or unfitted the fetters of some of the prisoners. Although it was forbidden to the sentries and keepers to speak to me, I soon managed to learn that all my accused friends from Kaminieç were in the same prison with myself, though lodged in different corridors.

One day, about noon, a great noise was heard at the entrance of my cell, the door opened, and a man appeared before me in the undress of a general officer, surrounded by generals and aides-de-camp, all in full uniform, who stood back respectfully in the corridor. The man had a tall figure, grey hair cut like a brush, an oval face without any moustaches, and very piercing eyes: his left sleeve was fastened up to one of the breast buttons of his coat, and the loss of an arm which this indicated convinced me that I now beheld no less a person than the Governor-General of Volhynia, Podolia, and the Ukraine, Prince Bibikov.* He took off his cap, pushed the door close, without however shutting it, sat down on the chair, and made me a sign to reseat myself on the mattress from which I had risen. During the conversation which followed he seemed very much annoyed at the bad air of the cell, and turned mechanically to the high window several times, as if to breathe freely. He addressed me in French.

'You probably guess who I am?'

* Prince Bibikov had his arm carried away at the battle of Borodino: all over Poland the answer is current, which he once made to a Polish lady, who on her knees implored a pardon for her son: 'The hand which signs pardons, madam, I left at Borodino.'

'I believe that I have the honour of speaking to the Governor-General, Prince Bibikov.'

'Your name is Piotrowski; you are a native of the Ukraine; you took part in the revolt of 1831, you emigrated to France. You afterwards returned to Kaminieç under the name of Catharo.'

'Yes, your Excellency.'

'You pretend that your return had no other object than that of revisiting your native land; but when after 1831 the Emperor granted an amnesty, why did you not avail yourself of it?'

'I do not wish to say anything that might be displeasing to your Excellency, but at the same time the manner in which this amnesty was drawn up was not of the nature to encourage us. Furthermore, the amnesty only applied to subjects of the kingdom, the inhabitants of the detached and outlying provinces were deprived of it; and to conclude, before asking pardon, one must feel that one has been guilty.'

'Who gave you that English passport?'

'I found it in the street.'

'You spent more than a month in Hungary; you see that I am well informed about you. Why did you go there?'

'To make my traces more difficult to follow, and to shorten the journey.'

'Oh! but you had some other reasons; you are a member of the Democratic Society.'

'I once formed a part of it, but I have withdrawn from it a long time ago.'

'You are an emissary of that society?'

'No.'

'Then in coming here you had no political mission?'

'Certainly, I had none.'

'Such assertions are not likely to improve your situation; I do not hide from you that it is a very unpleasant one; and only a sincere and complete confession can diminish your troubles, and above all make you worthy of the indulgence of the Emperor. You knew Konarski?'*

'No.'

'But you have heard of him?'

'Certainly, above all of the tortures inflicted upon him.'

'Your case is similar to that of Konarski, and only the sincerity of your confession can lessen its consequences. I do not wish to judge of your sentiments, I only wish to know whom you have known at Kaminieç, and in the provinces; I do not ask you to tell me what were your mutual plans, tell me only with whom were you acquainted.'

'Why, your Excellency, I knew almost everybody in Kaminieç, and in its neighbourhood.'

* A celebrated emissary, executed at Wilna, in 1841, after a long and cruel detention.

'That is not the question, and you know that it is not; the point is, who were your intimates?'

'I had none; it is true I was able to reveal my nationality to a few, and to ask their help and counsel; but your Excellency must fully understand why I ought not to name them.'

After some moments of silence, Prince Bibikov replied, 'I do not understand why the Poles and the Russians should hate and hurt each other for ever; we are all Slaves, brought together by origin, language, and manners, we ought to be united, and to march on together; and he who thinks otherwise does not understand the true interests of the two nations.'

'I am quite of your Excellency's way of thinking, and we indeed have no feeling of ill-will towards the Russian nation; but we aspire to be free, and as regards the government . . . .'

'I have no time to discuss this with you. I repeat it, your situation is a most critical one, but you can improve it sensibly by making a sincere avowal; I do not promise you complete or immediate liberty, for I never promise that which I am not sure of being able to perform, but I can intercede with the Emperor that he would give you permission to serve for the future in the army of the Caucasus. The Poles, like all the Slaves, are brave and courageous; you are still young, you are not wanting in intellect, you would very soon become an officer, and then your career would depend only on yourself.'

He pronounced these words in a loud and firm voice; then rising, he added, with a certain gentleness: 'For the rest, I do not ask for your secrets; tell me only the names of the persons by whom you were known. I have no wish to know what you said to them—their names are all that is required; and I do not even exact from you that you should give them in immediately. You are weak, and under impressions still too recent and too lively. When you wish to speak to me, send to say so by the orderly of the day; in the meantime, let me have a note from you, and put your biography on paper.' He made me a slight bow, and, as he went out, stopped at the door, and said, 'Have his chains taken off.'

Some minutes afterwards, the Commandant of the place came with a farrier to see me delivered from my chains; and this was the first and last benefit which I derived from the visit of the Governor-General; but it was a very great advantage, and I was truly grateful to him for it, for since my departure from Kaminieç I had not been able to take my boots off once. My legs were much bruised, yet I walked up and down my room the whole of that day; and I had almost a pleasure in the pain which the exercise gave me, for it proved that my feet were free.

Some weeks passed; and one evening, at a pretty late hour of the night, I saw a thing which had never yet entered my cell — it was a light. An aide-de-camp, followed by four soldiers, bid me rise, and follow him. Is the moment of execution arrived? I thought, as I threw round my cell a glance which had in it something of a farewell. Supported under my arms by the soldiers, I traversed the great court of the prison. The snow creaked under our feet, the night was very dark; but the keen and pure air, to which I was not accustomed, while it cut my breath, did me an indescribable amount of good; and while I believed that I was on the way to meet my fate, I felt, if I may so express it, a bitter-sweet delight in inhaling the fresh gusts of wind. I was led into a large room, which was feebly illuminated, and where officers of different ranks were seated at a large round table covered with green cloth; they smoked their cigars, talked in a loud voice, and laughed between times. This was the Commission of Inquiry.

Among these gentlemen it was with real joy that I recognised the face of Major Poloutkovskoï, and yet he it was who had arrested me! The person who presided, and who seemed to be chairman of the commission, was dressed in a plain black coat. He was a member of the third division of the Imperial Cabinet (the secret Police) and a Privy Councillor — in short, it was Pissarev, the *alter ego* of Prince Bibikov, a man of whom the remembrance is too terrible to be soon effaced in the detached provinces.

He made a sign to me to approach, allowed me to be seated near him, and began his questions in French, and in a very affable tone. Although with more of detail, they were identical with those which had been put to me by Prince Bibikov. I made the same answers — and such was the character of the many examinations which I underwent before the Commission of Inquiry.

As I was of noble birth, I found, one day, at one of the sittings of the Commission, the Marshal of the nobility of the province. His presence was demanded by the laws; but he seemed to suffer from his office, and evidently only went through a painful formality, while he addressed me in Polish and put a few questions as to my family and connections. On the whole, these gentlemen seldom failed to treat me with consideration, in spite of the silence and the negatives with which I met their demands. One day, the president even said to me, 'You must find the time in prison pass very slowly; my library is at your disposal, if you wish to have some books. Do you prefer travels or novels?'

'Will you have the kindness to let me have a Bible?'

'A Bible!' he replied, looking at me with an odd expression; 'upon my word, I have not got such a thing; but I can procure one for you.' And he did send me a Bible, after which time I no longer felt that I was alone.

Those of my fellow-countrymen to whom the very names of Prince Bibikov and of M. Pissarev recall the sorrows of so many families, the blood and tears of so many noble victims, and of three provinces all outraged and oppressed under the pressure of the most haughty and rapacious of tyrannies, will no doubt be astonished — it may be, shocked — at what I have just related. Yet such undoubtedly was the conduct of these two men towards myself. I ought also here to declare that no attempt was ever made to inflict on me any of the tortures to which so many Poles have been subjected in Russian prisons — more than one of my fellow-accused being, alas! among the number. It is true that I was several times threatened with such measures, but the threat was never put into execution.

The inquest dragged out its length however, and I soon received the blessed permission to walk in the corridors every day for one hour — care being taken to clear them at that time of every living soul, except the two sentries. The corridor was narrow, dark, and damp; but at least I could satisfy the imperious necessity for exercise which I had felt, and I could also talk in secret from time to time with the sentries. If these soldiers chanced to be Poles — which they very often were, being even men whc had served with us in our army of 1831 — they always showed me more compassion, while they maintained also a far greater show of reserve. The Russian soldiers acted I think more from curiosity; but what surprised me most was the frequency with which I was asked whether I had never met, in foreign countries, with the Grand Duke Constantine, whom they firmly believed to be living in France or in England, and who should one day return to deliver them from Nicholas. I found however that I must renounce the real pleasure which I felt in talking to my sentries. One day the jailer surprised one of them in conversation with me. He was led off to receive sixty blows with the rods, and the cries of the unhappy man under punishment presently reached my ears.

I ought to say something in this place of my neighbours, viz. of those who inhabited the cells opposite my prison. Those who were implicated in my affair were lodged in another part of the fortress, and I never had any communication with them. Once only I caught a glimpse of the judge, Zawadzki, and I hardly recognised him again, for the man formerly so strong and very corpulent was reduced to a perfect skeleton. My neighbours in the corridor were not political criminals. One of them, a soldier named Toumanov, awaited in irons the execution of his sentence of four thousand blows with the rods, which had been passed on him for some insubordination to his superiors. He had no fear, counted on the 'toughness of his hide,' as he expressed it, cursed the Tzar, his officers, and his fate, and sang a great deal, especially an air of which the words began, 'March to the sacking of Poland!' When the moment of his execution arrived, his jailers made many brutal jests at his expense. 'Now then, Toumanov, the devil will get your soul to-day; you will never live through the thing.' The unhappy wretch replied, with coarser oaths, 'I tell you I mean to live through it, and we will have a glass together yet before I am off to Siberia! I shall be better there than serving the Tzar.' I heard afterwards from these same jailers that after two of the four thousand blows he fell senseless on the snow, which was red with his blood, and was carried back to prison. If he survived he was liable to receive, at some future day, the other half of his sentence!

The next of my neighbours was a peasant of the district of Poitava, short in stature, but of immense strength. He had deserted from the army, taken to the woods and a wild life among them, where he had killed several men. He also, when led away to punishment (for his sentence was the knout and penal servitude for life), replied to the hideous comments of his keepers, that he was not afraid. The third prisoner, like the two first, was also in chains, a young handsome soldier, who, while on a march with his battalion, had stopped at a village and loitered behind for a whole week, being 'bewitched by a woman.' The poor boy had then come of his own accord to give himself up, and he now expected his trial. His character seemed to be both good and gentle, and he was in the habit of singing an air of which the melody, though slightly monotonous, was so sweet and plaintive that I could not listen to him without emotion — such sweet tones could hardly have come from a vicious heart. When he left our prison I never was able to hear what became of him, but I regretted him and that plaintive strain which had so often charmed my ears. His cell was soon occupied again — by a subaltern convicted of having set fire to a magazine of forage which was under his care, the motive being the wish to conceal a certain deficit which had occurred. He had now gone mad, but in general his mania was of the inoffensive and quiet kind. He talked constantly, prepared for death, and exhorted his absent mistress to place over his remains a black cross, of which he described the shape and ornaments with the greatest exactness. Another day he complained that a gnat had stung him — that all the blood had been sucked out of his body, and that only water had been left. A *pope* was sent for, who recited a great number of prayers by way of exorcising him; but at last one day the prisoner would not permit him to leave the cell. A psalter in one hand and a crucifix in the other, the madman repeated, without ceasing, 'Little father (*batiouchka*), *I* will break your head for you if you do not immediately give me the holy communion.' The pope manœuvred cleverly so as to reach the door, assuring him that he was going to fetch the pyx; he then saved himself by making a rush, abandoning his crucifix and his psalter. On the following day the governor of the citadel had the maniac's cell opened, though he took care himself to remain in the corridor. The prisoner, standing at the threshold, made him a sign to enter. 'Come, your Excellency, I have a secret to whisper in your ear;' but his Excellency was more prudent than the *pope*. Some soldiers soon advanced; they garotted and bound the poor fool, and they carried him off to the hospital.

In his place arrived a Circassian — a free lance of the Caucasus, who, having been taken prisoner and employed in the works of the fortress, had tried to make good his escape along with two countrymen of his own, his fellow-sufferers. Pursued by the troops, they defended themselves for a long time with their spades, which were their only weapons. One succeeded in escaping, one was killed by a thrust with a bayonet, the third fell into the hands of the soldiers and became my opposite neighbour. He was called 'a mountain prince,' and, with hands and feet in fetters, he was almost always to be seen seated on his couch, gloomy and silent, and with a proud look on his face. I never failed to make him a respectful bow when, in walking up and down the corridor, I passed the loophole in his cell.

In the meantime, weeks grew to months, and as the months succeeded each other, the cold of winter had given place to the heats of July. The stifling air of my prison reduced me to a state of extreme nervous irritability, which broke out over every trifle, and at night I could not sleep. I had forgotten to notice one permanent suffering in my captivity, of which the intensity can never be appreciated, except by those who may have made a personal trial of it: I mean the order given to the sentry to watch all my actions through the window in my door. No one can imagine what an indescribable torture it is to a man to see and to know that a watch is kept upon every movement. That strange eye, impassable and implacable, which meets yours at every moment — that eye which follows you everywhere and at all times — becomes to you a sort of infernal providence; and I abandon the task of making any one understand what it is that the prisoner feels who from the instant that he wakes in the morning sees from his bed those two eyes pointed towards him like two stilettos. Will it be believed, from the earliest dawn I longed for the night, even after a night which had been already very long and rayless; for then at least I was protected from those two eyes. Sometimes, impatient and distracted, I would go up to the loophole and oppose my feverish glare to those two persecuting eyes; and then I laughed like a savage, when I obliged the man to turn away for a moment.

It was in this state of extreme irritation that I received one day a visit from an aide-de-camp, accompanied by another official, by the jailer, and by some soldiers. He desired me to rise, and to undress.

'But I am already undressed!'

'No; but you must be stripped.'

'Why?'

'I have orders to take a complete description of you, and to note down any marks you may have about your person.'

'But that is something barbarous and savage! the description of my features ought to suffice!'

'My orders are precise, and I beg of you to undress.'

So there was no help for it.

If I had been better acquainted with the usages and customs in Russian proceedings of the sort, this notification ought to have enlightened me as to the nature of the punishment to which I was going to be condemned, as well as upon the fact that my sentence was imminent, such examinations being a preliminary to deportation. However, I was so far from having any idea of this, that when some days later I was again summoned before the Commission of Inquiry, I anticipated nothing more than one of those interminable examinations which had already become so familiar to me; but the unaccustomed solemnity of those who were present soon gave me a presentiment that something extraordinary was coming, and before long my sentence was read out. This sentence, which was long and minutely drawn up, finished with 'the pain of death,' commuted, however, by Prince Bibikov, for that of penal servitude in Siberia for the term of my natural life. I was, in addition, degraded from the ranks of the nobility, and I was to make the journey in fetters. After having heard this document, I was ordered to write at the bottom of the paper the following words: 'Rufin Piotrowski heard this sentence on the 29th of July, O. S. 1844.'

I was immediately conducted to the dwelling of the commandant, where I was to take my old travelling clothes, and have my feet put in irons. To my horror, they presented me with the same rusty bars which had caused my torment all the way to Kiow. In vain I besought and implored the commandant to give me another set of chains, he would not consent to do so; and all that I could obtain from him was an order given to the gendarmes who were to be my convoy, that the tight foot-rings were to be enlarged at one of the nearest stations. I was not permitted either to revisit my cell or my companions in the corridor; I was marched down into the courtyard, where a *kibitka* with three horses was in waiting, and I took my seat there between two gendarmes whose muskets were loaded. The doors of the fortress closed behind the *kibitka*, and before me opened the way to Siberia.

CHAPTER IV.

OF DEPORTATION AND THE LIFE OF AN EXILE IN SIBERIA.

THE *KNOUT* AND THE *PLÈTE*—RUNNING THE GAUNTLET—GANGS OF EXILES—GRAND-DUCHESS MARIE—THE JOURNEY—RUSSIAN ALMS—A 'POPE'—THE RUSSIAN SOLDIER—OMSK—PRINCE GORTCHAKOV—EKATERINSKI-ZAVOD.

TO be exempt from corporal chastisement is one of the privileges of a Russian noble; and in cases of deportation a member of the nobility should not be obliged to make the journey on foot, or in a gang of convicts. This does not prevent the torture being applied to political prisoners, even when nobles, during the progress of an examination; yet their sentence is in general in accordance with the laws, and it is seldom that the statutes are set aside, as they were in the case of the Polish prince Roman Sanguszko, to whose sentence the Emperor Nicholas undoubtedly added with his own hand the order that the prince's journey should be made *on foot.* Thanks to the accident of my birth, I had never known the ordinary aggravations of such a lot as mine had now become, I mean the knout, the *plète,* and the march in a gang; but as many of my countrymen have undergone such punishments, and as I also should forfeit (so said the decree against me) my right of being exempt from them when I reached my destination, I shall give some more precise details upon the subject, albeit a sad one.

The knout is a strip of hide, a thong which is steeped in some preparation, and strongly glazed as it were with metal filings. By this process it becomes both heavy and extremely hard, but before it hardens care is taken to double down the edges, which are left thin on purpose, and in this way a groove runs the whole length of the thong, except the upper part, which is supple, and winds round the hand of the executioner; to the other end a small iron hook is fastened. Falling on the bare back of the sufferer the knout comes down on its concave side, of which the edges cut like a knife. The thong thus lies in the flesh, and the operator does not lift it up, but draws it towards himself horizontally, so that the hook tears off long strips. If the executioner has not been bribed, and does his business conscientiously, the person under punishment loses consciousness after the third stroke, and sometimes dies under the fifth. A peculiarity of the Russian law may be also noted here, which orders that the number of blows from the knout shall always be an unequal one! The scaffold on which the sufferer is placed is called in Russ 'a mare' (*kobyla*). It is an inclined plane, to which the man is tied with his back uncovered. The head is firmly fastened to the upper part, the feet to the lower end, and the hands, which are also knotted together, go round below the plank; any movement of the body becoming in this way impossible. After receiving the prescribed number of strokes, the poor wretch is untied, and on his knees undergoes the punishment of being *marked.* The letters *vor* (meaning thief, or malefactor) are printed in sharp-pointed letters on a stamp, which the executioner drives into the forehead and into both cheeks, and while the blood runs, a black mixture, of which gunpowder is an ingredient, is rubbed into the wounds; they heal, but the bluish mark left remains for life. In old days, after thus marking a man, they sometimes tore off his nostrils with iron pincers; but a *ùkase* of the last years of Alexander I. definitively abolished this additional piece of barbarity. I have myself encountered in Siberia more than one criminal thus hideously disfigured, but all dating from a time anterior to the publication of the *ukase* in question. As for those who had the triple inscription of *vor*, I have seen an incalculable number in Siberia; but I believe women cannot be punished in this way, and I never met with one who wore the triple brand.

The *plète,* so often and so erroneously confounded with the knout, is a less fearful instrument of punishment. Three stout thongs are weighted at the ends with balls of lead, the other extremity winds up the m of the executioner, and according to the law it ought to weigh from five to six pounds. When it comes down on the back it strikes like three sticks; it does not tear up the flesh like the knout, but the skin breaks under the blows, which make a lesion of the spinal column, break the ribs, and I have been told detach even the viscera from their places; and those who have suffered under the *plète*, if they have received any great number of lashes, generally fall into consumption and perish. In order to give himself greater purchase, the person wielding it makes a run and does not strike till close to 'the mare.' I have said that it is possible to gain over the operator, and in this case he can manage not to touch the instrument with the little finger of the hand. This lessens the blow, although the attention of the superintending officer is not attracted by the practice, and any reader by experimentalising with a stick may convince himself that it does so. If however the sentence stands for a great number of strokes, the executioner is then bribed to inflict the first with tremendous violence, and as much upon the sides as possible, so that life is sooner extinct, and death puts a speedier end to the sufferings of the victim.

A third species of punishment is running the gauntlet (*skvos-stroï*, literally 'through the ranks'); it is generally reserved for soldiers, and yet many of my countrymen have suffered thus for political offences. It is inflicted with long rods newly cut, which have been steeped in water for some days to make them more pliant. Soldiers are arranged in two files, but each man stands at some distance from the other, so that all may strike with a long swing without being in each other's way. The condemned person, stripped to the waist, passes through the ranks, his hands are tied in front upon a musket of which the bayonet rests on his chest; the butt-end is held by the soldier who leads him. He walks slowly, receiving the rods on his back and shoulders, and if he faints and falls he is picked up again. A *ukase* of Peter the Great fixes the maximum of blows at twelve thousand, but it is seldom that more than two thousand are given at one time, unless for the sake of 'setting an example;' in general, after two thousand the patient is carried off to the hospital, and when healed of his wounds he pays the rest of his penalty.

After such patients as these have recovered a little health and strength in a military hospital, they are hurried off to some one of the head-quarters of the empire, where a large number being assembled, they are classed according to their sentences, whether of simple transportation (*possilenié*), or of hard labour in the public works (*katorga*). Thus classified, they are told off into gangs of a hundred at the least, and of two hundred and fifty at the greatest computation. The gangs thus formed then separate for Siberia, and the time which is spent on the road is one of the greatest elements of suffering in their painful lot. For example, to go from Kiow to Tobolsk requires a long year; and if the gang has a farther destination (say the mines of Nertchinsk, in the government of Irkoutsk), the journey will take more than two years. Criminals condemned to hard labour are placed under a stronger escort, and under a more severe watch than those who are simply deported, and they generally form a brigade by themselves. I met many of these caravans on my journey, and they travelled in the following order. In front rode a Cossack at a walk, completely armed, and with a lance in his hand; after him came men either singly or chained together by hands and feet; these were followed by twenty, all fastened at the wrists to long iron rods; the next were fettered in the same way, with their feet chained in addition, but the women, as far as I could judge, did not wear any irons. On both sides of the gang marched soldiers with loaded arms, while some Cossacks rode up and down. After the prisoners, and in the first carriage, one might see the officer in charge with his head down, and smoking his pipe; the other carriages brought the baggage and the sick, who wore a collar by which they could be chained to a pole fixed in the vehicle.

My heart felt ready to break every time that I met a company of the sort, and the sight of the women was most trying. A mournful silence reigned in their groups, and it was only broken by the dull noise of their chains. No doubt these men were in general real malefactors, the off-scourings of any society; but who could say that among them there were none that were innocent, no political criminals, no countrymen of my own? Later, and when sojourning on the banks of the Irtiche, I had for my companions two political exiles like myself, Siésieki and Syezewski: these men had done the whole distance on foot and in a gang, and they furnished me with every detail of their march. Thus, they told me that none of these unhappy creatures can stir in his sleep without awaking companions fastened to the same bar, and indeed without causing them sharp pain, if the movement should happen to be a rough one, as often is the case in sleep. At the times for halting and eating the prisoners are huddled together in a circle, while the foot soldiers watch them, and the Cossacks stray round them on horseback. The column walks for two days and rests on the third; and for this purpose, beyond Nijni-Novgorod, where the villages are few and far between, houses have been constructed to shelter the gangs at distances calculated to suit the recurrence of these days of rest. These buildings, long and low (for they are only one story high), extending in the middle of wide and desert plains, and only inhabited at intervals, are calculated to leave a strange impression. Military stations are also established at unequal distances along the route from Kiow to Smolensk, and even to Nertchinsk. In each of these stations is to be found an officer with a number of soldiers sufficient to replace the escort which arrives. The officer is in all cases responsible for the prisoners, and has over them a perfectly discretional power. He may punish them with the bastinado, the rods, and the *plète*; and abuses are, as may be supposed, inevitable, though, to the honour of humanity, it must be said that very many of these officers, far from making a cruel use of their dictatorship, often show themselves full of care and compassion for the unhappy beings whom they are obliged to conduct. At times of severe cold or of any great flood, the columns are obliged to stop at any station where they may happen to be. These expeditions are sent off in such a way that every week one gang enters Tobolsk as another leaves it to continue its march. At Tobolsk sits what is called the Commission of Deportation, whose business is to assign a definitive destination to each man, according to local convenience, or the necessities of the public works. It has been calculated that the number of transported persons amounts every year to little short of ten thousand.

I must give one more detail, supplied to me by the same Siesieki whom I have already mentioned. The train of which he formed a part was met near Moscow by the Duke of Leuchtenberg and his wife, Grand-Duchess Marie. The daughter of Nicholas, on learning that many Poles, condemned for political offences, were to be found in the column, had them pointed out to her, and remained for an hour in contemplation of the body; no word escaped her lips, but she dried continually the big tears which fell from her eyes. The Duke of Leuchtenberg approached Siesieki, asked him his name, and said that he should seek for his pardon at the hands of the Emperor. Did the Duke forget it, or did he not dare to ask? Nothing can be known; but this I know for certain, that, many a long day afterwards, I found Siesieki in Siberia, and that I was one day to leave him there.

Were not these strange meetings? Carried away in my *kibitka* towards the land from which no man returns, a convict on his way to work out his bitter sentence, I yet saw many shapes of misfortune worse than my own. I could see faces of men in such gangs as I have described, who, looking into mine, counted me as happy. Nay, I could say to myself, I too had only escaped this, the last and lowest stage of misery and shame, by means of the privilege which attached to my birth—a privilege which my own convictions disallowed, but which the Tzar himself maintained. Compared with the lot of this herd of the lost my state certainly was more endurable. I was sure to arrive soon, only too soon, at the place for which I was bound; I was not rivetted to any parricide, or to a malefactor, and my hands at least were free. The tight rings of my fetters alone caused me any suffering, and now I almost blushed to speak of them; but the pain was really great, and by dint of entreaties I prevailed on the soldiers to have the luckless rings let out at one of the halting places, which after all was only in accordance with the orders they had received at Kiow. At first, these guardians of mine had obstinately refused to meet any of my attempts at conversation with them, replying that they were forbidden to address me. However, I kept up with them, and I ended in humanising them. We soon talked freely, and drank together some glasses of that Russian brandy of which I was learning to appreciate the salutary and strengthening qualities. Neither of the men seemed to be bad-hearted in any way, and they were more distressed than pleased by the business in hand. One day, when, from sufferings of mind and bodily fatigue I fell sick, and was lying down at one of the posting-houses, I overheard the following conversation between them :

'Well, we are very unlucky: if we do not arrive at Omsk on the day appointed, we shall be beaten with rods; and if we hurry him too much, and he dies of it, we shall be beaten all the same; we are in very bad luck!'

They were continually haunted by the fear of my dying or committing suicide. When we had a river to cross, they sat by me in the boat, and held me by both arms, in case I should leap into the water; and at our meals they gave me meat cut into little squares, from which the bones had been carefully removed, and which I had to eat with a spoon.

Thus, without being positively cruel, these soldiers showed an astonishing indifference to my sad position. In the conversation, for instance, which I have just cited, it will be seen that they made an abstraction of me: I ceased to be a man, a creature of God, suffering in body and in misery of mind; I was only a dangerous charge, to be got rid of as quickly as possible; and the only thing they could find pity for was for themselves. But it was not in them alone that I had to remark a charity so nicely restricted, or such indifference to the pains of other men. At one of the places where we changed horses, the new postilion, a great rough fellow, came up to me and asked me:

'Are you a Pole? How many *kibitkas* are following you, then?'

'None.

'What! none? As soon as you see a *kibitka* with a Pole, one may always bet that there will be no end to them; these Poles must be in swarms, and yet I can't think how we are not come to the last of them by this time.'

At the same time I should be singularly ungrateful and unjust if I did not declare that such speeches as these were rare and exceptional, and that they stood out in contrast with the general manner of the country people towards me. These showed themselves full of compassion, and even of solicitude; and after entering Russia Proper, as I advanced by degrees into the interior, I never ceased to receive from them unequivocal marks of their sympathy and pity. How often was I not followed by travellers, especially by ladies, who pressed gifts of money on my acceptance! How often have I not seen at our halting places young girls stop and look at me with sadness, even with tearful eyes! One rich merchant, who was returning from the fair at Nijni-Novgorod, pressed upon me with real eagerness the sum of two hundred roubles, saying it was nothing for him to lose, and might be of the greatest use to me. If I always thought it right to refuse such presents, of which, moreover, I should have been doubtless deprived by the Russian authorities, I accepted without hesitation and with much gratitude the articles of food and drink brought to me on all sides by the inhabitants. It was rarely that the master of any posting-house failed to offer me either tea or brandy at the stations where we stopped; his wife or his daughters presented me with cakes, dried fish, or fruits, while the neighbours would hasten to do the same. At one of these stations, not far from Toula, I saw an official in a uniform arrive, and I was timidly offered by him a little parcel wrapped in a silk handkerchief. As he gave it me, he said, 'Accept this from my patron saint.' I could not make out his meaning; and as the sight of an uniform did not predispose me in his favour, I made a sign of refusing it.

'You are a Pole,' he said, colouring a little; 'and you are not acquainted with our customs. This is my birthday, and on such a day it is our bounden duty to share our goods with those who are in adversity; accept this then I beseech you, in the name of my saint.'

I could not resist a petition so touching and so Christian in its spirit. The parcel contained bread, salt, and a few coins; the money I gave to the guards, and I broke bread with the official, who asked me:

'Why are they taking you to Siberia?'

'Because I have thought and felt as a Pole.'

'You were right to do so, because you were in Poland; but why do the Poles wish to plant their ways of thinking in Russia? In the garrison of our town, there were about ten Poles incorporated into our army after the revolution of 1831. Will you believe it, Sir, these Poles excited our soldiers, persuaded them that they were very unhappy, that the Tzar was the cause of it, and that his authority was not lawful? Now what was the consequence of all this? They only made their own case worse, and they drew upon themselves all the severities of the Russian law. These Poles never reflected that every nation has, and ought to have, a government suited to its nature. Now the Russian people are rude, ignorant, and uncultivated; why think, when in such a state as this, of any other authority or of any political reforms whatever? However little we were to depart from the severity of our laws, we should see the life and fortunes of our citizens seriously endangered, and that before very long; we should have murders, fires, and rapine of all sorts. I know my nation too well. In time we may proceed to some changes, but it will not be very soon; and it is vain to think of it at the present moment.'

Very different was a scene which was acted not far from Kazan. There, on going into a station, I saw, to my great surprise, that with the character of post-master my landlord combined that of priest (*pope*). Surrounded by convivial peasants, the *batiouchka* was delivering a long peroration, while he swallowed great potations from a monstrous bottle of brandy which was on the table by which he was seated. I do not know by what sign he perceived that I was a Pole, but he rose immediately and turned the torrent of his eloquence upon me, deploring the seditious spirit of the Poles, their disobedience to the Tzar, and the misfortunes which they drew upon themselves and upon Russia. All these considerations did not however prevent his offering me a glass. I drank and prudently beat a retreat, while the *pope* made over my head an infinite number of signs of the cross. I really do not know whether a benediction was intended, or whether he hoped to drive out of me the evil spirit of revolt.

Although thus an object of a general commiseration, which showed itself by the touching offerings of the poor, and even in the enigmatical benedictions of a tipsy priest, I nevertheless could practise charity in my turn, for many begged from me. One day in particular I can recall. It was, if I mistake not, at Saransk, as, with fetters on my feet, I stood waiting for a relay of horses, that I saw a man stretch out his hand towards me and ask for alms. He had on a military cap, and the many medals on his coat showed that he had served in several campaigns. He was, in fact, a soldier discharged from the service, and even I could recognise that he had once been in the Imperial Guard. What a strange contrast was here! A faithful and deserving servant of the Tzar begging his bread from a man who, a rebel to this same Tzar, was condemned by him to labour as a felon among felons! Without doubt, the most hapless being in the universe, more unhappy than even the convicts of Siberia, is the soldier of the Emperor of all the Russias. I do not speak of those twenty or five-and-twenty years of service which try his health and wear out his strength; I speak not either of the thousands of blows which he receives during his long martyrdom; but if, at the end of so many years passed under arms and under the rod, he were in his old age protected from want and misery, it would be well. At the most, however, the Russian government grants to some decrepid and attenuated victim of military discipline permission to settle upon the crown lands at some thousands of *verstes* from his family, and from the place of his birth, without even giving him what is wanted for reclaiming the fields from which he is to scrape a living. If he marries he is obliged to remit to the Emperor every male child who attains the age of ten years; and thus he has the assurance that there is prepared for his son a life and an old age as miserable as his own. But it must not be supposed that all veterans are provided for even after this fashion. By far the greater number are told off to the fortresses or to the prisons of the government, or else sent back to their old homes, where they survive, old, poor, and unfit for work, as burdens upon families to whom they have become all but strangers; though the government, in giving them their discharge, has taken care to stipulate that there they shall neither be permitted to beg, nor allow their beards to grow. Unfortunately, this last order is more easily carried out than the first.

With the exception of that enforced halt which was occasioned by the illness I have mentioned, we continued our course without stopping anywhere except for our meals and to change horses. Day and night we drove, sleeping as we sat in the *kibitka*, only that my slumbers there were less profound than those of my keepers, for at each jolt of the carriage (and such jolts were incessant) my chains were shaken and knocked against my feet, so that I was obliged to draw them up and hold them always in my hands. Often in this plight and tormented by sleeplessness I sat alongside of my guardians, who slept so heavily that more than once I caught their caps for them when they were on the point of losing them from the wind; and I could not help smiling as I looked at them, and thought that I might be fairly said to be outwatching my watchers. The journey was monotonous, in spite of its giddy and headlong pace, or rather this very pace made it monotonous by confounding all impressions and preventing any contemplation of the outside world. Going at the rate of about sixty-six *verstes* or *kilometres* a day, I had traversed in succession the governments of Tchernigov, Orel, Toula, Riazan, Vladimir, Nijni-Novgorod, Kazan, Viatka and Perm ; I had passed the mountain chains of Oural and Tobolsk, and I found myself, at the end of twenty days, transported from the fertile plains of Poland to the very centre of Siberia-West ; and that without, so to speak, any remembrance of the people or of the country which I left behind me. At one of the last stations short of Omsk, while a relay was being procured, a soldier passed, and stopping in front of me began to whistle an air which made me quiver — Dombrowski's air, 'No, never shall Poland perish !' The man was a compatriot of Mazovia, a soldier of 1831, an old brother in arms, now incorporated into the army of Siberia. He stole furtively up to me and had only time to say, 'What are our people about ? What do they think of us in France ?'

At last, late in the night of August 20, 1844, we stopped before a sort of castle. 'Who goes there ?' cried the sentry from the top of the bastion. 'An unhappy one,' replied the postillion of our *kibitka*. Immediately the gates swung wide, and we were in Omsk. After the lapse of about twenty minutes, and with all the feverish promptitude which distinguishes the public service of Russia, a report of my arrival reached the commandant of the fortress, and Prince Gortchakov, the Governor-General of Western Siberia. The order was sent back to have me conveyed to the station of the guard, close to the prince's residence, and there I was installed, having for my companion an officer under arrest in this room, for some infraction of discipline. He was quite a young man of good family, hardly twenty, good looking, pleasant and gay, speaking French, and communicating something of his own good humour to all who came near him. When I said that I was a Pole, he gave me a more than hearty reception, pressing tea on me, and putting himself to inconvenience in order to prepare a bed for me. In spite of the fatigue of the long journey, I spent the greater part of that night in talking with him, for I found much pleasure in his gay and natural conversation. He knew the country well, and could give me information which was at once precise in itself and of the greatest use to me; but what most enchanted me was his unrolling before me a first-rate map of Siberia. This I examined with feverish curiosity; I had all the marks explained to me, I studied and strove to fix in my memory the different routes and watersheds of the country. My heart beat violently, and I could not take my eyes off the map.

At last the officer noticed my agitation. 'Ah!' he said, 'I fear you meditate an evasion! pray, pray do not think of it, it is perfectly impossible. Many of your countrymen have tried it, and those may be said to have been happy who, tracked on every side, tortured by hunger, and maddened by despair, have yet been able to escape the consequences of their crazy undertaking by a timely suicide. The consequences are certain to be the knout and a life of misery such as I have no words to describe to you. For God's sake, put all such thoughts out of your mind!'

I asked my companion what was the cause of his detention.

'Far be it from me to know,' he replied. 'This is not the first time that I take off my hat to these walls. It is a pleasure that comes my way at least twice a month. We have a colonel of the old school, quite a martinet in discipline; and then, as you see, I have the luck, or the bad luck, to be always in the most giddy spirits, and he puts me very often under arrest, to see if it will make a wise man of me. What makes him more angry is that I never ask him about anything, and he says, that that is insolence, and that I have too much liberty of thought (*volnodoumstoo*).'

He spoke to me afterwards of his intention to change his regiment, because his colonel had decidedly taken a dislike to him. He expected to be sent among the subjugated tribes of the Kirghis, whose language he was learning, by talking with those of the natives who happened to be prisoners in this castle. The next morning he had one of these sons of the desert, a Khan, to breakfast with me; and thus I had for the first time an opportunity of seeing a representative of those warlike and nomadic races which occupy the steppes beyond Orenbourg.

The next day, at eight o'clock in the morning, I was visited by the commandant, Colonel De Grawe, a worthy old gentleman of alarming corpulence but very obliging manners, and who was of Swedish extraction. 'What a pity, what a pity,' he never ceased repeating, 'that once free, and in a foreign country, you ever took it into your head to come back!' After him came the prefect of police in Omsk, M. Nalabardine — tall, thin, dry, straight as an arrow, tight as a cord, with a long face and little eyes, which were piercing and sunk. He seemed a mixture of the Cossack, Kirghis and Tartar races. There was something of a vulture in his physiognomy; and, indeed, I learnt afterwards that he really was cruel and rapacious in the extreme. Yet this man had some involuntary feeling. He asked me how it was that I had dared to return to Poland without the permission of the Tzar; and when I replied that I had yielded only to the pangs of home sickness, he cried, with a voice which was unsteady with emotion, 'Ah! native country, native land, thou art indeed a beloved thing!'

At midday I was desired to wait on Prince Gortchakov, and shown into a large waiting-room, where a number of persons in his employment sat writing. After some minutes, several of them rose, and, holding out their hands to me, addressed me in Polish. They were young Poles, political prisoners, who worked at desks in the government offices. Encouraged by their example, the Russians present also had the courage to approach me, and to ask me about my lot; and from them I learnt that this was a very decisive moment for me. I have stated before that the Commission of Deportation held its permanent sittings at Tobolsk; that it received the gangs, and assigned to each of the condemned his future and final destination; but as I had not made the journey in a gang, it was not the commission at Tobolsk, but the Governor-General of Siberia, residing at Omsk, who was to point out my *settlement*. Now this was a very important matter to me, because he might, for example, order me to work out my sentence of penal servitude in any of the government works or factories of the neighbourhood; or else he might send me to dig in the mines of Nertchinsk. The hell of a Siberian convict has, alas! many circles; and the question of determining which of them should be my fate was precisely the one which was being discussed in the adjoining room, where the Governor-General's Council was sitting. They told me I might pin my hopes chiefly on the presence at the board of M. Kapoustine, an official of the highest rank and greatest influence about the Prince—a man of generous instincts, and who always pleaded in favour of deported persons convicted on political grounds. All of a sudden, a sound was heard, everybody looked hard at the page before him, and Prince Gortchakov appeared at the door of the room. He came forward a step or two, fixed his eyes on me for some seconds, then turning his back, he returned to his own apartments, without having addressed me. An hour passed away in waiting in this cruel suspense. At last we saw M. Kapoustine of the Council leave the inner room. He announced to me, with a polite and kindly manner, that I was to be sent to the works at the government distilleries, at Ekaterinski-Zavod (established by the Empress Catherine), in the district of Tara, on the banks of the Irtiche, at the distance of rather more than 300 kilometres from Omsk. Hardly had he ceased speaking and departed, than the clerks began to offer me their congratulations. I bade farewell to them, as well as to the two poor gendarmes who had brought me from Kiow; then, stepping into a *kibitka* which waited at the gate, I was whirled away to the final term of my travels.

CHAPTER V.

THE KATORGA.

COMPANIONS IN EXILE — THE 'KATORGA' — A MURDERER — THE FELONS — KANTIER — PAY AND PUNISHMENTS — THE COUNTING-HOUSE.

ABOUT ten o'clock of a cold morning, for it was now the 4th of October, I saw before me the outlines of a village composed of two hundred miserable houses, all built of wood, lying near the river Irtiche, and situated in a vast plain. Further back, upon a rising ground, and in the middle of a fir wood, the buildings of a factory were visible. This was Ekaterinski-Zavod. I was introduced into the counting-house (*kazionnaia kantora*), and the *smotritel*, that is to say, the inspector of the establishment, soon arrived; for to M. Aramilski the gendarme had already carried all the papers which concerned me. He made me strip to the waist before all the persons present, thus verifying the description drawn up at Kiow, which he had in his hand. He then ordered me to be inscribed in the register of convict labourers, not under my name but under my number.

I was then to be taken to the station-house; and he added, as he went out, without even having addressed me, 'he will work with chains on his feet.'

When he was out of hearing, a young man, who, through all this business, had continued writing like the other clerks in the office, rose and threw himself into my arms. It was Charles Bogdaszewski of Cracow, who, implicated in the affair of Erenberg the poet, had been condemned for three years to hard labour, and to deportation for the term of his natural life. Some moments afterwards, we were joined by John Siesieki of Lublin, another political offender. They spoke quickly, and with an emotion which they did not disguise. They conjured me to show myself patient and submissive in every way, and not to rebel at anything. It was only thus that I could arrive in time at being employed in the office, instead of having to do the hard and severe work of the factory itself; and at this price, above all, I could purchase an immunity from those corporal punishments to which every labouring convict is liable. I cannot describe what was the character of this broken and breathless colloquy, or the shiver which ran through my frame when I heard Polish lips speaking, as of a matter of course, of their fear of blows and of the rods. They left me, but it was to make haste to use their influence with the under-officials of the establishment, with the treasurer and the forester, that they might induce the *smotritel* to go back from the order, which seemed inconceivable to them, that I should work in irons, such a measure not being in use here even in the case of murderers. I learnt later what was the meaning of this unusual severity. At the bottom of my certificated sentence, Prince Gortchakov had added with his own hand, 'A special watch must be kept upon Piotrowski;' and this extraordinary recommendation had made a deep impression on M. Aramilski. 'Since I have been superintendent,' he said to the forester, 'nothing of the sort ever occurred to me; this must be some diplomate' (*eto dolgène byt kakoï diplomat*).

The station-house, to which I was immediately directed, was full of soldiers, many of them Poles who had fought in our war of independence. These seized the least excuse to come up to me and ask me in whispers what had become of Poland, what was happening in Europe, and whether there were any hopes? (*Son Nadzieje?*)

Worn out with fatigue and by many emotions, I stretched myself on a bench, and for two hours I remained plunged in a gloomy reverie. All of a sudden I saw standing in front of me a strong truculent-looking man, whose ignoble expression did not belie in any way the triple mark of *vor* which was printed on his forehead and on both cheeks. He addressed me thus, 'Get up, you must go and work.' This was the overseer of the convicts, a felon of distinction himself! Oh, my

God! Thou alone didst hear the cry of my soul, when for the first time I was ordered about by an abject being like this! At these words of his I darted a look at him in return which seemed to express all the desolate indignation of my spirit. I do not know that it was so, but he stepped back, dropped his eyes, and said with a sad air, 'Well, what can I do? They order me, and I must execute my orders.' My breast heaved, I pressed my head between my hands, for my brain felt on fire, a cold sweat burst out all over me, and at last I breathed again. 'Let us go,' I said, as I rose up, and I went out, following the overseer.

He led me to a large forge close to the refining house, my feet were placed in the anvil and my irons struck off, a deliverance which I owed to the humane offices of my two countrymen; and thus for the first time since I had left Kiow I was able to pull off my own boots! I was then taken to a building which was only in part finished, a kiln for drying the malt. The roof was not completed, and the wood-work had to be cleared of a vast quantity of chips, litter and offensive refuse, with which it was covered. I mounted by a ladder, and was followed by the overseer, and by a soldier, who had orders for the future never to let me out of his sight. On the roof I found another convict, whose labours I was to share. A broom and a shovel were put into my hands by my colleague, and by the overseer I was shown how to use them. The air was cold, the sky clouded and dark, and the task imposed certainly not a severe one; but in order to avoid any remonstrances, and to escape being either spoken to or looked at, I worked away without ever stopping or so much as lifting my eyes, and was soon drenched with perspiration. Alas! I was weak, and what was more, I was weeping!

In his course of daily inspection M. Aramilski also came up upon the roof where I was at work, followed by other officials of the establishment. I continued to sweep without turning round, and I avoided their eyes as much as if I had been a criminal. Some time after they had left, the overseer said, 'Now rest.' I seated myself on a heap of sweepings alongside of my companion, a young man, who was tall and well-made, but who had the triple mark on his face, and who seemed of an easy cheerful temper. Overcoming the hesitation which I felt, I spoke first.

'Have you been long in these works?'

'Three years.'

'To how many years' labour are you sentenced?'

'For life!'

'What was your crime?'

'I killed my master.'

I shuddered, but went on:

'Without doubt it was an accident, you did not intend to kill him?'

'Why, for the matter of that I did not *plan* it,' he said with a sneering look; 'I had an axe hanging at my girdle, I took it in both my hands and split his head open for him.'

I was chilled with horror. After a few moments' silence I said:

'But why did you kill him so cruelly?'

'Why? not for fun, you may be sure. No, our master was a bad man, very cruel, who overworked us and beat us incessantly, almost to death; and to deliver the neighbourhood from a ruffian like that I took upon myself to kill him, and I did so. It was God's providence that I did not die under the knout, and now I am much happier and better off at this *katorga* (penal labour) than I ever was at home. The only thing that I regret is my young wife, whom I had to leave; she is young and pretty, and will soon find another husband.'

'But you ought to repent of the sin of having slain a man.'

'*That* was not a man! That was a devil!'

We soon after this went to work again, and did not stop till nightfall.

I returned to the guard-house, and there my two countrymen came under an escort to visit me, the *smotritel* having given leave for this indulgence. We conversed together in a low voice, and in the middle of all the racket made by the soldiers and convicts we related to each other the chief events of our lives. These poor friends did not cease exhorting me to absolute patience and submission. They conjured me to master my temper, to suppress all exhibitions of it, and not to despair of seeing myself soon raised to a position which would be by comparison more happy, and which they themselves now occupied — thanks to their patient and irreproachable conduct. We embraced tenderly, then separated, and I fell asleep. Thus ended my first day of convict labour and of convict life: how many more of the same succeeded it and resembled it!

I rose with the sun to go to the works, at eight I had breakfast, from twelve to one we had an hour in the barracks for dinner and rest, and then we worked till dark. The occupations were often varied according to the wants of the establishment or the inclinations and temper of the inspector. By day and by night I was associated with the other felons, and always under the eye of the overseer and of the soldier in charge of my person. On some days I swept the courtyards; sometimes I carried wood and drew water; sometimes, again, I might be sent to hew wood for fagots, and to stack them in symmetrical piles; and this last employment in the open air, in the autumnal and winter months, in rain and snow, and in the icy temperature of Siberia, was the most trying of any. Long, gloomy, and mournful were the days, and it is needless to dwell on them any further.

The dominant feeling in my mind was the wish to avoid any discussion or wrangle with my superiors or with the overseers. Such an occurrence would have brought about a terrible catastrophe, for I had made a vow that I would not submit to corporal punishment, and that I would resist it, whether at the price of my own life or of that of others; and for this reason I worked beyond what was asked of me, and beyond my own strength. I must do myself the justice to add that I neglected no effort to conquer my feelings and moments of impatience, and I must do my superiors the justice to say of them that they were neither teasing nor gratuitously and wickedly unkind. Severe and hard as they often were, they never treated me with the capricious rudeness of despots, while the convicts who were my colleagues treated me with a deference, I might almost say a kindness, for which I was heartily grateful. They did not annoy me with any of those cruel jests by which the bad even in very different ranks of life often insult any one superior to themselves whom misfortune has brought down to their own level. More than once I have known them offer to help me at some work which they thought was too heavy for me, or they would change with me, taking my task and giving me their own, if it happened to be a lighter one. From a very early stage they ceased to speak to me with '*thee*' and '*thou*,' and called me 'Sir;' and certainly unmerited misfortune ought to command the respect of untutored men, even of savages, where they, in spite of bravado and seared consciences, feel themselves to be really criminals. With the exception of a very few political offenders like myself, all the convicts at Ekaterinski-Zavod (to the number of three hundred souls) were really malefactors. One would have murdered a wayfarer, another had committed a horrible rape, another would be an utterer of false coin, another both a thief and a housebreaker. As a daily intercourse with such men was inevitable, I had neither a false shame nor a misplaced pride in my dealings with them. I often talked to these strange companions, studied their characters, and heard from them their different histories and the events of their lives. I am certainly not about to become the historian of these heroes of the bagnio; but I will give one tale, which is not without interest, and which shows that a false Byronism of deed and thought was not unrepresented among them.

One of our felons, Kantier by name, was sentenced to hard labour for life. He was still young, a man short of stature, but strongly built, of a clear and dark but pale complexion; he had black and burning eyes, and his whole physiognomy bespoke a firm and daring disposition. He had been clerk to a wine merchant at St. Petersburg; and when I asked him one day what was the cause of his sentence and punishment, he replied, 'It is because I killed the girl with whom I was in love. I suspected her of being unfaithful to me. I had suffered horribly, and I was determined to be revenged upon her. In order to execute my design with greater ease, I pretended to make it up with her;

and, by dint of coaxing, got her to promise, on a certain holiday, to go on an excursion into the country with me. She hesitated about it a long time, as if she had had a presentiment of some mischief; but at last she consented, upon the condition that she might bring a female friend along with her. *That* did not suit my plans very well, but I had to put up with it. On the appointed day we started, all three of us. Armed with a pistol and a dagger, I walked alongside of my mistress and talked to her. She had never seemed to me either so pretty or so loving as she did then; but that only added to my jealousy and my thirst for revenge. More than once I was on the point of dispatching her, but her face disarmed me. At last I stopped; it was in a field; I pointed out something in the view to my sweetheart which made her turn away her head. At that moment I put the pistol to her temple, and pulled the trigger. My hand shook, and I only wounded her; the friend screamed and ran. She, slightly hurt and stunned by the shot, turned round two or three times, then, throwing herself on her knees before me, "Forgive me!" she cried in a voice so touching and heartrending that I shuddered. But I answered by sinking the dagger into her heart, the weapon going in up to its hilt. She fell down stiff and dead. I stabbed her in the breast with my knife, and then ran to give myself up to the police; and here I am, after the knout, for life. . . . .'

'But are you not sorry for having killed her? Does not your conscience reproach you bitterly for such a crime?'

'Yes, I am sorry for her. I shall never forget her as long as I live, and I shall never love any one else; but as to my conscience, I thought I was quite right in killing her.'

'But, if it were possible for her to be alive and come back to you, you surely would not do so by her again?'

'She made me first the happiest and then the most miserable of men; and, if she could come back, I should certainly kill her again.'

'Then, you mean to say you think you have committed no crime?'

'Where is the crime? She took away my peace, and I took away her life; she was the most to blame of the two.'

I must now say something about our village, and about the organisation of the factory. The government distillery at Ekaterinski-Zavod was founded in the reign of Catherine II., whose name it bears; and the population consists of the descendants of former convicts. All the interests of the village were centred in the distillery, which produces annually from two to three million of *litres* of alcohol, and furnishes brandy to the country over a district of one or two thousand *verstes*. The distillery was farmed by two rich merchants of the government of Simbirsk, M. Orlov and

M. Alexeiev, who must have realised a considerable profit upon it, because, besides the price which they paid as rent, and the augmented charges of pay to the convict labourers, they had contracted for the pay of the commanding officer and the keep of the garrison, viz. of a hundred and one persons; and they were necessarily obliged to give constant and valuable presents to the inspector and other government officials. The inspector generally allowed them about half the force of convict labourers for the distillery; the other half was employed in the public service, as in road-making and mending, in the construction of government buildings, and in sanitary works. Each of us received in money three francs a month, and ninety pounds' weight of corn, the sale of which in the village was to furnish us with food; but the gentlemen who farmed or rented the distillery from the crown, in order to encourage their work-people, raised the pay up to five, eight, and even ten francs a month; the men employed in barrelling the spirit being paid by the piece, and thus gaining more than the rest. In this way, it was advantageous for the convicts to be in the employment of the distillery, for they received a better salary, and were less likely to encounter the trying interference of the government officials; but, in any case of insubordination or idleness, the distillers or their representative were obliged to refer to the inspector, who ordered the punishment to be inflicted. This, I mean, was the case when it was a question of the stick and the rods; as for blows and cuffs, the convicts got plenty of them from everybody alike. The greater number of convicts lived in barracks; the more favoured were allowed to lodge in the village: but then they had to pay for the bed and board of the soldier who lived there and watched them. From all this it will be seen that, by those who had any education, the counting-house and office of the factory were the posts especially desired, and that those who occupied them were thought most worthy of envy; but it is needless to add that all were alike in the eye of the law, that these steps or grades could not give any acquired rights, and that at the good pleasure of the inspector, or *smotritel*, one might be at any moment 'removed to other functions.'

Thanks to the constant care with which I acquitted myself of the tasks imposed upon me, thanks to the mastery which I had gained over myself, and of which I certainly should not at one time have believed myself capable, I passed, in the following year, not only into the service of the lessees, but also was employed in their office; and in this way I ceased to be in the constant society of persons who were unreclaimed, and who lacked culture both morally and intellectually. I received wages to the extent of ten francs a month, and my occupation was in every way less painful than any former ones had been. I went to my desk at eight in the morning, and I remained in the counting-house till mid-day, where I was again from two in the afternoon to ten or eleven at night; and although work was not pressing, and one was not really wanted, yet it was incumbent on me to be always present. During the long hours of ennui I wrote, took notes, and abandoned myself to meditations, during which plans for the future slowly ripened in my mind. My office, it happened, was the rendezvous of a great number of travellers, who frequented it both for the sale of grain and in order to buy spirituous liquors; they were peasants, townsfolk, merchants, Russians, Tartars, Jews, and Kirghis. If I was very scant of speech, and short in my communication with the official, with the other convicts, and with the custom-house officers, I acquired, on the contrary, with a curiosity that never flagged, from all these passing travellers, all that was to be learnt of the peculiarities of Siberia. I spoke to men some of whom had been to Berezov, others at Nertchinsk, others had penetrated to the frontiers of China, to Kamtschatka, to the steppes of the Kirghis, even into Boukhara; and thus, without passing the threshold of my office, I learnt to know Siberia, its nearest and its furthest details. The knowledge thus acquired was to be of great value to me afterwards, in forming the plan for my evasion.

One of my fellow-countrymen, Wysocki, was head clerk in the counting-house of the distillery; but my great ally there was the young Russian, Stépan Bazanov, manager of the factory for the lessees, whose relative he was. He was a lad of twenty or upwards, brave and upright, whose only weakness was the most naïve adoration for the Emperor Nicholas. He never would or could admit that Nicholas did wrong; all the wrong, according to him, was owing to the Boyards, and he declared that, were it not for the intervention of the nobility, the Tzar would make his people the happiest in the world; and I am bound to say that, as far as my experience has gone, this opinion is a pretty general one in Russia, among the people, though not among the 'staroviertsi.' What most disposed me to like Bazanov was that he confided his love griefs to me. The poor boy, who was lamentably uneducated in every way, had fallen violently in love with a cousin of his own; but the Orlovs put difficulties in the way of the union which he so much desired. Fancy hearing a lover's confidences in an accursed place like this where convicts worked! though to be sure the man who made them to me knew that he was free, and that he did not awake every morning to fear the stick and the rods!

I must say that the thought of being exposed at any moment, for any trivial cause, and at the beck of any official, to treatment as shameful as it is terrible, created in me a gloomy and fierce temper, and that, in spite of the relative and very appreciable improvement in my case, I was kept in a state of continual tension. I could not forget the subject, there was no way of doing so;

the punishments daily inflicted on some one or other of the convicts, all my own equals in the social hierarchy of the place, sent up a cry of *cras tibi*, enough to drive anyone mad with despair. Moreover, the familiarities to which the superiors often admit their deported labourers have a dangerous side. There is no real trust to be placed in the caprices of a man invested with arbitrary powers. His favours are likely to be capricious also, for these men are generally of low minds and manners; and it amuses them to make a sport of their fellow-creatures, raising them one day only in order to humiliate them more deeply hereafter. This is a snare into which many Poles, who like myself have been carried to Siberia, are apt to fall; into which indeed they have fallen. Their education, their manners, the noble nature of their misfortunes, all attract to them a certain consideration, and sometimes even win for them the good graces of their masters. Thus they rise above the level of the common herd of the lost, and they beguile themselves with the illusion that in this way they are reintegrated into society. But the moment of awakening from this dream soon comes, and the deported man, rudely reminded of his real state, may be called happy if he is reminded of it only by word of mouth! Some years before my arrival at Ekaterinski-Zavod, there was a Russian general, N——, who had been condemned by Nicholas to penal servitude in Siberia. The *smotritel*, respecting the high position and the advanced age of the prisoner, set him to the lightest and least painful tasks, and admitted him to society and his table. Unluckily, the general sometimes forgot himself (especially if he drank a little too much), and, taking up the tone of a senior and superior officer, showed himself recalcitrant. The inspector then had him chained to the furnace of the distillery, and obliged him for a month or a fortnight, during the extreme cold of winter, to keep up the fires. The general, overheated and covered with sweat and ashes, promised to amend, and recommenced his familiarities with the *smotritel* and other functionaries, only to find himself again another time by the furnace. Having spent several years in this way at the *katorga*, he was pardoned by the Tzar, and restored to his old rank as a general officer.

One other amelioration took place in my lot, and that even before I was told off for a clerkship in the counting-house, and it was, in my estimation, a benefit as great as even that great improvement on my former labours. The inspector gave me leave to live out of barracks; and thus I was able to leave behind me that habitation which was the ordinary dwelling of felons, and which was the scene of their drinking and of their infamous debaucheries. I dwelt henceforth, along with my two fellow-clerks and fellow-countrymen, in Siésieki's house. Thanks to the length of his long sojourn at Ekaterinski-Zavod, this exile had scraped together, out of his slender salary, enough money to construct a small wooden house, which was not complete as yet, and indeed was not even roofed in; but thither notwithstanding we carried our household goods. The wind whistled through numberless chinks, but as wood cost next to nothing, we piled up a great fire on the earth every night; and there we could feel not only that we were at home, but that we were delivered from the horrible company of the common criminals; although it must not be forgotten that we were watched, and that we had to pay for the soldiers who mounted a ceaseless guard upon our persons. Ah! if that little house is still standing, and shelters perhaps at this moment some unhappy and deported brother, let him know that he is not the first or the only one who within its modest walls has wept as he invoked a distant and a beloved land! My friend Siésieki had been, he told me, a prisoner in the citadel of Warsaw along with the hapless Lévitoux, and had thus been, so to speak, an eyewitness of his horrible death. Their cells opened into the same corridor; and more than once Lévitoux, when returning covered with blood from the inquest and the torture, would call to him, 'I cannot bear it any longer, I know that I shall go mad, and then I shall speak in spite of myself!' This fear haunted him continually; but one day, on his return from one of these *blood-baths*, as he called them, he said to his companion through the window in his door, that he begged he would keep awake till about eleven that evening. Siésieki, without, however, attaching much importance to this request, complied with it, and did not go to bed or lie down: about ten at night he saw a great light in Lévitoux's cell. The sentry called, 'Fire! fire!' but before the jailer could be fetched, or the keys of the cell found, some time was of course allowed to elapse. The door was opened, a dense smoke filled the corridor, and the poor fellow had just expired upon the straw mattress, to which he had set fire with his own hands by means of his night-light. Through his cell window my friend beheld the burnt corpse, and saw the soldiers drag it along the corridor by the feet, a horrible spectacle, with the head knocking upon the flags. It is said that at the news of such a finale even Nicholas was moved, and gave orders that in future political offenders should not be proceeded against with so much severity; also, ever since this event, no person detained for a political cause, and supposed to be gravely implicated in one, is ever allowed a light in his room.

Siésieki had made, as I related before, the whole of the journey to Siberia on foot, and had formed one of a gang. When he first arrived at our factory, he had been put to the hardest labour, in company with the other convicts; but some years later the forester required the services of a clever and safe servant, and Siésieki was attached to his department, the more readily because he added the qualifications of a good sportsman and a good shot to those of being a clever and an honest man. It may easily be guessed that the inspector and other functionaries profited by the first-fruits of his chase, and that at that price he gained permission to carry a gun. Indeed he was often absent on leave for a week at a time, a proceeding of which we once felt the inconvenience, for as Bogdaszewski and I were obliged to be all day at the office, he ought to have been there to watch our house; but profiting by one of his long absences some one robbed us! Our door was broken in and our provisions of tea and corn stolen, a loss which to us was no slight one.

In the neighbourhood lived several deported Poles, dwelling in Siberia as simple exiles. They used to avail themselves of some saint's day or holiday to visit us, for, with permission of the authorities, they were able to make excursions to Ekaterinski-Zavod. From them we learnt the fate of many other exiles, and we would invoke together the names of the thousands of our dead who had laid down their lives in this land of expiation. The great event, however, of our monotonous existence was the arrival among us of a Polish and Roman Catholic priest. Four of our clergy are permitted by the Russian government to traverse every part of Siberia. Once a year in this way they visit the different establishments where the political offenders dwell, and offer to them the rites and the consolations of their faith. The arrival of one of these servants of

God is made known in each district a few days beforehand, and the faithful collect from different points. The priest during his stay celebrates a mass, gives the Holy Communion, and consecrates the graves of those who during the year have passed into their rest. No honest, and above all no Christian mind, can fail to appreciate the devotion of these four poor priests. It cannot be too much admired, for it carries them along their ceaseless travels, and supports them as, in their sledges, they journey through the intense cold of Siberia, from Tobolsk to Kamtschatka, and from Nertchinsk to the Polar Sea. The father who visited us in 1845 was a Dominican from Samogitia; but he forbore to wear the gown of his order for fear of outraging the Greek orthodoxy of the natives of Siberia. The inspector had the kindness to allow us to hold service in his room, which was the most spacious one in the village. We all went to confession, and then approached the Lord's Table. The crowd was great, for exiles and Polish soldiers arrived from very great distances—even those Poles who were not Roman Catholics did not fail to come with joy to the sacred service, for, whether Catholics or not, to them the mass spoke of the native land so hallowed by them and by all her children.

CHAPTER VI.

SIBERIA.

SIBERIA — HARDSHIPS OF DEPORTATION — BREAKING THE BAN — THE ABBÉ SIEROCINSKI—HIS CONSPIRACY—HIS EXECUTION.

IN this way I had mounted quickly from the lowest to the highest status to which a convict can rise in this establishment of ours on the banks of the Irtiche; and by the beginning of the year 1846 I might almost have fancied myself merely as a recruit of the omnipotent bureaucracy of Russia, sadly banished to these distant realms beneath an inhospitable sky. Very different was this time from the terrible winter of 1844, when I swept the gutters, hewed or carried wood, and lived under one roof with all the offscourings of the human race! And, alas! how many of my brothers, groaning at this moment in the mines of Nertchinsk or in gangs under the lash — how many indeed of those who had been condemned to a punishment less severe than my own, would have thought themselves happy in the position which I had gained at Ekaterinski-Zavod as early as 1846; and from which, however, I was perfectly determined to slip away, at the risk even of encountering the knout and the mysterious dungeons of Akatouia!

The word Siberia embraces a variety of miseries and of trials which the nomenclature (already very rich) of the Russian penal code is yet far from being able to define or even to specify. The two principal categories, deportation (*possilenié*) and penal labour (*katorga*), only indicate, so to speak, the two great exterior lines of an immense *vagueness*, which can be filled up at will. Everything is arbitrary in a sentence which is applied and interpreted by a host of dictators, by a commission at Tobolsk, by a Governor-General in Siberia, by the first and the last comer, by an inspector and by an overseer.

It is one thing to be deported to Viatka, to Tobolsk, or even to Omsk; it is another thing to be sent to Bérézov, as was our warm-hearted Madame Félinska, or to Kamschatka, like Beniowski or General Kopeç, and so many illustrious compatriots; it is another thing, again, to serve in the army of the Caucasus, with the right of promotion, that is to say, with the possibility and the hope of being one day protected from corporal punishments, or of being placed in a Cossack regiment, and sent to the Kirghis frontier. One may get off with the *katorga* in some of the factories or government distilleries, as I did at Ekaterinski-Zavod; but how many miserable beings labour in the horrible mines at Nertchinsk, with irons on their feet, and only hoping for some falling in of the mine to put an end quickly to a life which has nothing more to hope or to expect in this world. The verdigris mines are those which are the most dreaded. The disciplined gangs of Orenbourg, and other places, have the reputation of leading a life yet more awful than that at Nertchinsk. There the rod and the bastinado are the daily bread of our poor students and artisans, who are in general banished thither. There remains the fortress of Akatouia, not far from Nertchinsk, the last punishment reserved for the greatest criminals, and for convicts who revolt, or are taken in the attempt to break their ban. Here it was that Peter Wysoçki, after the bad success of his conspiracy in Siberia, was at last shut up. I know nothing of this mysterious place, and I can say nothing about it, for I have never seen any one who had penetrated its mystery; but I only know that, throughout Siberia, the very name is pronounced with an indescribable terror.

The contempt which the inhabitants of the country very naturally have for the felon, falls back also upon the man who is simply deported; and the exile may often hear himself insulted with the name of *varnak*, an indigenous expression which conveys a concentrated notion of abjectness and infamy. He who is deported has no civil rights, his deposition cannot be taken in any court of justice, and his wife, if he has left one in his native country, may contract a second marriage, because he is counted among the dead. But the legislator who laid down this last law with regard to the exile defeated his own object, which is to increase, by any means, the population of Siberia. The convict or the exiles in its regions can only marry into the worst class, and among the least respectable of its inhabitants; and what is more, his children, if any are born to him, must always remain serfs of the crown. It is true that it is permitted to a wife to follow her husband into Siberia, and that the most pitiless measures have not prevented our seeing such instances of devotion as those of Princess Troubetskoï and Madame Koszakiewicz, with many other Polish ladies; but then the law forbids her again to leave the country, and her children born in this land of exile become, in like manner, royal serfs; and we must point out that there is a peculiarity in amnesties which, even when granted, only apply to the parents. Any children of theirs that have seen the light in Siberia cannot profit by the pardon, but require a special decree. To the Emperor Nicholas, however, these many and sad restrictions did not seem sufficient. In the month of December 1845, he issued a general order for Siberia, which, among many other aggravating clauses, declared all deported persons to be incapable of possessing any property whatever, even chattels and personalty; and ordered that all who were sentenced to penal servitude should, without any exceptions whatever, live in barracks. This command caused a general consternation throughout the country, and the very officials themselves were heard to declare that it was as cruel as it was inopportune, inconvenient, and all but impracticable. I do not know if it ever was rigorously carried into effect; but I may say that these new measures went for a great deal in determining my resolution to fly from Siberia; for I preferred exposing myself to every danger rather than consent voluntarily to return, and be reinstalled in the barracks of the felons.

However hard life in Siberia must of necessity appear to persons under political sentences, I must confess that ordinary criminals do not complain of their lot, and that they sometimes appear to prefer it to their former condition. Serfs and soldiers especially, even when at hard labour, have often said to us, 'What have we to regret? we worked just as hard where we were before, and we were beaten much oftener.' And yet these very men are, in many instances, not less ready to brave the knout and the most terrible punishments, by breaking their ban—so powerful in man is the love of liberty and the love of his own hearth. During my journey in Siberia I had already remarked, and was struck by the fact, that numberless fields of turnips edged the roads on both sides, and that in more than one place these turnips seemed to have been torn up, while the plantations bore the marks of footsteps. I learnt afterwards that the natives keep up the supply of roots on purpose;

and that they are intended for the use of fugitives, and to serve them as food during their nocturnal flights. In villages and hamlets along the high roads the inhabitants take pains to place over night, on their window-ledges, bread, salt, and jars of milk, supplies which are destined for the same persons; and the natives do all this quite as much from self-interest as from charity, for the great trunk roads of Siberia are marauded by runaway convicts, and no man can imagine or describe what perils, what sufferings, and what privations these desperate wretches undergo in order to escape detection. Those who have been branded generally use vitriol or cantharides to get rid of the obnoxious letters; but they seldom fail of being apprehended, and the best fate that can await them is that they should henceforth lead a savage life in the woods, where they become, or rather are again, robbers.

If among the ordinary felons in Siberia the temptation to flight is so strong, among the political exiles and among my fellow-countrymen that temptation is very seldom yielded to. The fear of the knout, and of all corporal punishments, is naturally far stronger among educated persons, or those whose lot is comparatively easy; then, too, the very imperfect knowledge of the language, the routes, and the manners of the country, all unite to dissuade the Poles from so desperate an attempt. The resource which remains for the Russian peasant in his flight does not apply or offer itself to the

Pole; for him it is no object to be lost in the boundless woods, or to hide in some obscure community for life. To obtain his ends, the Pole must reach and cross the confines of another country; and the immensity of the distances to be traversed before this can be achieved is well calculated to make him lose all hope. At the same time, attempts to rise in a body and thus effect their joint deliverance are not at all rare among political exiles. The exploits of Beniowski are remembered by all, and they appeal to many spirits; so that we hear sometimes of a conspiracy, of which the object is to force its way, by dint of arms and numbers, to Persia, China, or simply across the Steppes. Sometimes we have even had the wish to make Siberia itself rise in revolt against the rule of the Tzar. Peter Wysoçki, who first gave the signal of our revolution in 1831, and who, being taken in battle by the Russians, was deported to Nertchinsk, formed such a plan as this; and he expiated his temerity in the fortress of Akatouia. Something similar to his was the conspiracy of the Abbé Sierocinski, so celebrated ever since in Siberian annals. I arrived at Ekaterinski-Zavod some years after that bloody tragedy had been played out; but I have been near Omsk, the stage on which it was acted; I have seen both the eye-witnesses and many of the actors in it, and I have collected from their lips the following details of the dismal story, and I can vouch for their perfect truthfulness.

Previous to the opening scene of our revolution, the Abbé Sierocinski had been superior of the convent of St. Basil, at Owrucz, in Volhynia, and at the same time director of the schools in that place. He took an active part in the movements and political agitation of 1831, and finally fell into the hands of the Russians, when the Emperor Nicholas despatched him to Siberia to serve as a private in one of the regiments of Cossacks; and thus for several years did the former superior of a convent, mounted and in a Cossack dress, pursue the Kirghis of the Steppes with a lance in his hand and with a sabre at his side. Now there existed at Omsk a military college, and one day, being in want of a professor, the authorities bethought themselves of the ex-Basilian, whose capabilities were well known, and who was therefore, especially on account of his knowledge of French and German, recalled from his life on the Steppes. Thus the old head of a convent and the old Cossack became by order of the government a professor in the military school of Omsk, although he did not cease to be a private and to belong to his former regiment. In his new position Sierocinski soon gained all hearts and obtained a large number of acquaintances and friends. His physical constitution was delicate and nervous, but he was gifted by nature with a spirit of rare enterprise and with great courage. He conceived the idea of a vast Siberian conspiracy, into which should be drawn all the exiles, all the soldiers in garrison, and many of those officers in whose minds the ideas and the sufferings of Pestel still survived, while he wished the natives of the country, the Russians, and even the Tatars to take a part in it. There is no doubt that the elements of revolution and revolt are not wanting in Siberia; how and why it is so would take me too long to explain in this place, but those who know the country well are fully aware of this feature in it. Discontent is very general, although the causes and the degrees of it are sundry and manifold, and differ so widely as to be almost contradictory. It is only by the presence of the garrisons that the country is kept safe within the iron-bound circle of the empire. Yet it was precisely in the garrisons themselves that Sierocinski sought and found the great number of sympathisers. His plan was to seize, by means of the conspirators and old deported soldiers, upon the fortresses and principal strongholds; this they were to do at a given signal, and then they were to await the progress of events; while in case of check or defeat they were to retire under arms into the Kirghis Steppes of the *Khanat* of Tachken, where there were many Catholics, or into Boukhara, and from thence press on into the English territories in the East Indian peninsula. The centre of the conspiracy was at Omsk, where they had all the artillery of the place at their disposal. The signal for a general rising was given; but on the very eve of the day on which it was to take place, three of the conspirators revealed everything to the commandant of the place, the same Colonel Degrawe whom I mentioned on my way through Omsk. Sierocinski and his accomplices were seized that same night, and couriers started off in all directions to give orders for arresting an endless number of persons. Thus was the plot discovered at the very moment when it was to have taken effect, and an enquiry began which lasted for a long time. Two commissions, selected and sent down the one after the other, were dissolved without coming to any decision, so obscure and so complicated was the whole affair; and it was only a third board, composed of persons chosen and despatched expressly from St. Petersburg, which succeeded in bringing the trial to an end. By order of the Emperor Nicholas, the Abbé Sierocinski and five of his principal accomplices, among whom was an officer of the wars of the empire more than sixty years of age, by name Gorski, and another Russian, Mélédine, were sentenced to receive each seven thousand lashes (with the rods) and 'without mercy;' in fact, the sentence consisted exactly of these five words, 'Seven thousand lashes without mercy' (*bez postchadi*). The other persons under arrest, about one thousand in all, were condemned some to three thousand, some to two thousand, some to one thousand five hundred lashes and to hard labour for life, while others were simply sent to work in the penal settlements.

The day of execution arrived; it was at Omsk, in the month of March 1837. General Galafeïev, who was celebrated for his cruelty, and who had been sent down from the capital by reason of this shining quality, was at the head of the dismal procession. By daybreak two whole battalions were drawn up in a great open space near the town; one of these was destined to officiate on the principal culprits, the other on those condemned to a smaller number of lashes. I do not intend to detail in all its minutiæ the butchery of that terrible day; I shall but notice the fate of Sierocinski and his five companions. They were led upon the ground, their sentence read out, and they began to run the gauntlet (*skvosstroï*): the blows fell, as the imperial order directed, *without mercy*, and the cries of the sufferers went up to heaven. None of them lived to receive the prescribed number of lashes. All (and they were executed one after the other) after passing through the ranks twice or thrice fell upon the snow, which was crimson with their blood, and then expired. The Abbé Sierocinski had been purposely reserved to the last, in order that he might witness the sufferings of all his friends. When his turn came, and they had stripped him and tied his hands to the bayonet, the surgeon of the battalion came up to him and offered him a flask containing some strengthening drops, but he refused them, saying, 'You may drink my blood, but I will not drink your drops, and I do not want them!' The signal was given, the fatal march began, and the old superior of the Basilian convent chaunted in a loud clear voice, '*Miserere mei, Deus, secundum magnam misericordiam tuam.*' General Galafeïev called to those who struck, 'Harder! harder!' (*pok repché*), and for several minutes the priest's chaunt rose above the whistling of the rods and the *pok repché* cries of the commanding officer . . . . Sierocinski had only passed once through the ranks, that is to say, he had only received one thousand blows, when he fell upon the snow bathed in his own blood, and senseless. In vain they attempted to place him on his feet. He was then laid on a tumbril prepared beforehand for the purpose, and fastened to a support in such a way as to let the blows fall on his back and shoulders, and thus a second time he passed along. When this second passage was gone through, his groans and screams were still audible; but they got gradually weaker, though he did not expire till after the fourth turn; the last three thousand lashes were only laid upon a corpse.

A common grave soon received those who were either killed that day or whose deaths followed soon after their punishments; both Russians and Poles perished, and were buried thus. The friends and relations of those who lie there were permitted to place the symbol of our faith over that memorable tomb; and as late as 1846 one might still behold a great wooden crucifix that stretched its black arms across the steppes, sharply defined against the sparkling and spotless whiteness of their snows.

CHAPTER VII.

THE FLIGHT.

AN ATTEMPTED FLIGHT — MY ROUTE — MY FUNDS — MY DRESS — THE SLEDGE — A RUSSIAN THEFT — THE JOURNEY — IRBITE — ON FOOT — A NIGHT'S LODGING — DANGER — COLD AND FAMINE — PAOUDA — THE IZBOUCHKA — THE CREST OF THE OURALS — LOST IN THE FOREST — SLEEP — ALMS — VELIKI-OUSTIONG.

THERE had been passed by the Emperor Nicholas, in the autumn of the year 1845, a decree, which I have already referred to, and of which the object was to aggravate the condition of the exiles in Siberia, by tightening round them the fetters which time and custom had slackened, and which become loose through the sheer impossibility of enforcing in all its strictness the severe law of the *katorga.* Commissions nominated for the purpose now visited all the penal settlements, and proposed new measures of severity in these places; and the enforced cohabitation in the barracks of all convicts, without any exceptions whatever, was the first point in which it was thought possible and desirable to yield to the present savage disposition of the Tzar. All this induced me to persist in the project which I had already conceived, and which had been long fructifying in my mind. At the very moment in which I had signed at Kiow the formula of the sentence which condemned me to convict labour for the rest of my natural life, I had formed the determination of flying from such an accursed sojourn and lot; and a vague hope of being again seen in the land of the living and among free men had entered my mind. The hard work to which I was set, during the first period of my *katorga*, was not calculated to encourage me; but my hopes rose as soon as I was able to have more relations with men and things, that is, as soon as I became a clerk in the counting-house of the establishment at Ekaterinski-Zavod; and, as early as the summer of 1845, I made two attempts, both of which were frustrated at the very outset, without, however, awakening any suspicion as to my intentions.

It was in the month of June that I noticed a little boat, which lay on the banks of the Irtiche, or floated on its waters, and which was very often forgotten, and not drawn up at night. I thought that I might take advantage of this skiff, and let the stream carry me to Tobolsk; but hardly had I, on one dark night, untied the boat, and given one or two strokes with the oars, than the moon broke through the clouds, flooding the landscape with a dangerous light; and at the same time I heard the sound of the inspector's (*smotritel*) voice, as he walked on the banks, with one or two of the other officials. It was all over with me for that time, and I gently crept back to land. In the following month I espied the same skiff, and in a much more favourable situation — upon a lake, at some distance from our factory, which, through a canal, communicated with the Irtiche. But this second attempt miscarried also, and that by reason of an unsurmountable and natural obstacle; for, at nightfall, the air at this time of year becomes so suddenly cooled that dense columns of vapour are caught up, and they are so thick and so close that one cannot see or distinguish anything at the distance of two feet — a phenomenon which is not uncommon in summer on the waters of Siberia. In vain now did I push my boat to every side and in every direction. The fog prevented my finding the opening of the canal into the Irtiche, and only as the day began to dawn did I discover the issue so long and so vainly sought. It was then too late, and I thought myself lucky in being able to get back to my lodging without let or hindrance; and from that time I abandoned every thought of confiding myself to the inclement waters of the Irtiche, but I set myself not the less persistently to ripen and consolidate the plans for my intended flight.

The first point to be considered, and upon which I had first to fix my attention, was the direction I ought to select for my perilous journey. The trunk road, which was the most natural, and presented itself before all the others, and which, from the heart of Siberia, would have taken me into the centre of Russia Proper, was, as I saw at once, the one least fitted for my purpose. The law there maintains a constant and active watch, and is assisted very often both by the zeal and by the rapacity of the natives, who sometimes find it profitable to take a shot from behind a hedge at some convict breaking through his ban. Indeed, among the people, especially among the Tatars, there is a popular saying, 'He who kills a squirrel only gets one skin, but he who kills a *varnak* gets three — his coat, his shirt, and his skin.' Many other routes, of course, were to be found, and in very different directions. I could traverse Eastern Siberia, by Irkoutsk and Nertchinsk, as far as the Sea of Okhotsk, and there seek some vessel, which would have carried me to the ports of the United States or to California. I might turn towards the south, crossing the steppes of the Kirghis, and arriving in Boukhara, whence I could reach the confines of British India. On the other side, the Oural River, if I had the good fortune to touch its source, might have carried me on its waters into the Caspian Sea, and allowed me to take refuge in Daghestan, among the Circassians. Finally, a fourth route remained to me, by which, after crossing the Oural chain, and reaching Oufa, in the government of Orenbourg, I might find the Volga, at a point somewhat lower than that at which a canal unites it with the Don, and the latter river would have led me to the Sea of Azov; and then, according to my wish, I might have repaired either to Turkey in Europe or to Turkey in Asia, or even into the western parts of Circassia. For reasons which it would take me too long to set down here, I found that I ought to give up all and each of these four tracks; and I resolved to seek for my liberty by way of the north, and across the Oural Mountains, and to press on over the steppes of Petchora and Archangel. This path was the least frequented, and for this reason only it was the safest. Moreover, it had the immense advantage of being the shortest; for, if I once touched at Archangel, it appeared to me an impossibility that, among the four or five thousand ships in the port, mostly all foreign ones, not one should be found willing to take on board a political refugee, flying from the *katorga*. It was then to these districts of the far north, and to the shores and borders of the White Sea, that I now directed my most minute investigations, although I also lost no opportunity of acquiring information as to any of the other directions, in case chance or fate should impel me in their way. Our bagnio was cosmopolitan enough in its character, and soon, from convicts gathered from all parts of the empire, I acquired a very exact knowledge of the manners and customs of all the Russias; but my conversations with the merchants and travellers, who, from north and south, from east and from west, passed through or frequented Ekaterinski-Zavod, chiefly helped to complete the education of a scholar who appeared to be careless and apathetic, but who was really greedy for every bit of information he could extract.

The exile who combines in his mind different plans of escape is absorbed in an amazing variety of calculations about very small matters, and it is only the sum total of his thoughts and designs which can present any objects of interest to the reader. Slowly and with difficulty I succeeded in gathering together the articles which I knew to be indispensable to my journey. Among these, and in the first rank, figured a passport. Of these documents there are two kinds in use among the Siberians, for these people have the taste, which is common among all the Russians, for making long peregrinations in the empire. There is first a pass, which is good only for distances comparatively short, and which has only a short time to run; there is also the passport of great importance, which is a very different matter, being issued by the higher powers and on stamped paper — it is known as the *plakatny*. I succeeded in forging both the one and the other, for, by men who have once learnt to like and to cultivate them, certain arts are carried on and plied even in the convicts' barrack; and thus it was that I obtained from a friend, a clever coiner of false money, and in return for a few roubles, a capital seal with the arms of his imperial majesty. Then as to the sheet of stamped paper, it was easy for me to appropriate one from the mass which I blackened every day in the office for the public use, and thus I had a *plakatny* at my service. Slowly and with difficulty too I procured the dress and the accessories needful for my disguise, which was to be effected both morally and physically, for I had to transform myself into a native, a 'man of Siberia' (*sbirski tchelovièk*), as they say in Russia. Ever since my arrival at Ekaterinski-Zavod, or rather even before that time, and from the time I left Kiow, I had purposely allowed my beard to grow, and it had now got to a respectable and perfectly orthodox length. After many attempts I furthermore became possessed of a wig, a Siberian one, be it understood — one of those sheepskins with the curls inside, which are worn in this country to keep out the intense cold; and, thanks to these means, I trusted to make my personal appearance such as was most unlikely to be recognised. In the last place, I may mention that, after deducting the cost of these articles, there remained to me the sum of 180 roubles (in assignats *), that is, about 200 francs — a very slender sum for so long a journey, and one which, through a sad accident, was yet to be greatly diminished.

I had not disguised from myself in any way the difficulties of my undertaking, nor yet the dangers to which at every step I was to be exposed. I also knew

* Paper currency.

that I could not even reckon on the poignard which I carried as a last and perfectly reliable means of safety, for, in spite of much that one hears, it is not always in one's power to put an end to one's life. I might be arrested in my sleep, or in some one of those times of moral prostration which follow on very prolonged effort and tension of body or of mind, and when a man, by loss of nervous power, is prevented from disposing of his existence. One thought, however, sustained me, and while it added greatly to the difficulties of my situation, it much lightened my conscience — it was the vow I had made not to reveal my secret to a single human being until, standing on a free soil, I could do so with safety to them. I determined not to ask for help, protection, or advice from any living soul until I had passed the limits of the Tzar's dominions, and rather to give up my own hoped-for salvation than to become the cause of peril and suffering to one of my fellow-men. During my stay at Kaminieç I had implicated more than one of my poor compatriots in my own bitter lot, but then I believed myself to be on a mission for the general weal: now, the only object I had in view was my personal safety at the time, and my freedom hereafter; and I resolved that, for their accomplishment, I would rely on no one but on myself. God has vouchsafed to me the strength to persevere in this resolution to the end. It seemed to me to be the only honest and justifiable course; and it has perhaps been on account of this vow, made from the very starting point, that He has extended over me His protecting Arm.

By the last days of January my preparations were finished, and the time seemed peculiarly favourable for my start, because there was soon to be held at Terbite, at the foot of the Oural range, one of those great fairs which are peculiar to Eastern Russia, where centres of trade are few and far between. The immense distances which have to be crossed, and the difficulties in the way of even the most ordinary communications between one place and another, make fairs of this sort a real *colluvies gentium*, and the roads are covered with innumerable trains of merchandise, and with a great concourse of travellers. Flattering myself with the hope that I might be lost in such a movement of people and tribes, I lost no time in profiting by the circumstance, and on February 8th, 1846, I set out.

I had on three shirts, the coloured one being, after the Russian fashion, pulled over the trowsers: I had a waistcoat and trowsers of thick cloth, and over all a little burnous (*armiak*) of sheepskin, well tallowed, which hung down to my knees, while great boots with tops strongly tarred completed my costume. A girdle of red, white, and black worsted was tied round my waist, and over my wig I had one of those red velvet caps, edged with fur, which are worn on holiday time by Siberian peasants of any affluence, and by commercial travellers. Besides all this, I was wrapped in a wide pelisse, of which the collar, turned up and tied by a red handkerchief round the neck, served less to keep out the cold than to hide my face. I carried a bag in my hand, and in it I had put a second pair of boots, a fourth shirt, a pair of blue trowsers, such as are worn in the country in summer, some bread, and some dried fish. A large dagger was slipped into the sheath of my right boot; my money was under my waistcoat in assignats of five or ten roubles; and, to conclude, in my hands, which were covered with stout gloves of skin, with the hair inside, I held a strong knotted stick.

Thus equipped I stole away at eventide from the settlement of Ekaterinski-Zavod by a cross-road. It was freezing very hard, and the rime which hung in the air sparkled in the moonlight. I soon passed my Rubicon, the Irtiche, whose frozen shield I crunched under my feet, and with hasty steps, which the weight of my dress alone checked, I took the road to Tara, a small market town at about twelve kilomètres from the place where I had been kept. The winter nights, I said to myself, are very long in Siberia; how many miles shall I be able to make before daylight appears to make them aware of my flight? and what shall I do when it dawns?

I had hardly crossed the Irtiche when I heard the sound of a sledge coming up behind me. I shuddered, but determined to await the nocturnal traveller, and, as happened more than once during my hazardous wanderings, that which I dreaded as a danger became the unexpected means of saving myself. 'Where are you going?' asked the peasant who drove the sledge, and who had drawn up beside me.

'To Tara. Where do you come from?'

'From the hamlet of Zalivina. Give me sixty kopeks (tenpence) and I will take you to Tara, for I am going there myself.'

'No; that is too dear, but I will give you fifty kopeks if you like to take me for that.'

'Well, so be it; look sharp, my friend!'

I seated myself beside him, and we started at a gallop. My companion was in a hurry to get home; the road covered by snow, which the frost had hardened, was as smooth as a mirror, and the piercing cold seemed to give wings to the horses. At the end of half an hour we were at Tara, where my peasant put me down in one of the streets of the town and went his way. Now alone, I went up to the first posting-house, and called in Russian fashion through the window, as loud as I could:

'Have you any horses?'

'Where are they to go?'

'To the fair at Irbite.'

'Yes, we have some.'

'A pair?'

'Yes, a pair.'

'How much a verste?'

'Eight kopeks.'

'I won't give so much; say six kopeks.'

'What can we say? Done! Presently.'

In a few minutes the horses were ready and put to a sledge. 'Where do you come from?' they asked me.

'From Tomsk: I am a clerk of N——' (I named somebody), my principal has gone on before me to Irbite; but, you see, I had to stay behind for some little affairs of my own, and now I am horribly late, and I am afraid my chief will be angry; if you will drive quickly you shall have something for yourself.'

The peasant whistled, and the horses went off like an arrow. Suddenly the sky became overcast, and a heavy snow falling, the peasant not only lost his way but could not find it again. After having wandered about in many wrong directions, we were obliged to halt and pass the rest of the night in the forest. I pretended to be furiously angry, and my driver, full of excuses, began to ask my pardon. I shall not attempt to describe the agony of that night, passed as it was sitting in a sledge, in the middle of a snow storm, and at the distance of at most four leagues from Ekaterinski-Zavod: at every moment I seemed to hear the bells of the *kibitkas* that were in full pursuit of me. At last the day began to redden in the east. 'Now, go back to Tara,' I said to the peasant; 'I will take another sledge there, and you, you fool! shall not have a farthing, and I will hand you over to the police for having made me lose my time in this way.' The countryman, much abashed, turned to go back to Tara, but hardly had we gone a verste when he stopped, looked all round, and pointing out some traces of a road under the heap of snow, he cried:

'There is the road we ought to have taken!'

'Get on, then,' I said, 'and thank God!'

From this moment my man did his best to make up for the lost time; but a horrible idea crossed my mind, I remembered our hapless Colonel Wysoçki, who, after having been detained as I was the whole night in a wood, was given up to the gendarmes by his driver. Perhaps my peasant, I said to myself, meditates to betray me in like manner, and my hand mechanically sought my dagger; but it was a vain terror and an unjust suspicion. He soon stopped at a friend's house, where I had some tea, and where I was provided at the same rate with horses to continue my journey. Thus I went on my way, changing horses at very reasonable sums, until I arrived late at night at a village called Soldatskaïa, where I became the victim of a theft as audacious on the part of the thief as it was painful to me. I happened to have no change to pay the driver, and along with him I squeezed my way into a pot-house where there were a number of tipsy people, for it was near the end of the carnival. I pulled two or three bank notes from under my waistcoat, and I was going to give them to the landlord to get them changed, when a sudden move in the crowd, whether purposely or not I cannot say, shoved me back from the table on which I had laid down the papers, and they were carried off in a second. In vain I called out, the thief was not to be discovered, and as I did not dare really to summon the police to my assistance, I was obliged to resign myself to my fate, although I had lost some forty roubles in notes, and (what added much more to my regrets, I might almost say to my terror) two papers had disappeared with them, which were of inestimable value to me, the one a memorandum on which I had marked with the greatest minuteness all the towns and villages through which I had to pass on my way to Archangel, the other that passport on stamped paper which it had cost me so much trouble to fabricate . . . . . .

Thus, at the commencement, and in the first day of my flight, I had lost a quarter of the small sum which I had saved for my travels, the note which was to have been the map and guide of my wanderings, and the *plakatny*, the only document which I could show to disarm the first suspicions of any curious persons. I was in despair!

One thing above all others was I believe the main cause of the success of the perilous task of my evasion, compelling me to persevere in spite of all obstacles and mistakes, and obliging me to take courage in spite of myself — this was the manifest impossibility of abandoning my undertaking. Having once fled from Ekaterinski-Zavod, I should certainly incur the same fate, whether captured at Tara or among the Oural Mountains, among the steppes of Petchora or in the port of Archangel, while every step I took brought me nearer to safety and deliverance. Thus no room was left for hesitation or regret, and, in spite of the irreparable loss which I had just sustained, I held on my way, and soon, striking into the high road to Irbite, I found, in the sudden animation of the landscape, a sight calculated to distract my eyes, and to inspire my mind with a certain degree of confidence. All over that vast and snow-covered plain, to the left of which ever since I passed Tioumen the wooded slopes of the Oural chain began to be defined, swarmed an innumerable mass of sledges, either going or returning from the fair. They were full of goods and *yamstchiks* (or peasants who undertake to carry merchandise), and were whirled along by those Siberian horses whose pace is only to be equalled by the skill of their drivers. The month of February is a harvest time for the dwellers in these districts, who make, by the hire of their horses and sledges at the time of the fair at Irbite, the largest of their yearly gains. They display then all the good humour and the noisy gaiety which can animate an active population at the end of the dead season of the year. I mingled my voice with the sharp cries and piercing calls of the *yamstchiks*; I greeted every passenger, regarding each in the bottom of my heart as an involuntary auxiliary of my flight, for the more the number of men, horses, and sledges increased, the more I took courage. How, I asked myself, could they distinguish in this vast crowd of merchants, bagmen, clerks and peasants one solitary political criminal who seeks his liberty by flight? how pursue me through this moving and ever-changing Babel? It would be about as likely and as useful to try (as we say in our proverb of the Ukraine) 'to follow and catch the wind upon the steppes.'

In order to make the reader understand how rapid was my flight, which differed in no way from the pace of the other Siberians on the road, it will suffice to say that, on the third day of my evasion, and in spite of having spent a night in the forest of Tara, I found myself, late in the evening, at the gates of Irbite, 4,000 kilometres distant from Ekaterinski-Zavod. 'Stop, and show your passport!' called the sentry; luckily, he added immediately, 'Give me twenty kopeks, and through with you.' It may be imagined with what alacrity I satisfied the demands of a law so opportunely modified, and I soon reached an inn, where at first I was refused admittance, because there was no room. After some time, however, I was received, on declaring that I only wished to pass one night on the premises, being sure, I said, of finding out next day where my master was, with whom I was to lodge for the rest of the time. I went out soon after, pretending to go to the police station, and, when I reappeared, said I had left my papers there, and would have them returned to me next day. The *izba*, or large room in which we all sat, was as full of *yamstchiks* as it could hold, and the smell of tar was enough to stifle one. I talked much of my principal, of *our* affairs, and did my best to share in a noisy meal of Siberian dishes; that is to say, of turnip soup, dried fish, oatmeal gruel mixed with oil, and pickled cabbages. When the repast was over, each man paid his share of the reckoning to the landlord, and then prepared a bed for himself as best he could in the *izba*. Some stretched themselves upon the stove, some on straw, some on the ground, some on benches, and some under them. I did as I saw the others do, but sleep never came near my eyes; so many hopes and so many fears chased each other through my mind, that rest was impossible.

Very early in the morning I rose, and, like all my companions, performed, in the most orthodox fashion, the three bows which every one is expected to make to the holy images that never fail to occupy the corners of a Russian dwelling; then, taking my bag on my back, I went out under pretence of seeking my principal. In spite of the earliness of the hour, the square was already very animated. Irbite is a town of a tolerably pleasing appearance, in spite of its houses being built entirely of wood. The streets are wide, the squares and market-places spacious. On every side stood booths constructed after the national fashion of thin planks, and intended to last only during the fair. Sledges, drawn up like regiments, contained bales of goods; and those which had been already emptied were now piled up in heaps, one on the top of the other. I am sure that there were several thousands of these vehicles. For my part, I did little more than go across the town, as many reasons weighed with me, and prevented my stopping there for any length of time — the chief reason being my fear of meeting some one of the many acquaintances I had made at Ekaterinski-Zavod. I had no wish to put my disguise to the proof, unless there was an absolute necessity for so doing. I therefore bought some loaves of bread and some salt in a shop, put them into my bag, and left the town by an opposite gate from the one by which I had entered it, and where the sentry did not, luckily, think it right to ask me any questions whatever. The expenses which I had incurred in hiring horses to Irbite, as well as the theft of which I had been the victim, had seriously diminished my slender finances; and at this moment I stood possessed of no more than 75 roubles in assignats, and how was I to reach France by means of so small a sum? It was clear that for the future I must trust to my own legs, not to say to my own hands also, if I chanced to come in the way of earning anything in my travels.

The winter of this year, 1846, was one of great severity, and the snow fell in such quantities that I saw more than one pretty solidly built house fall in from its weight; indeed, within the memory of the Siberians, there had not been so hard a winter. On the morning, however, of the day on which I left Irbite, the air appeared to me to be rather milder; but then the snow began to fall, and it came down in such style, so thick and so heavy, that I could not see where I was going. It was a strange sensation to stand thus alone in the middle of these wastes, of which the silence is almost always unbroken, and to be covered with snow flakes, from which I vainly tried to shake myself free, while walking became very fatiguing in the soft heaps which got bigger at every moment. I managed, however, not to lose my way, and every now and then a *yamstchik* or two, driving past in his sledge, helped to clear it before me again, till, about mid-day, the snow began to cease, and my march became less impeded. As a general rule, I avoided the villages, but when it was necessary to pass one, I walked straight along the street, as if I belonged to the country, and did not require to ask my way; and if grave doubts arose in my mind as to which road to take, it was only at the last house of the hamlet that I ventured to ask any questions. When I felt hungry, I pulled a piece of frozen bread out of my bag, and ate it as I walked along, or sat resting at the foot of a tree, in the most remote part of a wood. When I was thirsty, I sought to slake my thirst at the holes in the ice on pools and ponds, which the Siberians constantly make in order to water their cattle; or, sometimes I had to content myself with letting snow dissolve in my mouth, although that plan was far from being a satisfactory one. My first day on foot out of Irbite was very trying, and the evening found me completely exhausted. My heavy dress had added greatly to my distress in walking, and yet I knew that I dared not part with it. When night fell, I sought the heart of the forest, and there prepared a sleeping-place for myself. I knew how the Ostiaks cover themselves when asleep in their frozen deserts. They simply scoop out a deep hole in a big snow wreath, and there find a bed, which, though certainly hard, is not the less a perfectly warm one. I did in like fashion, and soon found the repose of which I stood greatly in need.

On waking next morning, I felt extremely uncomfortable, and found that my feet were frozen. Not quite familiar with the niceties of Ostiak bed making, I had been imprudent enough, in covering myself with my pelisse, to keep the furry side next to my body, and the heat thus developed had completely melted the snow, and exposed my feet to the low temperature of the dawn. I resolved to profit by this lesson for the future, and, in the meantime, tried to bring the circulation back by walking and running, in which I was, fortunately, successful. By mid-day, to my sorrow, the wind rose very high — a truly Siberian wind, dry and icy, seeming to blind one as it cuts one's eyes, and sweeping the heaps of snow before it, so as to obliterate in a few minutes every trace of the best beaten road. The natives are accustomed, as soon as winter sets in, to mark their tracks on each side by pines and pine branches stuck into the snow at short distances from one another; but this season the avalanches had been so numerous that, in most places, they more than hid the signal branches. I presently perceived that I had completely lost my way. Plunging about in the snow up to my waist, sometimes up to my neck, I began to think I must perish there from hunger and from cold; but by evening I came on a road again, and, mercifully for me, it was the very one I ought to take, and for which I was in search. It was quite late, when I saw a small detached cottage, near a village, with a young woman standing on its doorstep. The hope of finding a resting-place got the better of all my hesitation; I went up to the woman, and asked her if she would give me a night's lodging. She made no difficulty about it, and took me into the *izba*, where her old mother sat. I made her the usual greeting, and, in reply to the usual questions 'where I came from,' and 'whether the Lord God was leading me?' I replied that I came from the government of Tobolsk, and that I was on my way to Bohotole, to look for work. The establishment at Bohotole is an iron foundry belonging to the Russian government, and situated far north of Verkhouterie, among the Oural Mountains; it attracts great numbers of workpeople from the provinces of Perm and of Tobolsk. While the women prepared some food for me, I spread my clothes and my linen before the fire, and, having dried them, and appeased my hunger, I stretched myself on a bench with an indescribable sense of comfort and happiness. I believed that I had neglected no precautions, for, after repeating to myself my Catholic prayers, I had made the orthodox triple salutation, or *poklony*, to the holy images; and yet some suspicions had been awakened in the minds of these women. I learnt afterwards that the sight of the linen I had tried to dry was the exciting cause; they thought me too well provided to be a Russian artisan, for I had no less than four shirts!

Sleep was just stealing upon me, when I heard some whisperings that disturbed me; and, all of a sudden, in came three peasants, one of whom said in a low voice:

'Where is he?'

The younger of the women pointed to where I lay. Presently, I was first called, and then roughly shaken up by these men, who asked if I had a passport. I was obliged to make some answer, so, sitting up, I retorted:

'And what right have you to ask for my passport? Are any of you *golova* (an official)?'

'It is true that we are not; we are only the inhabitants of the place.'

'And, as inhabitants of the place, what right have you to attack houses, and to walk in to ask for passports? How am I to know who you are, and whether you are not likely enough to steal my papers? But, keep yourselves easy, you will find presently with whom you have to do.'

'But I tell you we are neighbours, country folks here.'

'Is that true?' said I, turning to the mistress of the house; and on getting a sign from her in the affirmative, I went on, "Well then, in that case, I will answer you. My name is Lavrenti Kouzmine, of the government of Tobolsk, and I am going to the iron foundries at Bohotole to look for work; and this is not the first time, by any means, that I have been this way.'

I then went into more circumstantial details, and concluded by exhibiting my passport. It was a mere pass, since, alas! my *plakatny* no longer existed, and it never could have imposed upon any official; but as it had a seal, the sight of that essential convinced this portion of the public, who then began to ask me a hundred questions about the fair at Irbite, and many other things. At last they departed, having wished me a good night's rest, and excusing themselves for having troubled me by saying, 'You see it was very excusable, because we thought it was a case of a runaway convict: they sometimes pass this way.' The remainder of the night passed tranquilly away; and on the following morning, I took leave of the two women whose hospitality had so nearly proved fatal to me.

The incident which I have just related carried with

it one sad conviction, which was, that I could not reckon on a shelter for any future nights without clearly exposing myself to very serious dangers, and that, until things should take a new turn, the Ostiak couch must be my only bed; and so with the Ostiak couch I contented myself, during the whole of my journey across the Oural Mountains, and until my arrival at Véliki-Oustiong — that is to say, from the middle of February to the first days of the month of April 1846. Three or four times only did I venture to crave hospitality for the night in some lonely hut; and that was only because I was exhausted by some fifteen or twenty days passed in the forest, and my strength was so far gone that I was hardly conscious of what I was, what I said, or what I did. All the other nights I contented myself with digging an earth for sleeping in — only I had become more cunning, and I had also acquired a greater dexterity in preparing my nocturnal refuge. I had noticed that, in the depths of the forests, the snow hardly reaches to the foot of the great trees; and that, as it accumulates, it still leaves an empty space round the trunk, which soon becomes a pretty deep cavity. I let myself slip down the stem of the tree into the hollow thus formed, which was not unlike a well. Having arrived at the bottom, I tried with my stick to throw some of the snow out of the aperture at the top, and thus made a vault, which covered and sheltered me perfectly. But very often I could not manage these nightly buildings; the snow would be too light and dry, or, at another time, the roof thus laboriously contrived would fall in with a crash. I had then to seat myself close to the tree; and leaning my back against its trunk, thus slept, or rather dozed, for the night. When the cold became so great that I felt my limbs growing numbed, I had to get up, and run hither and thither. It was too dark either to follow or to find the road; but exercise, at all risks, I must have, to revive my animal heat. On more than one occasion, I have lain down tired, and simply let myself be covered by the falling snow; this was, perhaps, the warmest cover of any; but I always found it difficult, in the morning, to shake myself loose of this white winding-sheet. By degrees, I got accustomed to this way of sleeping; and sometimes, when night fell, I would find myself turning into the thickest part of the woods, as to some familiar resting-place; though at other times, I must confess, this savage life seemed to me all but unbearable. The absence of any human dwellings, the want of warm victuals — sometimes even of frozen bread (my only food, for days together) — would make me feel that, not very far from my side, there lay in wait for me those two hideous spectres — Cold and Famine — whose names we are so apt to take in vain at every little trifle which makes us uncomfortable! In such moments, what I most dreaded were the sudden attacks of sleep, which would come on me unawares. These I knew full well to be the forerunners of death, and against them I struggled with all the little strength that remained to me. The craving for something warm to eat or drink was very great; and it was often with the utmost difficulty that I refrained from going into some hut, to beg a little of the turnip broth which they make so much in Siberia.

After leaving behind me Verkhouterie — the last town (it is a wooden one) which I was to pass on my way to the eastern slopes of the Ourals, and where I took good care not to stop, I fell in with six young Russians — a meeting which was very fortunate for me, as from them I obtained various pieces of useful information. By their dress, and indeed by their speech, I saw that they did not belong to this part of the country, and that they were not even Siberians. When I asked them, they told me that they came from the government of Archangel, from the district of Mezen, on the very borders of the Frozen Sea; and that they were on their way to the province of Tobolsk, to push their fortunes as veterinary surgeons. These young men had pleasant faces, very fair complexions, and hair so light as to have a silvery tinge, like well-dressed flax. Indeed, had they not had clear blue eyes, they might have passed for Albinos. They told me that the country from which they came was very poor — miserably poor. In short, nothing grew there, either wheat, oats, or barley; and the inhabitants lived on fish, getting bread only from Archangel. The sight of men who had come so far, and come on foot, gave me fresh courage and hope. I, in my turn, could give them many details about Siberia (though not about the districts in which I had dwelt), and I told them where they were likely to find the greatest number of horses. Nature seems often to play strange games in distributing men as she does over this globe. To these miserable dwellers on the most remote shores of the Frozen Sea, Siberia appears as a land of promise—the Eldorado of their dreams of happiness; and thither they emigrate in bands, and in whole families, to look for more lucrative labour, and in search of a more clement sky.

I do not know how many days I may have spent in thus climbing the woody but snow-clad heights of the Oural chain. The uniformity of the way, and the repetition of the same accidents of travel made me at last lose all count of time. I only know that at Paouda, far set in the heart of the mountains, I dared for the second time since I had left Irbite to sleep in a human dwelling, and that then for the third time since that date I tasted some warm food. Even this little good fortune I owed to a happy chance. I passed through the village very late in the evening, and as I went by a house in which the lights still burnt, I suddenly heard a voice call, 'Who goes there?'

'A traveller.'

'Have you far to go?'

'Oh, very very far.'

'Well, if you like, you may turn in and sleep with us for the night.'

'The good God reward you! But shall I not trouble you?'

'How trouble us? No one is gone to bed yet.'

I crossed the hospitable threshold, and found in the house two kind worthy beings, a husband and his wife. They gave me a modest Siberian meal, which to me seemed a feast fit for Lucullus; but what I enjoyed most was the being able to take off my clothes, which I had not been able to do for so many nights, while I camped under the stars. They asked me a good many questions, and I was ready to reply to them, saying that I belonged to the district of Tobolsk, and that I was on my way to Solikamsk, on the other side of the Ourals, that I had a relation there, and that the times being hard, he had written to me that I might find work in the salt works there. These good folks then began to talk of their own lot, and to complain of it heartily. It appeared that they were 'peasants of the works' (*pozavodskoïe krestyany*), or serfs, liable from generation to generation to be impressed for statute labour in the different government factories, of which there are a great many in the Oural districts. Formerly there were works at Paouda itself, but since they had been done away with, the serfs were now obliged to go to labour as far as

Bohotole; from this liability neither women nor persons above the age of fourteen years are exempt, and it may be supposed that such conditions were severely felt. On the next day my hosts would not let me depart till I had breakfasted with them, and they steadily refused to accept of the money which I pressed upon them. What a warm and hearty farewell did we take of each other! but my ease of mind vanished when the good man of the house, just as he parted from me, and was giving me some final instructions as to my road, added, 'at any rate, a little beyond Paouda you will come to the military station; they will ask for your papers there, and they will not fail to give you all the information you can require.'

It may be believed that I neglected no efforts not to come in the way of any such sources of knowledge. I struck aside and went by hill and by dale, now and then up to my neck in snow, and did not regain the high road till I had left the tutelary guard station far behind me. Thus I went on for several days, only buying bread at rare intervals at the *izbouchka*, which at great distances from one another and from time to time I met with on my way.

Izbouchka are little houses built at great intervals for the accommodation of travellers, and are to be found from the Oural Mountains to Veliki-Oustiong; you find there bread, salt fish, turnips, radishes, cabbages and *kvass* (a liquor made from cider), and sometimes, though rarely, brandy. In some of these inns, that is to say, in the more spacious ones, there is to be found hay and corn for the horses. Their owners buy in the provisions, and it is said make a good profit on these strange hotels, which in general are kept by one old man, or by a couple as miserable as they are decrepid. One evening I met a train of *yamstchiks* who were on their way back from the fair at Irbite, and were halting to rest their horses; but I did not remain with them. I knew that I was nearing the summit of the Oural range, and a superstitious feeling impelled me towards it as to the culminating point of my fate. At last I reached the top of the pass. It was a fine night; the moon illuminated with its full splendour a glorious but fantastic scene, where the gnarled shadows of the trees, and of gigantic masses of rocks, were flung far upon the immense expanse of snow. A silence so solemn as to be almost religious in its unbroken stillness reigned around, except when at times a dry metallic sound struck upon the ear as the stones cracked and split from the intensity of the frost; and yet nature, rude and wild as she appeared to me at this time, and under this dress, was to me, alas! a friend more pitiful than any of the civilised beings around; *she*, at least, never asked me for my passport! It was with difficulty that I kept my mind from dwelling on spirits from another world, from recurring to the fairy sprites and other tales to which I had been accustomed during my childhood in the Ukraine, so much were they recalled by the strange and sinister-looking forms which the moon revealed, while in her rays their outlines assumed monstrous proportions. Indeed, in the eyes of any Ukraine child might not I myself have easily passed for no less a person than the 'great demon of the night,' as I stood there in my strange dress, beard, eyebrows, and moustaches, all crusted with frosty rime, wandering thus among the shadows of the forest, myself but another shade?

From any more prolonged contemplation of the landscape cold obliged me to abstain, and I soon began to descend the western slopes of that immense barrier which nature has interposed between Siberia and Russia in Europe. During the course of next day the *yamstchiks* came up with me again, and I had an opportunity of seeing with what marvellous skill they drive their horses along roads which are all but impracticable. They had thirty sledges, to each of which a solitary horse was harnessed, and the whole string was driven by seven *yamstchiks*. The way was narrow and hedged on each side by walls of snow as high as a man, and in these both men and horses would occasionally disappear. When one train met another coming in the opposite direction, the train which was the smaller, or the least heavily laden, would then plunge into the snowy wall; and I do not exaggerate when I say that sometimes after a plunge the horses' ears alone remained visible.

Having completed this peculiar evolution, the drivers of both trains would then apply themselves to pulling both sledges and horses out of the wreath. But even these occurrences were as nothing compared to the accidents caused by the bogs and quagmires which are so frequent on these routes. The horses, however, are perfectly accustomed to all obstacles, and they throw themselves into the ravines, and then allow themselves to be extricated by their drivers. The difficulties of the passage of the Oural chain are so great that these intrepid men cannot make more than twenty verstes a day, and as far as Véliki-Oustiong I found all along the wayside the corpses of horses that had given in from fatigue. What the *yamstchiks* themselves seem capable of enduring in the way of privations and fatigues is something truly incredible.

I reached Solikamsk in the beginning of March. It lies at the foot of the western declivity of the mountains. Without making any stay there I pursued my way by the steppe of Petchora, tending towards Véliki-Oustiong, by way of Tcherdine, Kaï, Lalsk and Nochel. The country was no longer hilly, but there was now as before the same immensity of snow, the same thick woods, the same winds and storms of ice; for me also there were the same weary marches and the same furtive purchases of bread at the unfrequent *izbouchka*, and the same earths toilsomely constructed for each night's repose. One discovery, however, was an unspeakable boon to me. I had remarked that in these depopulated regions the foot travellers, who were so few and far between, were in the habit, when overtaken by night in the woods, of lighting a large fire, and of keeping it blazing till daybreak. I did this several times, and the flaming logs in the middle of a frozen desert not only warmed but cheered me; but this would not do for a roadside diversion, and I only ventured on it when deep in the forest.

I always steered clear of the towns which lay in my way; but one day, when, to avoid Tcherdine, I had wandered long in the woods, I completely lost my way, and had not a notion to which side to direct my steps. A hurricane of snow made me literally pirouette, and covered me all over with its flakes, while, as a climax to my misfortunes, I had no more bread in my bag. I rolled in the snow with convulsive movements; I could not sleep, but I prayed for death. When day again dawned, the sky cleared, the weather was fair, my pains had abated, but my strength was utterly exhausted. I strove to guide my course by the sun, or by noticing the moss which grew on the north sides of the trees, and dragged myself on for a while by help of my stick, till the pangs of hunger again attacked me. Wearied with the strife, and with a face bathed in tears of weakness, hunger, and despair, I let myself drop at the root of a tree. By degrees sleep stole upon me, and it was accompanied by a humming noise in my head, which threw all my ideas into the wildest confusion. Strange to say, I became totally insensible, and only the tearing pains inside gave me any sense of life. How long I lay in this state I know not; I was suddenly roused from it by a strong man's voice. I opened my eyes, a stranger stood before me.

'What are you doing there?'

'I have lost my way.'

'Where do you come from?'

'From Tcherdine; I am on a pilgrimage to Solovetsk; but the storm made me lose my way, and I have had nothing to eat for several days.'

'I am not surprised at it; we belong to this part of the country, and yet we often lose our way; you should never have set out in such weather: drink a little of this.'

He put a wooden bottle to my lips; I drank a mouthful of brandy, which revived me instantly, but so burned the stomach that it made me start with pain till I executed a perfect tarentelle.

'Come, be quiet, can't you!' cried the stranger, and he offered me some bread and dried fish, which I devoured with a sort of frenzy; I then sat down again at the foot of my tree, and my companion seated himself alongside of me. He was a trapper by profession (*promychlennik*), and after having secured his prey, he was returning home, with his gun slung over his shoulder, and with pattens on his feet. When I got a little calmer, he offered to conduct me to the neighbouring *izbouchka*. 'I thank you with all my heart; may the good Lord reward you for all you have done!'

'So we are a Christian, are we? Well, step on now, and never give in!'

I got up with great difficulty, for my head was swimming round; but summoning all my strength I followed my leader, and I steadied myself from time to time on his arm, till at length we stood once more on the road from which I had wandered, and there the trapper, having commended me to God, left me, disappearing into the thickets. I could see the *izbouchka* at some distance, and so great was my joy at the sight of it, that I believe I should have walked up to it, had I known that gendarmes were waiting at the door to arrest me. I managed to get as far as the said door, but when I had crossed the threshold, my strength failed me, I fell on the ground, and rolled under a bench. Then, after a dead faint of some minutes, I came to myself again, and asked to have something warm to eat or drink. Some turnip soup was given to me, but this, although tormented by hunger, I was hardly able to swallow, and towards midday I fell asleep on a bench, where I slept till about the same hour on the following day, when my landlord in alarm shook me up. He was a kind honest man, and his affability towards me was redoubled when he heard that I was on a pious pilgrimage, as far as the Holy Isle in the White

Sea. I was still quite wet, and my garments had to be dried at the stove; but sleep, rest and warmth had already cured me. I was able to eat something, and start again on my travels, sorely against the wishes of mine host, who begged me to rest one day longer in his house. I had to give some reasons to account for persisting in my resolution, and I promised him solemnly that on my return from the goal of my pilgrimage I would pay him a second visit.

These *izbouchka* were a constant source of temptation to me during my arduous journey to Véliki-Oustiong. How often, after many days of walking, have I passed before one of those hospitable abodes, and had to struggle with the longing I felt, not for a night's shelter, as that was a happiness which I could not aspire, but at least for some of that warm broth which my stomach, weary of frozen bread, salt fish, and kvass, implored. At such times I held a sort of tragi-comic dispute with myself, and my good and my evil genius seemed to contend within me.

One day, having entered one of these huts to buy some bread, I found there a tall hale old man, with a silvery beard, and a girl of about eighteen, with a pleasing face, who was rocking a child, and singing as she rocked in order to put her infant more readily to sleep. The old man made me pay very dear for the bread, charging six kopeks for the pound; and I sat down to eat some, adding to it a little salt, and washing it down with some mouthfuls of *kvass*. As I did so, he looked at me with complete indifference, and contented himself with asking me one or two insignificant questions. The young woman, who was his granddaughter, regarded me with an emotion which was quite visible; and hardly had the man absented himself for a moment, than she jumped upon a stool, and reaching up to a shelf, took down two large cakes of wheaten flour mixed with butter and cheese, which she furtively pushed under my pelisse, and then went back to her cradle, humming her song all the time. I shall never lose the memory of this charitable action, done as it was with an inimitable grace, and with all the haste and trepidation of crime.

I refrain from wearying the reader by any further account of that long journey to Véliki-Oustiong, for the frightful monotony of the hours was only broken by meetings which I at once welcomed and dreaded, with *yamtschiks* and pilgrims. I will only mention one incident, which may give some idea of the state of my mind and nerves. One day, in the forest, I saw a man running towards me, with a look of the greatest terror: 'Do not go any further,' he cried, 'there are two brigands in pursuit of me at this moment!' I tried to get him to stop so that we might present a double resistance to these robbers, but he continued his flight at a great pace. Left alone, I armed myself with a cudgel, and thus advanced to meet the enemy in question. Will it be believed, the sensation I then had was one of pleasure? Here was a danger, but it had nothing to do with a passport. Here were men who had as much to fear as I had myself, and to whom I represented law and order; but I never had the satisfaction of making their acquaintance! And I missed the brigands, as in the Oural Mountains I had also missed the bears that play so fine a part in the narratives of the natives, for neither on the one nor yet on the other side of the chain did I meet any of the redoubtable animals.

I reached Véliki-Oustiong on some day in the first fortnight in the month of April 1846, and there I intended to alter the style of my travelling costume. I had left Irbite on the 13th of February; therefore, for about two months I had led, in the woods and among the snow, a life which might truly be called the life of a savage.

CHAPTER VIII.

THE PILGRIM AND THE PILGRIMAGE.

PILGRIMAGES — THE BOHOMOLETS — MANNERS AND CUSTOMS IN VÉLIKI-OUSTIONG — ON THE DVINA — ARCHANGEL.

LONG, however, before reaching Véliki-Oustiong I had decided upon the part which it now behoved me to play. As I had been a commercial traveller as far as Irbite, thence through all my wanderings in the Ourals I had called myself a workman looking for employment in the foundries at Bohotole, or in the salt works at Solikamsk. But I had no sooner left the last-named town behind me than I gradually assumed the manners and the attributes of a pilgrim, on his way to pay his devotions to the holy images of the convent of Solovetsk, in the White Sea. Thus, I became a *bohomolets*, according to the phrase which is thus consecrated in the country, and which literally means 'a worshipper of God.' The worship of holy images and pictures obtains largely in Russia, where four spots enjoy a peculiar renown, and attract an infinite number of visitors. These are Kiow,

Moscow, Véliki-Novgorod and the convent of Solovetsk. Many Russians, even some of the richest merchants, make the tour of all these four places in succession, a journey which is performed on foot, and occupies several years. I actually met at Onega two women, of whom one was still quite young, who had courageously performed the whole of this round, and were then on their way back to their native districts beyond the Oural Mountains, and beyond Verhouterie in the government of Irkutsk. The greater number of the pilgrims content themselves, as a general rule, with visiting the sanctuary which is nearest to them; and thus thousands of the faithful from all the northern countries, and from Siberia itself, annually repair to the convent of Solovetsk, the journey thither being generally made in winter, because the roads at all other times of the year are impassable.

These *bohomolets*, both men and women, are everywhere welcomed and well received, although it will happen that among their ranks an occasional rogue will be found making year after year a lucrative trade out of his peripatetic piety. Indeed, the Russian peasant regards the entrance of a *bohomolets* into his house as a benison, and not content with extending to him alms and a cordial hospitality, he often confides money to a pilgrim, meaning it to be deposited in the sanctuary, and there expended on his account in burning tapers, accompanied by vicarious prayers. I have been myself compelled in my character of a pilgrim to take charge of the pious deposits and tithes of the poor.

I was induced to adopt this disguise as much by the hope of uniting myself to some one of the pilgrim bands as by the universal respect paid to their character, and by the small chance that under their dress I should be exposed to any demands for my passport. While traversing the steppes of Petchora I had met several such companies on the way to Véliki-Oustiong, but while claiming fellowship with them I carefully avoided incorporating myself into their ranks. Too great an acquaintance might, I feared, betray me to them; but I had the opportunities of furtively studying their devotional habits. At last, having reached Véliki-Oustiong, I thought myself sure enough of my part to be able without risk of detection to attempt a way of life in common with one of these bands of 'worshippers of God.' We were in the town, and I found myself sufficiently embarrassed as I stood alone in the great market-place, where, by good luck, a young man in a citizen's dress stepped out of a shop, and came up to me as he said, 'You are a *bohomolets* going to the monastery of Solovetsk.'

'Yes.'

'Well, I am going there too; have you got a lodging?'

'Not yet, I have only just arrived.'

'Then come along with me. Our numbers are great already, it is true, but there will be room enough for you. Our hostess is a good woman, she cooks for us and bakes our bread; I have just been buying flour and groats,' and he pointed to the sack which was on his shoulder. I made haste to follow my guide, whose name was Maxime, and who was a native of the government of Viatka. We soon reached our dwelling-place, and there in two *izba* were crowded together upwards of twenty pilgrims of both sexes. No one mentioned my passport, and the landlady was so complaisant as to prepare my bread for me, while I soon established friendly relations with my companions as well as with the many other pious travellers who filled the town, to the number of two thousand, for they all awaited there the breaking up of the ice of the Dvina, when on rafts and in barges they would make their way to Archangel. What odd, curious, and instructive faces I might have studied among my fellows! There might be seen the most sincere asceticism wholly detached from sense and sin, and specimens of that well-considered and adjusted piety which trims between the interests of both worlds. There was every degree between a beatitude which savoured of idiotcy, and the most astute and hypocritical imposture, so that Leonardo da Vinci might have found models among the ample collection, as well for his Apostles as for his Judas. I could not, of course, escape from the natural consequences of my situation; and there was no help for it, when, especially through the Passion Week, I had to take part in the innumerable nasal canticles raised by my brethren in the *izba*, and furthermore when I was compelled to repair every day to join with them in matins and in even-song, not to speak of making the sign of the cross about a thousand times, with *poklony* by the hundred, or of carrying lighted candles, and of kissing the hand of the *popes*. The sight of these priests always gave me an uneasy twinge, for I feared lest some day I might be requested to repeat the Russian creed, of which I was absolutely and profoundly ignorant. But, luckily, my *poklony*, executed with zeal and dexterity, served me in good stead — a gymnastic exercise which, as exacted by Russian orthodoxy, let me say, is a sufficiently fatiguing one, as anyone will experience who tries to touch the ground with his forehead a hundred times running, and that too without bending his knees. My inward religious feelings suffered from such mummery, but at least I managed to avoid having to confess to one of the *popes*, which I did under pretence of having fulfilled that duty a few days previously at Lalsk; and when once the Holy Week had passed, this high pressure devotion appeared to subside a little, though the psalms and stations observed in the churches still occupied a great deal of our time; and I personally was far from regretting the long hours thus spent in the sacred edifices, which were resting places infinitely preferable to our *izba*.

I had ample leisure to inspect Véliki-Oustiong, and, with the exception of Archangel, it is the Russian town with which I am best acquainted. Built almost entirely of brick, it has, however, especially on the banks of the Suchona, some handsome houses; but its greatest ornament consists of course in its churches, which are painted yellow, and crowned with zinc roofs coloured green. I think that I counted not fewer than twenty-two of these; and there are also two convents, one for monks (*tcherntsé*), dedicated to Saint Michael; the other for nuns, which is without the walls. I regret to say that the life and conversation of the latter body, especially of its younger members, did not appear to me to be highly edifying.

Although the population of Oustiong does not exceed 15,000 souls, the town has, notwithstanding, some commercial importance — being, in truth, the natural depôt for all the different products of the countries of Viatka, Perm, Vologda and of Siberia. These products, which consist, for the most part, in grain of all sorts, flax, hemp, tallow, salt meat, tar, wood, and furs, &c., accumulate at Véliki-Oustiong, to be transported thence, through the Dvina, to Archangel, and to be shipped from that port in vessels bound for all the quarters of the globe. It also happens that numbers of sailors and boatmen assemble there, to await the opening of the Dvina, and then to conduct the merchandise in barges, of which there are many thousand, and of which the owners are called *prikastchiki*. Now, these contractors allow the *bohomolets* to have a free passage in their boats, provided they victual themselves for the voyage, and bring with them a sufficient supply of flour, groats, and dried fish; while any pilgrim who is willing to take an oar receives fifteen roubles (in paper) from the *prikastchiki*, who are only too glad of such an offer, as there is often a great want of hands. I had never yet handled an oar in a large barge; but I undertook this labour, in the hope of adding a little to my finances. I had spent precisely fifteen roubles since I left Irbite. Bread in those regions was cheap, and during the passage of the Ourals, and on my further march, I had never had any occasion to incur foolish expenses; but I was, nevertheless, very thankful to have the means of bringing my viaticum back to its original figure of seventy-five roubles. So, on the first day on which the Dvina was navigable, I, along with my fellow-pilgrims, struck a bargain with one of these boat-owners — glad to escape, at last, from Véliki-Oustiong, where I had spent a whole month in interminable devotions, and where I had been miserable from *ennui* and restlessness. One proposition with regard to my voyage troubled me a little, I was to remit my passport to the *prikastchiki*, and he, as was customary in these passages, was to keep it for me, and return it when we landed. The hurry and bustle of our embarkation reassured me, however, a little; and, indeed, the master did but give one glance at my unhappy little pass, when the sight of its seal seemed to content him; and thus, on the 10th of May, 1846, I found myself installed in the barge, ready to start and drop down the Dvina to Archangel.

A Dvina boat is a sufficiently curious piece of construction, and, seen from any distance, mostly resembles a house, or a floating barn. There is no art in guiding it. Everything is left to the muscular labours of the crew, and each craft requires from forty to sixty boatmen. The number of the oars varies from thirty to forty, and they do not pretend to be anything but small fir trees. Among the many curious parts of these boats, which are intended to serve either as magazines for the wares or shelter for the passengers and crews by night, I will only mention one great chest, of rough deals, placed on four pile-heads on the roof, and filled with clay to the middle. This is the kitchen, and fire is kept up in it during the whole day; while, on two great beams, fastened transversely to the sides of the case, and over wooden pins, hang the pots in which the food is prepared. We carried our baggage on board in the evening, and slept there all the first night, till, at day-break, the *nosnik* — that is to say, the master of the vessel — cried, with a loud voice, 'Be seated, and pray to God!' Everyone then assembled on the deck, and after preserving for a moment a devotional attitude, worthy of a Mussulman, each man rose, crossed himself repeatedly, and made his *poklony*. When the prayers were finished, every living soul on board, from the master to the poorest of the *bohomolets*, threw a piece of copper money into the stream, to render the Dvina propitious to their course along its breast.

The aspect of the river, covered with many boats and rafts, is a very animated one. After any lengthened halt, and at the moment of again getting under weigh, one hears again the cry, 'Be seated, and worship God!' The crew goes through the accustomed exercise, while signs of the cross and the *poklony* went on vigorously, whenever we hove in sight of any of the many little chapels which abound on both banks of the Dvina. During a calm, the barge was allowed to float with the stream, and then both passengers and crew would rest, sing, or converse. I was struck with the great lack of ideas and sentiment which was apparent in the songs of our company, in spite of their generally possessing a sweet and graceful melody; and these are common characteristics of Russian popular airs. If the wind rose, or if we neared any dangerous part of the river, the boatmen would then exert themselves; and they displayed both agility and strength. I, for my part, strove diligently to acquit myself of the duties of my task; and I may say, without flattery, that I soon acquired superior dexterity in handling the oar, and in steering. Thus I had the satisfaction of being applauded by the old helmsman, and of hearing the name of Lavrenti (my assumed cognomen) invoked in all moments of difficulty. In spite of our diligence, the barge stuck twice in shoal water, and then our united efforts were required, for ten or twelve hours, before we could make her float, and get her off again. One frequent amusement of the voyage was being boarded very often by little skiffs, filled by women and children, who asked us for alms. They sang one of the sweetest and most plaintive melodies that I ever heard in my life, of which the refrain always was the words—'Little fathers, little mothers, give us bread!'—'*Batiouchki, diadiouchki, daïtie khlebtsa!*' No one on board, either crew or pilgrims, could refuse the request; and these beggars would then strike up another song, and wish us a good and a happy journey.

Our navigation of the Dvina lasted a fortnight. Gradually, as we approached Archangel, I saw that the nights became shorter—the last one, indeed, was marked by an interval of only two hours between the setting of the sun and its rising again; and during that time also, any one might have read or written without difficulty. When at last the towers of Archangel began to glitter in the early morning beams, the whole crew gave a shout of delight, while the boatmen hastened to throw into the stream the big chest full of earth, which had served as our kitchen range. The other boats did the same with their respective kitchens, for this, it appears, is a time-honoured observance. The rowers, in like manner, break off the ends of their oars, with a prodigious noise—another strange custom among the navigators of the Dvina; and when, at last, we reached the landing-place, each man had his passport restored to him, and received from the *prikastchik* the fifteen roubles which he had gained by the labour of his hands.

Thus I was in Archangel! I touched the shores of that bay of the White Sea, which, in all my weary wanderings in the Ourals, had appeared to my mind's eye as the haven of refuge! I now beheld those flags fluttering on vessels of deliverance, of which a vague and fairy-like impression had often risen, like a *Fata Morgana*, to cheer me on my Ostiak couch in the heart of the lonely forest. Ah, how grateful to my eyes were those pendants, barred with stripes of many hues — to eyes which for so many months had dwelt only on vast desert expanses of snow! How ardent and sincere was the thanksgiving which I now recited among my fellow 'worshippers of God,' who were thankful, like myself, to have reached the end of pilgrimage!

I knew, however, that I must avoid making any over-hasty step, and in order to act out my part, I repaired with my companions to the station of Solovetsk (*Solovetski dvorets*), that is to say, to the huge buildings erected in Archangel itself, by the monks of the convent in the Holy Isle, for the accommodation of the pilgrims. There, as was the custom, I left my slender baggage in the hands of the porter, and I was truly thankful to remark that no inquiries as to passports were addressed to those who arrived. In spite of the large number of its *izba*, the house was crammed with inmates, and I could find only a small corner in the highest part of the barn; and this I had to share with an elderly devotee of the other sex, whom piety certainly did not render a more lovely object, while on all the following days, no sooner did one party of *bohomolets* leave the establishment on its way to the Holy Isle, than another arrived from Véliki-Oustiong, and in this way the caravanserai was constantly as full as it could be. The natural consequences of such an agglomeration of persons, of such a mixture of all ages and of both sexes, are more easily to be guessed than described; and it is much to be wished that, between the paradise of the Holy Isle and the hell of these *Solovetski dvorets*, there should be some place of purgatory, for it would conduce greatly to the morals and to the sanitary well-being of those concerned. I need not say that the chants and processions of Véliki-Oustiong were resumed here with a marked increase of fervour; and on the day after our arrival I had *to assist* in the chapel (*tserkiew*) of the establishment at many strange acts of devotion, such as are not to be met with except in the churches of the orthodox. This chapel was filled with *bohomolets*, some of whom were having prayers read over their heads, others had the benefit of Akathisti (Antiphones) in the same way, while others again crouched, and bore the gospels on their backs. The gospel in this case is a huge folio tome, about two feet in length, and printed in large antique type; the boards are two solid planks of wood, and encrusted upon them are the Twelve Apostles in silver. The execution is very massive, and the officiating *pope* has great difficulty in lifting so heavy a book. The man who wishes to have the gospels read upon him must stoop, but not kneel, until his head serves as a sort of desk. It is true, that several *bohomolets* may put their purses and their heads together for this service of devotion, but then the grace, like the weight, is distributed among them; and he who wishes to receive it in all its efficacy, endeavours to make of his individual person, and for a quarter of an hour, one of those quaint cariatides of the faith. Everything is bought and sold in the Russian church, and according to the size of the offering, whether greater or smaller, the *pope* on these occasions either reads out the gospel of the day with sonorous gravity and unction, or mumbles it over in haste with contemptuous carelessness; and it requires both the strong convictions and the strong neck of a Russian peasant to submit to such religious exercises. But what miracles will not piety perform! One of my companions in our lodging-house, a peasant of Viatka, had complained of violent pains in his head, but after having gone through this operation with the Evangel, and having had his neck swelled by it, till the veins of both neck and face seemed ready to burst, he assured me, as we left the chapel, that it was as if some one had lifted off with their hands the horrible pains from which he had suffered: 'Praise be to God' (*Slava Bokow*).

The occupations of a fervent *bohomolets* did not, however, prevent my wandering about the town. Archangel has a population of not much more than twenty thousand; but its port and commercial business give it an air of great animation. The town proper is joined by a wooden bridge over the Dvina with the island of Solonbal—a sort of suburb, in which has arisen the palace of the Governor. Many churches and some good houses in brick decorate this city, which is mainly constructed of wood. One single wide street, which extends through the whole length of Archangel, is paved: all its other streets and lanes are excessively dirty and muddy, for the *toundra*, or marshy clay upon which, like St. Petersburg, this city has been built, crops up in all directions. In one of the squares rises a colossal statue of Lomonossov. To this rhetorician and celebrated grammarian is traced the origin of a national literature in Russia, under the reign of the Tzarina Elizabeth, the daughter of Peter the Great.

The chief, and indeed, the only object which I had in view in this town may easily be guessed. Although the season had only begun, about twenty vessels were already in the bay; but among the different flags which waved from their masts, I was not able to discover one with the tri-coloured emblem. The absence of this ensign was in itself of bad augury to me. The ships were, for the most part, English; there were also some from Holland, Sweden and Hamburg, but not one French. I very soon perceived also that on the deck of every vessel walked a Russian soldier, a vigilant witness, whose eye it was impossible to elude, for this watch was not taken off even at night; while sentries posted at short distances from one another formed an unconquerable barricade along the quays of the harbour, and obliged all who came and all who went to give an account of themselves. How, then, with these sentries on the alert, could I make a signal to any captain or seaman! A crowd of idlers and foot passengers crossed the quays, and added to the difficulty of any such attempt. How then could I, if any seafaring man should pass, accost him in French or in German —I, in my *bohomolet's* dress, and surrounded by any number of people! Must I not surely draw all eyes upon myself, and bring about an immediate arrest! I continued, nevertheless, to wander up and down the quays, in the hope that some favourable opportunity would present itself; but, alas! none such came. And thus I was obliged again to turn my steps to the *dvorets*, where, by this time, I was expected to join in the pious exercises of the rest. On the second day, all those who had reached Archangel with me embarked for the Holy Island; but I, pretending excessive fatigue, did not accompany them, and again betook myself to the harbour. I sauntered up and down by the edge of the water which I had hoped was to have set me free; I even saw some ships that had finished taking their cargo on board, a sign that they would soon set sail and depart. My heart beat violently; my breast heaved, and I could hardly repress the cry, 'Save me! Do not abandon me thus!' At last I accosted some seamen, busy with the hawsers which still fastened a ship to the pier. In spite of the extreme danger thus incurred, I ventured a few words in French; they only raised their heads and stared at me with amazement. I tried German, but with as little success; till, finally, they burst into a loud laugh, and I had to slip away as quietly as I might, for a crowd had already collected round me. On the following day my efforts had no better result, and I shall not describe either the torment of those three days, or the different attempts I made to reach any of the outward bound vessels. In spite of the severity of the season, I did not hesitate even to bathe in the harbour, hoping thus to approach some one of the ships; but nothing came of it, and no chance of escape offered itself to me. Late on the third day I returned to the *dvorets*, and there turned over in my mind all the circumstances of my present state, and I finished by arriving at the heart-breaking conviction that I could no longer reckon upon the port of Archangel. Already some surprise was excited that, as a *bohomolets*, I had so strangely delayed my departure for the Holy Isle, and to remain any longer in the town, to await the arrival of some French trader, would have been to order my own arrest. Had I not assumed the character of a pilgrim, I might perhaps have ventured into some *café* of public resort, and I might have flattered myself with the hope of making the acquaintance of some foreign captain; but in my peasant's dress how could I present myself in any such place? Ah! that last night passed in the caravanserai of the pilgrims, how dark, and how sad it was! It was the thought, it had been the hope, of Archangel which had given me strength to meet the greatest dangers, and to endure the most terrible privations. And now, having reached the object of all my efforts, I was to find that they had been all in vain, and that I must fly from the city which I had so long persisted in greeting as the place of my final deliverance.

CHAPTER IX.

THE WHITE SEA.

THE MONASTERY OF SOLOVETSK—THE PRISONER OF SOLOVETSK—HETERODOXY AND ORTHODOXY—THE PROMONTORY—A FURTHER JOURNEY.

I DID not go as far as the monastery of Solovetsk, but I have collected a great number of details about that place of pilgrimage. In the White Sea, about 280 verstes to the westward of Archangel, there is a group of islands, and of these the largest bears the name of Solovetsk. Originally inhabited by the Fins, it was afterwards occupied by some intrepid trappers (*promylchlenniki*) of the ancient republic of Novgorod. It became afterwards the asylum of St. Zosimus, who built a cell there, and founded a little wooden chapel. Other cenobites succeeded him on that spot. A convent of monks (*tcherntsé*) was formed, and this foundation soon becoming celebrated for its miracles, was enriched by the offerings of the faithful, and was finally endowed with a fortress or stronghold, for the preservation of its treasures. With the republic of Novgorod,

Solovetsk and its monastery passed under the domination of the Tzars, who strengthened its fortifications. In the time of the false Demetrius, the partisans of Boris Godounov, along with their riches, took refuge in the castle of the Holy Isle, and there made an obstinate resistance 'to the most intrepid knights who held with the pretender:' thus saith tradition. May they, by any chance, have been *our* celebrated *Lissovians*—our hardy warriors of the seventeenth century. At any rate, this defence of the place added to the glory of the island, which, after Kiow, occupies the first place in the list of the holy places of the Russian Empire.

The situation of Solovetsk in a frozen region, and in one that is difficult of access, makes all culture there next to impossible. Latterly, and chiefly by reason of the labours of the monks, some vegetables, chiefly cabbages, have been raised on the island; but flour, wheat, groats, oil, and other articles of food only come thither from Archangel. The recluses can make *kvass* for themselves, and their manufacture has a peculiar celebrity. They also possess a mill, a few cattle, and even some horses. Close to their cloisters are large warehouses in which the pilgrims deposit their baggage, receiving a numbered ticket in exchange; but the buildings destined to shelter the *bohomolets* are a much greater affair, and their numbers are very considerable. There are large furnished rooms or halls with long tables and benches. There the faithful lodge, sleep, and eat their meals; the compartments of the men being separated from those for women. I have never heard the hospitality of the brotherhood spoken of but in terms of praise. During the repasts, a monk reads to the guests in each hall, out of the 'Lives of the Saints,' or recites some prayers. Every *bohomolets* has the right of being lodged and fed gratuitously for the three first nights. During that time he prays, goes to confession, lights and hold candles, and gets *akathisti* (antiphones) or gospels read over his head. There is a tariff for all these spiritual exercises, but the terms are very modest, though the visit to the tombs of St. Zosimus and of St. Savatyï have to be paid for separately. When the three days have expired, the pilgrim will be expected, if he stays longer, to provide for his own wants, and to pay for his lodging. A number of devout persons make a vow to remain on the island for whole years at a time, and these years they spend in acts of devotion and of penitence. Such guests are warmly welcomed by the brothers, but on the condition that they pay their own expenses, or make themselves useful in the convent by some occupation, and become workmen, gardeners, and the like.

As soon as the White Sea has become navigable, that is to say, by the first days of June, the pilgrims crowd into little boats, called *karbasses*, which, from Archangel, carry them to the Holy Isle. The price of the voyage is very small, but owing to the discomforts, and indeed to the dangers of a long crossing on a sea generally very rough, many *bohomolets* go on foot from Archangel, and skirt the shore till they reach a promontory opposite Solovetsk, from which it is separated by an arm of the sea not one verst in width, and only then do they commit themselves to the *karbasses.* No one can land on the island, except during the four months of June, July, August, and September, for by the beginning of October all navigation of the White Sea is prevented by the violence of its tempests, and still more by the ice which enters it from the Polar Sea. So from October to June there are no visitors at the convent.

It is a strange thing, and one perhaps not without significance, that alongside of the very house of God, the Tzars have built one for themselves — a mysterious prison, of which the *bohomolets* speak with the greatest terror, because no one knows what is the meaning or the use of it. Who may be the unhappy beings who are inclosed within these dungeon walls! No common criminals certainly, for *they* are sent to Siberia. And yet the prison of Solovetsk is certainly occupied, for sentries and keepers are always on duty, and at their posts. I have been told that some years ago an old man was seen there. He had a white beard, and had become blind from weeping. I do not pretend to give any guarantee for the truth of this tale, which has, however, been narrated by many; still less do I venture to vouch for the secret which has been whispered into my ear on more than one occasion; but they say that the blind prisoner of Solovetsk is a brother of Nicholas — that he is the Grand Duke Constantine himself. . . . !

But to return to my own history; on the day which followed the night in which I determined to abandon any further attempts at evasion from Archangel, I rose at daybreak, received my baggage from the porter of the *dvorets*, and declared to him my intention of pressing on to the monastery of Solovetsk. After having bought some bread and some salt, I crossed the Dvina, and struck away in the direction of the western promontory which faces the Holy Isle. The day was hot and fine, the country flat, but wild and deserted. By evening I reached a little hamlet, and there I decided to take a Russian bath, a measure which had become indispensable after my long sojourn among the saints. The Russians, even the lowest of the people, frequently use these baths on Saturdays, or on the eve of their festivals. The bath house is a simple wooden building, where you find a huge stove of about two yards square, formed of bricks or of unquarried stone, put together without any cement. There is no chimney, and the smoke goes out at the holes in the roof. As soon as these stoves are really heated, water is poured over them, and the steam which flies from them, filling the whole place, turns it into a bath room.

After leaving the stove, I felt a strange longing to drink some milk, and on going to get some in a hut pointed out by my host, I found two women, to whom I made my wants known, after having made the three signs of the cross, which are expected of one. They gave me very scant measure for the piece of money which I offered, and served me with a bad grace, for which I was not at first able to account. While I took some mouthfuls of the milk we began to converse, and at last I found the solution of the enigma. They belonged to the sect of the '*staroviertsi*,' or old believers, and by the way in which I made the sign of the cross they recognised in me an orthodoxy that was to be deplored. They did not conceal from me what was their regret, that a man of such piety, a *bohomolets*, should be thus wandering in the ways of certain perdition. They then showed me how truly to make sure of my salvation, and tired at last of differing with them, I ended in adopting their method. These good women were so happy, that they gave to their neophyte three fresh measures of milk, and refused payment for it. As they took leave of me, they offered fervent prayers to God that I might be preserved in the paths of conversion! But these prayers, alas! were not to be granted, for as soon as I returned to my landlord's dwelling, I was again obliged to cross myself in the orthodox fashion.

I continued my journey, walking for several days in

a marshy country, or through woods of stunted fir trees, where I was often obliged to spend the night. I became more and more aware of the polar nature of the climate. The sun hardly ever left us; and even during the short interval between his setting and his rising again, his level rays threw over the landscape a clearness of light which would have allowed one to execute the finest needlework. Night was only to be distinguished from day by the greater stillness which reigned over the face of nature. It is true, that the geographical ideas which had been acquired by me when I sat on a form in school had prepared me years before for this phenomenon, yet I felt as if in a dream on thus finding myself in regions where the sun never sets. The country, I found, became always poorer and more desolate, until, at last, I reached the coast; and after that, I continued to walk along the cliffs, where, for several days, the weather was extremely fine, and the sun so warm that I was obliged to take off my pelisse. But, before long, a heavy gale of wind rose; and the ocean, rolling in mountainous waves, and covered with snowy foam, seemed eager to justify its name of White Sea, and presented a spectacle at once mournful and admirably grand. The tempest lasted for several days. I hardly ever met a human being; but the sight of a serpent, which had been newly killed, showed me that in this country and in this latitude reptiles were not wanting.

On reaching a small village on the sea-shore, I found in a *possada*—that is to say, in a colony—a multitude of *bohomolets*, and, among others, my former companions from Véliki-Oustiong, who had set out, long before me, from Archangel, in *karbasses* bound for the Holy Island, but who had been driven by the storm to land and seek for shelter at this spot. One of the *karbasses* had been swamped, and every soul on board lost in the waves; and now these poor people awaited the laying of the tempest; but I left them, assuring them that I should reach the monastery much sooner and safer on foot than they would in their wretched little boats. Towards evening, the sea went down, and I had soon reached the promontory which faces the island of Solovetsk. Leaning on my staff, I stood for some moments contemplating the shores, and thinking of our old Lissoviens, who may, perhaps, have encamped on this very spot, while pushing their adventurous course to the extreme north. Then, turning to the left, and without waiting for a passage to the monastery, I struck into the road which would take me to Onega.

And, in truth, now that my attempts at Archangel had failed, this was the only route open to me; for a return to Archangel and Véliki-Oustiong, with a journey thence through the very heart of Russia Proper, was not to be thought of; and, again, there was nothing more natural than that a *bohomolets*, having accomplished his pilgrimage to Solovetsk, should turn to

Onega, and to the government of Olonets, so as to make the pious round of Novgorod and of Kiow, and there *salute the holy bones* — for such is the sanctified phraseology in use (*dla pokloniĕnïa swiatym mostcham*). I do not say that I yet saw what I ought to do on reaching Onega; but after the mistake about Archangel, I was not inclined to make any great plans, or to think of the morrow. I therefore resolutely pursued my way, skirting the western edge of the promontory, and walking, for several days, along a path which was bounded, on the one side, by the sea — on the other, by a low range of hillocks, densely covered with wood. Before me, I saw nothing but sands, heaths, and marshes; and one incident will, I think, suffice to give an idea of this desolate country. One day, having arrived at a *possada*, I could get no bread. The inhabitants had been without any for a week, because the bad weather had stopped the boats that came from Archangel; but, as an equivalent, I found some of the fresh herrings of the White Sea, which were of a good size and excellent flavour.

At Onega, I was not tempted to make any further experiments among the foreign ships that I saw at anchor in the port. In order to have made any attempts of the kind, with the slightest chance of success, it would have been necessary for me to pass several days in the town, where there was no crowd of pilgrims among whom I could hide, as at Véliki-

Oustiong and at Archangel, so as to conceal myself from the eyes of the Police. Moreover, I was still under the painful impression left by the discovery of my last bad reckoning, and I had decidedly more confidence in *terra firma*, which, as yet, had never deceived my hopes. Two land routes were open to me from Onega, and it was now time to choose between them. The one to the right would have led me, by the marshes of Laponia and the river Torneo, to the Swedish frontier; the other, to the left, trending across the government of Olonets, would take me, by Vytiégra, to the Gulf of Finland, and to the Baltic. Of these lines, the first was the most fatiguing — the second the most dangerous. Had I not already crossed the Ourals and the steppe of Petchora, I should certainly have taken an extreme northern direction to Laponia; but I now dreaded the privations, and the miseries with which I was too well acquainted. Wasted and disheartened, I had begun to fear hardships more than danger, and I decided in favour of Vytiégra.

Without, therefore, making too long a halt in Onega, I pushed towards the south, by skirting the banks of the river which also bears the name of Onega. Every now and then I met solitary pilgrims on their way to the monastery of Solovetsk, to whom naturally I could impart the latest intelligence about the island. I remember one old man in particular — small, withered, and white as a dove, but very fresh and hearty withal, who said to me, 'Can you doubt where I come from? I am from Kargopol . . . . . !' He pronounced the name with such pride, with such a sense of the greatness of his native town, that I really might have fancied that I heard the famous *civis Romanus*. Now Kargopol, which I soon reached, may truly be said to be one of the saddest little hamlets of a very sad country. Yet, in spite of the sombre and monotonous aspect of these districts, where marshes alternate with boundless woods, in spite of the enormous distances I had to traverse on foot, in spite of the discomforts incident to the condition of a fugitive who has always to fear gendarmes, inns, or any expenditure which exceeds the bare necessaries of life, this journey from Onega to Vytiégra was very far from being equal in suffering to that which I had made over the Ourals and the plain of Petchora. My character of a pilgrim gave me a certain assurance that I need no longer to the same extent avoid the dwellings of men. Besides, the season was milder; and when at nightfall I had to turn into some wood to sleep, I could find branches and green leaves enough to fashion a pretty soft bed. What most surprises me is, that, in all these nights passed in the solitude of the forests, I was never once disturbed by wild beasts. Sometimes, indeed, I was startled by the distant howling of the wolves, but none of these animals ever presented themselves to my eyes.

It must not, however, be supposed that, during this

expedition, I was not exposed to much tribulation, in spite of the really very exact knowledge which I possessed of the manners and customs of the country. Sometimes an adventure would be almost comic: as when, one day, not far from this celebrated Kargopol, I asked for food at a hut, and received for answer that they had nothing but *tolokno* to offer me.

'Well, let us have the *tolokno*,' I said, rather pleased than otherwise to make the acquaintance of a national dish, which I had often heard of, but never seen. My confusion, however, became great when the mistress of the house set down before me a jug of water, a spoon, and a small earthen jar half full of a dry and blackish flour. How was that to be eaten? How could I fail to betray that I was a stranger by my crying ignorance of a dish so common in Russia? I began to talk, as if for my life, about any nonsense that would divert their attention; but my hostess was not to be diverted, and she asked me why I did not eat, since I was so hungry?

'But perhaps you would like it better mixed with kvass (cider)?'

'Oh yes, with cider,' I replied, as much at a loss as before.

She brought some cider, and, luckily, poured it herself into the pot, stirring it with the spoon. The brown mass then swelled until it filled the jar, and made a paste, which I now knew how to eat. It was made of oats baked in an oven, which are then carefully sifted and pounded in meal, and, when mixed with water or cider it forms a substance so fairly palatable that I can recommend it especially to our brave highlanders of the Carpathians.

The district of Olonets is traversed in all directions by canals, formed to unite the different lakes and rivers of Onega, Ladoga, Vytiégra, Svir, &c.; and these form the principal means of communication between one place and another. For the preservation and inspection of these works, stations have been set down at different points, and these are constantly occupied by soldiers, the greater number of them being Poles, who have groaned under arms in the imperial service for the last sixteen years, that is to say, ever since 1831. From Archangel to Vytiégra I fell in with several of my unhappy countrymen, thus incorporated into military bodies, and generally found that, in spite of their long residence in the country, they spoke Russian very imperfectly. I often talked with them, pretending to be a native of Siberia, and thus drew from them an account of their sorrows. I remember, in particular, one sinister phrase which made me shudder. Hearing once the complaints made by a Pole of the hardships and fatigues of his life as a Russian soldier, I said to him what only a true Russian would have said:

'But, after all, you are not so very much beaten?'

'What! we are not beaten,' was the retort, accompanied by an almost savage laugh; 'you don't think we are beaten? as if anybody got the Tzar's bread to eat gratis!'

I frequently saw another sad sight in this country, namely, gangs (*partyé*) of Jewish children that were being driven to Archangel. It should be known that, whereas the Russian government in Poland only recruits among adult Christians, it takes boys of from ten to fifteen from the Jewish population, in order that, forgetting more perfectly their traditional religion and manners, they may become fit for military life, for which it seems that adult Israelites are not so well adapted. A great number of these young recruits are intended for the navy, and sent to the different ports of the White Sea, and, to me, the sight of these poor children, with their heads shaved, and wrapped in their little pelisses, was most pitiful; for the soldiers in charge of the gang drove them before them like a flock of sheep, and I was assured by the natives that many of them died by the way.

It was also in this department of Olonets that I saw another symptom of the moral state of Russia, which was in itself not less curious. I had gone into a cottage to ask my way; it was on the road from Kargopol to Vytiégra. I found in the hut an old man with a long white beard, and of respectable appearance, who, as soon as he began to talk to me, expressed such a hatred of the Tzar, the government, and the priests, that I had no difficulty in recognising in him a *starovier*, or old believer. Finding me to be a man well disposed to share his religious views, he ran on at great length, and finally shed tears over the persecution of the true faith. In order to prove to me that the manner of making the sign of the cross adopted ever since the reformation of Nicon (that is, the ordinary Russian fashion) was wholly heretical, he looked all round the outside of his house, locked the door, and, having taken an oath of secrecy from me, he drew from a hiding-place a little figure in copper, evidently a rough piece of old Byzantine workmanship, which certainly represented our Lord as giving the benediction with the two fore fingers of the right hand extended, as in the manner of the *staroviertsi*. 'They force us,' he continued, 'to go to the *tserkiev* of the heretics, where the *popes* oblige us to make the sign of the cross in their own way; but when we come back from the *tserkiev*, we pray to the true God, and we ask Him to forgive the great sin.' He afterwards drew from the same repository an old paper book, setting forth 'The History of the Patriarch Joseph, as betrayed and sold by his Brethren.' The good man proceeded to instruct me in these novelties, and shed some tears of emotion at the virtue of Joseph when tempted by the wife of Potiphar.

Scarcely had I reached Vytiégra than I was accosted on the quays by a peasant, who asked me where I was going.

'I am a *bohomolets,*' I replied. 'I am returning from the monastery of Solovetsk, and I am on my way to "*adore the sacred bones*" at Novgorod and at Kiow.'

'Then, I am your man,' he said. 'I will take you to St. Petersburg. My boat is small, but I have only my horse to take with me, and you can help me to row . . . it is not heavy.'

'I know that sort of work very well, and I know that it is not light; how much will you give me?'

We wrangled for a long time over the price, the sly villain having every mind to get the use of my arms, and not to pay for it; but at last we agreed that he should give me dressed victuals for the whole time of our voyage, and, so pleased was he with the bargain he had made, that he took me straight to a pothouse to drink a glass with him.

The project of going to St. Petersburg, into the very capital of Nicholas, was sufficiently strange, and, most certainly, it was not one which I had contemplated when I made sundry and manifold plans of evasion at Ekaterinski-Zavod; but, since leaving Archangel, I had been wandering pretty much on chance, with no other object than always to get near some sea or frontier, no matter which, and always to avoid remaining more than a few hours in any place where they were likely to ask me for my papers. Now the boat in question was to leave that very day; and there was something, even in the very strangeness of the enterprise, which seemed reassuring. Any capital appeared to me less dangerous than a small provincial town, and the event showed that I was not wrong in this calculation.

By evening the boat was slipped from her moorings, and the navigation began, which, by Vytiégra, the lake of Onega, the river Svir, the lake of Ladoga, and the Néva, was to conduct me to the very walls of St. Petersburg. We rowed day and night, or floated past innumerable canoes, boats and ships, with which the lakes and rivers were literally covered; but, above all, past rafts of wood, also intended to supply the wants of the metropolis, and which, in some places, completely obstructed the passage. We made a party of three — myself, the master, and his son, a stout young man, who, whenever we neared the banks, would get the horse out and fasten him to the boat, so as to help to draw it along. In spite of the smallness of the boat, its owner could not prevail on himself to refuse an occasional passenger, whom he would take up or put down at spots agreed upon; for how could he be expected to resist turning a penny from time to time? But these freights caused me the greatest distress, for the passengers could not be said to be members of any Temperance league, and I had to watch over the tipsiest ones, and once had even to jump into the water to pull out a poor wretch who had rolled overboard. As I do not wish to make myself appear better than I am, I must state here that I had a strong personal interest in the safety of these troublesome guests; for, had any disaster really occurred, we should have been obliged to stop, and report ourselves at the nearest police station, when the negotiation thereupon ensuing would, to a certainty, have been opened by a request for our papers; thus my charity was hardly of a very evangelical sort.

As we approached by degrees the end of our voyage, I became more absorbed in thought, and, above all, more anxious to learn something of the usages of St. Petersburg. Happily, we picked up at one of the stations several women, who, after paying visits to their relations, were returning to the capital, where they seemed to have lived for many years as servants and housemaids. My condition as a *bohomolets* obliged me to preach to them a degree of morality in conduct, which seemed only to excite their risibility. However, I did not preach entirely in vain, especially when I took under my protection an old woman, of whom these chambermaids had made a butt in a way that was really disgusting. She was an old peasant of Korélia, on her way to St. Petersburg, which she had never seen before, to visit a daughter, who plied her trade as a laundress in the city. She was immensely grateful to me for my protection, called me her '*batiouchka*' (little father), and soon offered me an assistance which can be called nothing less than providential.

After encountering a violent storm, during which

our women screamed horribly, and after leaving behind us Nova-Ladoga and Schlusselbourg, where Alexis Orlov strangled the unhappy Peter III., by the orders of Catharine the Great, we reached the quays of the capital, at about eight o'clock in the morning, and drew towards the shore opposite the Perspective Nevski. The servant girls jumped gaily from the boat, giving me a rendezvous *to preach to them*, and I was preparing to step on shore, feeling, I must confess, much at a loss what to do with myself, when the poor Korélian woman came up to me, and said, 'Just stay with me; I have sent to tell my daughter, and she will soon be down to fetch me, and will show you where you can get a cheap lodging.' It may be imagined with what eagerness I embraced her proposition; and oh, ineffable joy! while we waited a long time in the boat, no one came to ask for our papers. At last the laundress appeared; she kissed her mother affectionately, and took up her trunk, which she and I then carried between us, on a stick across our shoulders. Thus we set off, preceded by the good old soul herself, who carried on her head the earthen jar which had contained her food. And in this strange trim I entered the city of the Tzar!

We had to go through an endless number of streets, bridges, and lanes before we reached the place where the laundress lived; it was in a lodging-house of one story in height (*dom postoïaly*), where the poorest of the working-classes dwell, and where they came at night to sleep on a flock-bed (if they can get it), or if not, to lie, as the Russian phrase is, 'on the floor, with their fists for a pillow.' The swelled faces and the red noses of some who frequented this miserable abode, showed that many shapes of sin and distress harboured there. There were, however, regular lodgers, who let out to passengers rooms that they had furnished on this speculation, and my laundress was one of these. Unfortunately, her room was already occupied; but she recommended me to a neighbour, and a bargain was soon made at the rate of eight kopeks a-day. In order to avoid the critical moment, I asked my landlady immediately to show me the way to the Prefecture of Police, where passports were given and examined.

'Who are you,' asked my hostess.

'I am a *bohomolets*, from beyond Vologda; I am returning from Solovetsk, and going to Véliki-Novgorod, to worship the bones of the saints. . . . .'

'You do well; God be your help! Show me your passport.'

I handed to her my shabby little pass, repressing any show of anxiety; but she evidently could not read, and only looked at the stamp, then said to me: 'How long do you think of remaining here?'

'From three to five days at the most; I must just rest a little.'

'Then I will tell you what it is, it is perfectly useless for you to go to the Police?'

'Just as you please; I don't know the ways of this place. But why is it no use to go to the Police?'

'Well, you see, I should have to go with you, and that is too much trouble for me.'

'Why must you go?'

'Because, you see, the Police have lately become se plaguily exacting. Formerly, it used to suffice if the new-comer himself went to the Prefecture; but now nothing will serve them but to see his landlord along with him. Then there is always such a crowd of people at the office, that one has to wait ever so long before one's turn comes round. If one has a lodger for a month or a year, then it is worth one's pains to go through all this trouble and fatigue; but if he is only to stay a night or two, one would never gain a living, for the time would be spent in coming and going. One could not do a hand's-turn in one's own house at that rate, and people must live, you know; and it is but little bread that one gets from the Police. And that is why we prefer not to make any declaration, when the lodger only remains for a few days; we find it the best plan, and if at the Prefecture they do not hear all they might like to hear, I cannot say I think there is any harm done.'

I made no objection, it may be supposed; but installing myself in my room I remained there all the rest of the day, in spite of the insinuating discourse of my landlady, who proposed to me that I should go and see the illuminations, for that day was a high day in the capital. It was July 9, 1846, and they were celebrating the nuptials, or the betrothal (I do not quite know which), of a daughter of the Emperor Nicholas, the Grand-Duchess Olga, with the Prince of Wurtemberg!

The next day, however, I did go out, and I promenaded the town, of which the wide handsome streets seemed to me to be singularly deserted. I was meditating on the quickest way of leaving the place, and had determined, if need be, to swim to the shores of the Baltic, although any more convenient method, if it should arise, was not to be despised. I knew that a packet sailed from St. Petersburg to Havre, but what were the days of its sailing, where did it lie, and was its captain French or Russian? Grave questions, which I did not dare to put to any one for fear of compromising myself. I walked up and down the Néva, and read the inscriptions on the different red and yellow bills which were posted up on blank planks on each of the different steamers; but I could only read by stealth, for a peasant, 'a Russian man' (*rouski tchelovièk*) like me, must not make a display of learning! So I sauntered slowly and perused the inscriptions. One would be 'the vessel of his Majesty the Emperor,' another 'of His Highness the Prince Imperial,' 'of the Grand Duke Michael,' 'of Her Majesty the Empress, and the ladies of her court,' &c.

Evidently all of too high a class for me. I managed at last to discover less titled vessels; but then their destinations were not to my liking, and would not have suited me in any way. After having thus examined the whole length of the left bank of the Néva, I crossed the bridge in front of the statue of Peter the Great, and now pursued the stream along the right hand to its mouth. I stopped for a moment at the foot of the two gigantic sphinxes which are placed opposite the museum, and the sight of these strange Egyptian guests in the City of Ice made me lose myself for a moment in thought. Suddenly my eyes fell on an advertisement in large letters, which, stuck up near the mast of a steamboat, announced that that vessel was to sail for Riga on the following morning . . . .!

I trembled, and I had difficulty in suppressing the emotion I felt; but still, I thought, how was I to reach the steamer, how enter into parley with the captain of it? I saw a man, probably the pilot, walking on deck; his red shirt pulled on over his drawers was quite after the Russian fashion, but I did not dare to address him, and I contented myself with devouring him with my eyes. In the meantime the sun was sinking, and it was going on to seven o'clock in the evening, when suddenly the man in the red shirt looked up and said: —

'Do you by any chance want to go to Riga? If so, take your passage by us.'

'Certainly, I want to go to Riga; but how is a poor

man like me to go in the steamboat? That costs a great deal, it is not made for the like of us.'

'Why not; come along. A *moujik* like you won't be asked to pay a great deal.'

'How much?'

He named a sum, which I do not remember, but which astonished me at the time as being really very moderate.

'Well, will that suit you? What are you hesitating about now?'

'I only came here to-day, and the Police must *viser* my passport.'

'Then, let me tell you, you will have a three days' job of it with your Police, and our steamer sails to-morrow morning.'

'What can I do then?'

'Go without having it *visé*, to be sure.'

'Bah! suppose I get into trouble?'

'Idiot! Here is a *moujik* setting up to teach me! Have you got your passport with you? Let us see it.'

I drew from my pocket the pass which I kept carefully wrapped in a silk handkerchief, after the Russian plan; but the man did not even give himself the trouble of looking at it.

'Come to-morrow, at seven o'clock in the morning, and if you don't find me here, wait for me; and now be off as quick as you can.'

I returned joyously to my lodgings, and on the

following morning I was punctual to my appointment. Steam was already got up; my man perceived me, and said simply, 'Pay your money.' He then left me, and returned with a yellow ticket, of which I naturally pretended to ignore the signification. This extracted a second notice, as follows, 'Hold your tongue, *moujik*, and let us manage.' The bell rang three times, the barrier was opened, the passengers pressed and hurried in, while a rude shove from my friend sent me in along with the others. Some moments after the paddles went round, we were in motion; and I was as one that dreamed.

CHAPTER X.

THE RETURN TO PARIS.

THE MOUJIK'S PASSAGE — LITHUANIA — THE PRUSSIAN FRONTIER — KÖNIGSBERG — ARREST AND CAPTIVITY — BAIL — FLIGHT — ARRIVAL IN PARIS — THE END.

A PASSAGE in the steamer from St. Petersburg to Riga does not furnish a subject replete with many features of travel, not even when the traveller is a Siberian exile, flying from the *katorga*. Yet I had one little adventure, for ocean certainly was hostile to me. Thanks, I suppose, to the stupefaction caused by sea-sickness, I suddenly found myself in the first-class cabin — an intrusion which horrified and disgusted everyone. An elderly Russian lady in particular never ceased crying in French, 'Oh, this peasant will give us the plague! He corrupts the little air we have to breathe!' Some servants came, who brought me to my senses, and took me to my own quarters, where, squatting in a corner in the fore part of the ship, I kept to myself, and did not again see any of the passengers of distinction, unless their walk happened to bring them occasionally in my direction. Two Germans, seeing me making my breakfast on a bit of bread and an onion (which I did to keep up my part as a *moujik*, not less than also, alas! from motives of economy), said out loud, in their amiable language, 'One can see that that is a Russian hog.' Oddly enough, the only persons among the travellers who showed any interest in me, and who sometimes condescended to talk to me (without having a suspicion of my nationality), were two young men, both of them Poles. I often followed them with my eyes as they paced up and down the deck; how gladly would I have pressed their hands!

I shall pass rapidly over the rest of my journey from Riga, across Courland and Lithuania, as far as the Prussian frontier, and shall only say a few words about the new profession I assumed on quitting St. Petersburg. The character of a *bohomolets* could not any longer serve me, now that I was going in a contrary direction from Novgorod, and I was also about to cross countries which, like Courland or Samogitia, were either of Catholic or Protestant beliefs. I therefore proposed to pass for a *stchetinnik*, for such is the name for the Russian peasants so often met in those districts as well as in Lithuania and in the Ukraine, who, going from one village to another, buy hog's bristles on behalf of the merchants of Riga. This trade suited me admirably, for under pretence of inquiring whether my article was to be had or not, it allowed me to knock at many doors, and to ask my way. I went on foot, sleeping most frequently in the woods or in the cornfields, and the fine weather (it was July) was very favourable to me. I had likewise exchanged my winter trowsers for the summer suit of blue cotton which I had brought from Siberia; I renewed my linen and my boots, and I exchanged my pelisse with a tapster for a great-coat and a little cap, which, with a view to traversing Prussia, I carried with me in my bag, while as to my little bournouse of sheep-skin (*armiak*), that, like a true Russian peasant (*rouski tchelovièk*), I always wore, in spite of the warmth of summer.

My passage through Lithuania, across our *hallowed* Samogitia, was not void of emotion, or of sufficiently diverting scenes. How often was I not tempted to reveal my nationality to some one or other of my own country people, and to ask their advice or assistance! But I resisted every temptation, and I never belied my character as a Russian *stchetinnik*. One day, at Polonga, I wanted to buy a cheese in the market from a Samogitian woman; we could not agree about the price, and my respectable countrywoman, strong in lungs as any woman of *la Halle*, delivered herself of a sentiment about 'dogs of Muscovites,' which was certainly not of a highly Christian description. Had I even been ignorant of the meaning of her words, their sense was sufficiently explained by gestures, patent even to a *moujik*, and I was obliged forsooth to pretend to uphold the honour of Muscovy against the outrages of a Polish woman . . . .!

It was between Polonga and Kurszany that I determined to pass into Prussia. I had infinite trouble before I could procure, without betraying myself, any information as to the way or the extent to which the Russians watched their frontier, my best source of knowledge being a soldier belonging to the customs. Seeing him take a bath in the little bay of Polonga, I followed his example, hoping thus to begin a conversation. As soon as he said that he was a native of Pultava, I declared myself his countryman. There is always one simple way of getting a Russian soldier to talk, which is to start him about his grievances, and the hardships of his lot. Once on this theme my companion informed me of all the precautionary measures which had to be taken, by day and by night, by the customs on account of smugglers and rebels (*bountovstchiki*), for so fugitives are called, with details as to the strength and the weakness of the watch thus kept . . . . I must give one expression used by the soldier, than which nothing could have been more characteristic. I had naïvely asked him why the Prussians did not help to keep the frontier and hunt down the *rebels* and smugglers? 'That,' he answered, 'is just the pity of it all! These cursed Prussians will not take any trouble at the frontier, and so *all the burden falls on our poor Tzar* . . . .!'

The conclusion drawn by me from this valuable conversation was precisely contrary to what I had at first supposed, and I saw that it would be best that I should try to cross the boundary line in the day time; so, at two o'clock in the afternoon of that same day, having armed myself with my poignard, and commended my soul to God, I slipped into the corn. Then spying from the top of the rampart the moment during which both sentries on the station turned their backs on each other, I leapt the first of the three ditches which marked the frontier. No noise was made; I clambered through the brushwood, but as I reached the second ditch I was perceived. Shots were fired from guns on both sides, when, hardly conscious of what I was about, I slipped into the third ditch, then climbed up and leapt again. I lost sight of the soldiers, and was in a little wood. I was in Prussia!

Breathless and exhausted, I lay for many long hours hidden in the thicket without daring to stir; knowing the violence and eagerness of the Russians, I feared lest they should even pursue me into forbidden ground; but happily all was still, and a soft rain which began to fall tempered the suffocating heat of the day. It was time to think of a fresh disguise. The *moujik's* orthodox beard was not suitable in Prussia, where it would only have attracted attention; so at Polonga I had taken the precaution to buy a small mirror and a razor, which I got at a Jew's stall, while, as to soap, a piece of what I had brought from Siberia remained still in my bag. I hung the mirror up on a bush, and, profiting by the rain and, above all, by the dew on the leaves for moistening the soap, proceeded in this way, though still lying and on my elbow, to perform the civilising operation of shaving myself. It was a slow and a painful one, particularly on account of my uncomfortable position; but I effected it at last, not, however, without sundry cuts made in my cheeks. About the middle of the night I got up and went on my way again, dressed in the great coat and the little cap, with my trowsers falling over my boots. I knew very well that I was by no means out of danger, for a convention between Russia and Prussia, a cartel as it was called, then obliged the two powers to deliver over their mutual fugitives; and more than one, alas! of my compatriots had been thus brought back to the Russian frontier, after having succeeded, in spite of many and great dangers, in leaving it behind them. Still I had confidence in my star, the great matter for me now being to avoid inns, and to keep clear of gendarmes, a task which, thanks to the summer season, was not very difficult. As to the direction of my journey, I had no longer any hesitation about it. I must gain the Grand Duchy of Posen, and there, among my fellow-countrymen subject to the Prussian rule, but whose safety I could in no way compromise, I hoped to find all the help which the rapid diminution of my finances demanded. I was then ignorant of the massacres which had recently desolated Galicia, and I did not even know that in this very Duchy of Posen a vast conspiracy had been discovered; for it was not in the solitudes of the Oural chain, nor yet among the lowest of the Russian people, that I could have learnt these heavy and sad tidings.

I reached Memel, Tilsit and Königsberg successively without any obstacles. I walked by day, and slept under the stars; I was nowhere annoyed about my passport, and to the unfrequent questions of merchants and travellers I replied that I was a Frenchman, a cotton-spinner, returning from Russia. At last on July 27th, having reached Königsberg, I saw in the harbour a vessel that was to sail on the following day for Elbing. Tired of constant walking, I wished to profit by a means of transport which could be had for a moderate price, and which would have taken me nearly to the Grand Duchy of Posen, and to my friends. I determined therefore to remain in Königsberg till the following day. While waiting in this way I sauntered about the town, and as evening fell I sat down on a heap of stones near a dismantled house, meaning at night to wander away and sleep in the cornfields, and to return next morning before the vessel sailed. Alas! I had not reckoned on my bodily fatigue any more than on the exhaustion of my strength, and a certain carelessness had been engendered by the last period of comparative security. Upon this heap of stones I fell asleep, and slept deeply. When I awoke, roughly shaken by the arm by some man, it was a dark night. A stranger stood before me, a night-watcher of the town, as they are called. He asked me who I was, and whence I came? Drunk with sleep, I muttered some incoherent words, and when a sense of my danger finally recalled me to myself, it was in vain that, in my infamous German, I offered any explanations as to who I was, and how I came to be there; all my answers seemed suspicious. My complete ignorance of the place and the darkness of the night prevented me from beginning to struggle with him, or attempting to fly; I did feel for my dagger, but luckily I could not find it. The constable took hold of my arm, called his comrades, and carried me off by force to the nearest office. I was arrested . . . . !

The feeling which came over me when once more I found myself in a prison was one of shame, far more than of sadness or of despair. To have escaped from the *katorga*, to have crossed the Oural Mountains, to have slept for months in the snow in ostiak *earths*, to have endured so many sufferings and privations, to have leapt the Russian boundary line among the musket balls of soldiers, and now to be taken up by neither more nor less than a Prussian night constable! It really was too ridiculous, and I blushed for myself.

The next morning, about ten o'clock, I was taken to the Police office, and then commenced all the sad and abject necessities of simulation and dissimulation, which press on a man who has to elude the cognisance of the law. I pretended that I was a Frenchman, a cotton-spinner, who was on his way back from Russia, and who had lost his passport. I gave my addresses in both countries, but I could perceive that my declarations did not inspire any confidence. What hurt me most was to perceive in this first examination, and still more in some that followed it, that I was taken for a malefactor, who had some interest in concealing a crime. I demanded to be sent back to France, where I said I was ready to answer before public justice for all my actions, and to submit to the consequences of all and everything that could be discovered about me.

I was now remanded to the Blue Tower (Blaûer Thûrm), where for company I found a burger detained for fraudulent bankruptcy and other peccadilloes. The Blue Tower certainly was not horrible to a man who knew the insides of Russian prisons, not to speak of the *katorga*; but the uncertainty and the irritation caused by this sad interlude recalled some of the worst days of my existence during the last years. At last, after a month's detention, I was again called before the police; it was signified to me that all the addresses which I had given had been found to be incorrect, and that I now lay under the gravest suspicions. Tired of making false pretences, and above all of passing for a criminal trying to hide his identity, I begged to have a private interview with one of the high functionaries who examined me, and for the presence at it of M. Fleury, a Frenchman, naturalised at Königsberg for the last thirty years. He was *interpréte-juré*, and had always assisted at the enquiries. When left alone with these two gentlemen I told them frankly who I was, and I left my fate in their hands. I cannot describe the astonishment, the stupor, and, I must also add, the consternation of my two examiners on learning that before them stood a Pole, a political criminal escaped from the *katorga*, and returned from Siberia! The official at first could not say a word; at last he cried, 'But, miserable man! we must give you up; the convention is decisive! Oh, my God! why, why did you come here?'

'I wished to spare you both embarrassment and remorse, so why did you not send me on to France as I asked you?'

They made me give all the details of my flight; then the Prussian official left the room. M. Fleury stepped up to me and said, 'We cannot avoid giving you up to the Russians; quite recently several of your fellows have been sent back over the frontiers. There is only one likelihood of salvation for you, try to see the Count Eûlenberg, or at least to write to him. He is President of the government (Regierûngs Präsident), and almost everything depends on him. He is a good-hearted man — frank, generous, and beloved by all. Write to him, for Heaven's sake! Oh, what a pity! what a pity!'

On my return to prison I did write to Count Eûlenberg and also to our Abbé Kajsiewicz, in Paris, to obtain an attestation of my identity, because I perceived that they questioned among themselves whether I was not an emissary who had taken part in the late affairs in Posen. Since my revelation they treated me better in my prison, but I was not the less the object of a very strict watch. After ten days I got an answer from Count Eûlenberg, which was polite but vague, although the advice at the close of it, 'to have patience,' seemed to me to be some encouragement. The principal point of all the investigations was, had I or had I not shared in the business in Posen? On that head I felt perfectly at my ease; but my anguish of mind, nevertheless, was very great, and very often I had to say to myself that perhaps my most certain hope of being saved lay in my own dagger.

One day a gentleman presented himself at my prison; he gave his name as M. Kamke, a merchant of Königsberg, and he begged to know if I would accept of his bail. Astonished as well as touched at this unexpected offer, I asked for an explanation of it, and then learnt that the report of a Pole who had escaped from Siberia being arrested in the town had spread, and caused a general and lively emotion. The honest townsfolk of Königsberg, who had more than once been irritated at the working of the cartel with Russia, were grieved at the idea of seeing a man given up who had succeeded in eloping from Siberia, and who had braved so many dangers. Several steps had been taken in my behalf, and they hoped to find means to liberate me under bail given for me! Ah, how much good these words did! The acceptance of securities for me met with some opposition; but when summoned anew, on September 1st, I found with the Police this excellent M. Kamke, who coming up to me embraced me, and told me I was free. It really was so, and the official in charge of the inquest repeated the assurance to me. He asked if I wished to remain some time longer in Königsberg, and I replied in the affirmative, for I wished to thank my benefactors, the many persons who had interested themselves in my fate, particularly Count Eûlenberg. It also seemed to me to be good policy not to appear to be too anxious to leave Prussia. Alas! how suspicious I had become!

M. Kamke took me home in triumph, and for a week I found in his family an affectionate care, of which the remembrance can never be effaced. Suddenly, a week having barely elapsed since I had been allowed my liberty, I was again invited to attend at the police. I found there two functionaries whom I had met before. With a sad but kind manner, they informed me that orders had come from Berlin that I must be given up to Russia; they added that they had now nothing in their power but to give me time to fly from this danger at my own peril, and that they hoped God would protect my steps. I was profoundly touched by their generous proceedings, and I promised to do my utmost to save them any further trouble. I immediately informed M. Kamke and my protectors of this new incident, and my flight was speedily arranged. I took leave of my brave and true friends, and on the following day, September 9th, I was already on my way to Dantzig. I was furnished with letters to different persons in the German towns which I had to pass through, and everywhere the greatest zeal was shown to make my journey easy. I must be permitted to mention especially the good offices of the celebrated and generous bookseller of Leipsig, Robert Blûm, whom Prince Windischgrætz thought right to have shot at Vienna two years later. Thanks to Help which never failed me, I had speedily traversed the whole of Germany, and on September 22nd, 1846, I found myself again in Paris, in the city which I had left four years before.

Something more than a year had scarcely elapsed after my return to Paris, when the revolution of February broke out, and my country believed in a better future. But, alas! we soon saw our mistake. Once more I had hastened to my own land, and had just time to assist in Galicia at a fresh shipwreck of our hopes. It was during the leisure which expectations thus deceived had left to me, and while my memory retained the impression of what had recently passed, that I wrote down the greater part of these

'Recollections.' If I have not mentioned my poor brothers in misfortune, implicated in the affair at Kaminieç, it has certainly not been because I was then, or am now, indifferent to their lot; but because I have been able to learn very little of their fate, or of the nature of the sentences which were passed upon them. Some have already succumbed under their sorrows; others still groan in Siberia, in the Caucasus, or in the penal companies of Orenbourg.

May God have mercy upon the living, and upon the dead!

POLAND A CENTURY AFTER ITS DIVISION,

AND

THE AGITATION IN WARSAW.

May 1861.

POLAND

A CENTURY AFTER ITS DIVISION.

THE world is full of victimised races, to whose ill-fortune it becomes almost reconciled, since the marvellous discovery has been made that, at some time or another, these people may have deserved their fate; as if the strong, for their part, did not also commit faults; and as if, too, Justice went evermore hand in hand with Fortune. But whence, then, those crises of anarchy which are apparent, not only in a solitary instance, but in the most general relations? Whence those convulsions which make us present, as it were, at a confused disorganisation of all political order, in one headlong annihilation of all combinations, and of all foregone conclusions? These take their rise, most frequently, in some original defect lying at the very roots of the situation, in some previous violations which, although they leave the people unarmed, do not the less affect the governments themselves — which compel the first to a system of indefatigable revolt, and the second to a system of repression, which is always fatally increasing in weight, till, at last, there ensues one of those struggles in which contend all the rights, principles, and accumulated wrongs — all the causes long thought to be dormant, but which, now reawakened, make their appeal to that public opinion which has started up as a new power. The whole history of Poland is before us, to prove how much violence it costs, how many perpetually recurring struggles it requires, to make the suppression of a whole race a public right, before the fact of its suppression can be forced into the vague and terrible list of 'things that have been accomplished.'

It is now nearly a century since three Powers, united by the saddest and most dangerous of solidarities, laboured to this end. Frederick II. of Prussia and Catherine the Great of Russia rejoiced in the work as in an easy victory; but it carried remorse into the soul of Maria-Theresa of Austria, who called it 'a blot upon her reign,' to which she could not subscribe without casting a terrified glance into the future. Thrice was the partition renewed — in 1772, in 1793, and in 1795. It began by leaving us a shadow of independence, with the shadow of a king at Warsaw; and it finished by making everything disappear, even to the very name of Poland. At each dismemberment they believed that they had achieved success; each time, on the contrary, the injustice of the whole proceeding became more evident, till it was almost acknowledged to be so by the dividers themselves—each time the wound became more envenomed, and the struggle more serious between an always precarious domination, and the heroism of a race remodelled by misfortune. At the capital moment of the last dismemberment, in 1792, Poland did not yield without a struggle; she proclaimed her political aspirations in the Constitution of the 3rd of May 1791, and, led by Kosciusko, she reappeared upon the field of battle. The Polish hero was conquered at Macejowice, and the work, begun in 1772, seemed very nearly completed. Up to this time, however, it had only been an affair between Russia, Austria, and Prussia; and Europe had remained a stranger to this dismemberment of a nation.

At the end of the storms of the French Revolution, and of the Empire, in which the Poles had taken part with all their warlike humour, and during which, by the timid, ephemeral, and incomplete creation of a Grand-Duchy of Warsaw, they had for an instant believed that their country was reborn, the Congress of Vienna, after allowing hope to shine before the eyes of Poland, let her fall again under the triple yoke, and consecrated her dismemberment as an accomplished fact. This time, at least, success seemed sure—the partition had become a public right, and it formed a part of the constitution of Europe; yet, in reality, the question was very far from being set at rest. The treaties of 1815 only organised new strife, under new conditions; and a new weapon was placed in the hands of the Poles, by this species of homage paid to a nationality that no one ventured quite to kill, its titles being recognised, and stipulations being made in favour of its guarantees; while, at the same time, they dared not refuse its fragments to those who claimed them by right of prior occupation. The question, then, was so little settled, that at the first agitation it did not fail to come up again. In 1830, Poland made an immense effort for its own resurrection, an effort which for a moment sufficed to hold in check the power of Russia, and filled Europe with anxiety and emotion. Alone, and abandoned to her own resources, Poland must evidently succumb; she must sink under the weight of arms, still more under the weight of oppression. Then, surely, the last words had been said, the last resistance conquered, and all was really at an end. On the contrary, nothing was finished; and this is the curious point, the great moral, so to speak, of the events which for the last two months agitate Warsaw and all Polish countries. One hundred years after the first dismemberment, forty-five years after the treaties of 1815, thirty years after the revolution quelled at Warsaw by the arms of Russia, Poland rears her head, more agitated than ever, wounded but not tamed, and showing herself in two lights — the one, as regards her relations with the state of Europe; the other, as regards that internal labour, by which she has obstinately sought to remake for herself a moral life, and a new destiny, in spite of the darkest, and most painful trials.

What, then, really is the character of this situation, so suddenly revealed in Northern Europe by the strange drama of Warsaw, at the very moment when Italy has constituted herself anew, and when Hungary claims her old tradition of independence — when both in the West and in the East everything is in movement — when all questions of nationality, of public rights, and of universal balance, are making themselves heard at once? What is most strange in these events is, that all is spontaneous and unforeseen, though an eternal reason gives them being. This is the act of life in a people, which, finding itself one day united by one and the same feeling, spreads itself peaceably through the town, and then demands, what even treaties have not denied to it, respect for its nationality, and its own religion, the guarantee of its existence in regular institutions, the preservation of its own language, the right of interesting itself in its own affairs, of occupying itself in agriculture, in the education of its own children; the right, in a word, to live and to breathe. Nothing assuredly can be more dramatic than the meeting which during the last two months has taken place in Warsaw. It is no longer one between two sovereigns, but between two nations, which for the first time for thirty years find themselves publicly face to face, which have suddenly brought their disagreement into the broad daylight of European conflict, and which are now interrogating each other in this mysterious pause; two peoples, of which the one has no arms but its rights and its prayers, and of which the other has no danger but in the very excess of its own powers.

This, then, really is the situation which has disclosed itself in the heart of Poland since the 25th of February, the day upon which this new, touching, and heroic adventure began for a population which, to a certain extent, thus returns to public life, and which goes out to pray for its country and its dead. At first, Russia appears to have been visibly surprised at this unexpected manifestation on the part of Poland, in which she believed, perhaps, that no such vitality existed, and she was divided between the inquietude caused by the movement, and by the sense that concessions must be made. She has not the gift of always making the happiest resolutions; she yields when it would be natural to resist, and resists when it would be just to yield. She begins by giving up some of those officials who are most compromised, and she ends in dissolving those popular corporations of which she not only herself sanctioned the existence, but of which she had availed herself for a month, in order to maintain order. Thus, by a series of enigmatical and contradictory acts, in which, doubtless, there is as much embarrassment as calculation, she sets all hopes and all fears fermenting together. Popular manifestations follow one after the other. The question assumes greater proportions, the movement becomes graver and more complicated, and in a short time the whole affair has changed its aspect. The pressure imposed becomes heavier than ever, when pitted against a moral agitation which has been throughout innocent of any violence, so that it requires but a few days and an evolution of Russian policy to bring the situation to one of those issues, which Prince Repnin characterised in his day with inexorable bluntness, when he said, 'Unless we deny all sentiments of humanity, it is true that we cannot help recognising the right which the Poles have to complain. You would have full right to drive out the Russians, if you had the power; not having the power, you must submit.'

Such is the question truly stated by the victorious side, and certainly such is the question so often supposed to have been definitely settled, but which has never been resolved. After the bloody repression of the 8th of April, as after all those that went before, the problem of the destinies of Poland is not the less on foot. It springs out of these events, and is shaped by their character and their aims, in the midst of those conditions of universal transition in which the world of to-day finds itself placed.

What makes these new events so important, is that

they form part of a European situation, at the same time that they are the outward and visible signs of a profound and inward work, of which Russian Poland is the centre (most active and most prominent at present), but which has also revealed, in the Grand Duchy of Posen, in Galicia, in short, everywhere, that, in spite of treaties and congresses, Polish feeling, the last and indestructible tie of a riven country, still lives. This question of Poland has its roots deep in the past, and I am not ignorant that it is so. Whether politically or diplomatically, it goes back, like so many more, to the transactions of 1815, and when the attempt is made to draw closer the knot of European affairs, whence come the crises of which this question has been the unhappy and the perennial source? Is it not because these treaties have manifestly been an immense and avowed violation of an imprescriptable right, or rather the fatal and complaisant consecration of all previous violations? One of the most essential causes of the tribulation and disorder in the politics of the time—a cause which now appears in all its distinctness—is the ever-growing contradiction between the dispositions of the solemn act of Vienna and the real state to which the different parts of Poland are reduced; so that, if there have been, if there shall again be, revolutionists, we must settle this in our minds, that it is not the Poles who are such. An example has been given them in this matter, and they have been left with this sad conviction, that, according to the rights of 1815, they have the right on their side. It is, indeed, a curious thing that the people of Poland have been the 'last to step down into the arena of to-day at that name of "nationality" which serves as a watchword to all other revolting populations.' Yet Poland was the first and the only country in whose favour such a word was hinted at by the Congress of Vienna, when it was inscribed in treaties, as if to render a marked homage to heroic misfortune, and, while tempering by guarantees the way in which Poland was abandoned, to maintain the mockery of an ideal 'nationality,' in spite of territorial division.

Still more curious was the sort of universal disavowal made of the partition of Poland, at the moment in which it was announced as a new public right. M. de Talleyrand, the representative of the French king, called it 'the prelude to European convulsions;' and of all the questions that were to come before the Congress, he considered the Polish one to be 'the first, the greatest, the most eminently European, and, beyond comparison, before all the others in importance.' The Emperor Alexander of Russia, professing himself the renovator of Poland, was actuated either by ambition or by the vanity of appearing as a liberal prince, and, doubtless, also by sentiments of generosity; but this renovation offered itself to his mind under the shape of a kingdom which should be a feudatory of the Russian crown, while it still preserved the integrity of Poland.

Poland was a subject of remorse to Europe, and she inspired respect, without having strength enough to make herself truly and really respected. Hence the strange combinations adopted by the Congress of Vienna, which (while it delivered over the provinces of Poland to Austria, to Russia, and to Prussia) multiplied at the same time protecting guarantees, and laboured to maintain a national link between the different parts, by assuring to them a certain autonomy, as if the future could be secured by abandoning the present.

From one point of view, nothing can be stranger than the organised *whole*, of which the scattered elements are to be found in the final act of Vienna, and in the separate proceedings between Russia, Prussia, and Austria, under the sanction of Europe. In Galicia, Cracôw, escaping the general shipwreck, is constituted 'for all time coming' (*à perpétuité*) a free, neutral and independent town. The transformation of the Grand Duchy of Warsaw into the kingdom of Poland, under the Russian crown, leaves the name of the country still diplomatically existing, and it leaves it also as the nucleus of reconstruction, the centre of attraction. The Prussian division gets the name of Grand Duchy of Posen, that it may preserve a distinct character in the whole monarchy of Frederick II.; and the frontier on the Prussian side is defined, as well as on the Russian border. Finally (and here is the origin of the great debate in the eyes of diplomatic Europe), the three powers engage themselves, by their act at Vienna, to give to the Poles, their respective subjects, 'representation and such national institutions, arranged according to their modes of political existence, as each of the governments shall judge to be useful;' while, in order better to define the sense and meaning of these guaranteed institutions, the separate treaties add that these are intended to secure to the Poles 'the preservation of their nationality.'

Nor is this all. In default of political unity and of real independence, Poland is at least to keep the unity of her interests. Full liberty of trading, of transit, and of navigation, is established in all and between all the divisions of '*ancient Poland*;' and it must be noted that care was taken constantly to recall the old frontiers of 1772 as the natural frame for all combinations. The quality of 'a mixed subject' is recognised in those who have possessions in all the three provinces, and who, escaping all classification, remain, in spite of everything, *Poles*, as their civil individuality cannot be divided under three heads. Such, indeed, is the spirit which permeates this work (singular and incoherent as I do not deny that it is), that Austrians, Prussians and Russians, are qualified as *strangers* or *foreigners* in the article which treats of arrangements to be made for the regulation of commercial interests on Polish grounds; and by this title *they* are excluded from such benefits as only the Poles are entitled to enjoy. I shall not proceed further. Considering the transactions of 1815 as a whole, and putting them together, what do we find? We find a free town, the last remaining image of former independence. We find the name of one common country consecrated by treaty, and resting upon the kingdom newly called into being. We see our right to a nationality made superior to all territorial demarcations. We read, in the first place, of the autonomy of the different provinces that have been dealt out to new masters, and that the map of old Poland is to be adopted and acted upon in material life; and we have a sort of *Zollverein* of commerce and navigation, serving as the sketch for a confederacy. One would say that it looks as if Europe, not daring to be wholly just, had wished, at each step, to soften away by equity the violation of the independent existence of a nation; that, practically, she sought to reunite the national tie, which arbitrary right had recently broken; and that she was less occupied in resolving the question of the destinies of Poland, or putting an end to it by one act of sovereign power, than in leaving it in suspense, and handing it over to the future.

All that thus appears in some inert articles of the treaty, receives a sort of luminous and decisive confirmation from the interpretations of the times, from the commentaries of the sovereigns themselves, as well as from the first deeds done under the fresh impression of these events. No one knows what passed through the mind of the Emperor Alexander — through that mind at once so playful and so imperious, so full of liberal desires and of mysterious unrest, of generous instincts and of Byzantine duplicity; but he, at any rate, entered upon his part by not recoiling from such a beginning as would ensure his popularity. 'In truth,' he said to Lord Castlereagh, 'though at this moment the object is not to re-establish Poland in its integrity, there is nothing to prevent that being done some day, if Europe should desire it. To-day, such a thing would be premature. That country needs to be prepared for so great a change; and there is no better way of doing it than to erect into a kingdom one part of its territory, and in this to place such institutions as will make the principles of civilisation take root and fructify; they will then spread through the whole mass.' And, in truth, Alexander was the first who set to work, till he gave a charter to his new kingdom, the constitution of the 13th of May, 1815; and of this he himself expressed the sense, in a proclamation made to the Poles: 'A constitution suited to your wants and to your characters; the use of your language preserved in public transactions; offices and employments bestowed solely on Poles; liberty in commerce and in navigation; facilities of communication with such parts of ancient Poland as are subject to other powers; a national army; all means guaranteed to perfect your laws, with the free circulation of knowledge in your country — *these* are the advantages which you will enjoy under our rule, and under that of our successors; and *these*, also, you will transmit as a patriotic inheritance to your children and your children's children. . .'

The reader will remark here, that this is strictly the meaning of the Treaty of 1815; and three years later, in 1818, Alexander, when opening the first Polish Diet at Warsaw, still held the same language. 'Your restoration is defined,' he said, 'by the most solemn treaties, and sanctioned by a constitutional charter; and the inviolability of these exterior engagements and of this fundamental law henceforward assures to Poland an honourable rank among the nations of Europe.' The Emperor, moreover, seems to have so little questioned the guarantees of Europe, that he boasted of having won them for Poland, as one wins a victory, by a brilliant charge. 'I have made this kingdom,' he goes on to say —'I have established it on the most solid basis; for *I have obliged* the Powers of Europe to guarantee its existence by treaty.' At one moment, the successful autocrat had thoughts of going a step further, and of aggrandising the new kingdom by annexing to it the old Polish provinces incorporated with Russia, viz. Lithuania, Volhynia, and the Ukraine; for he had reserved the right of doing so, in his treaty with Austria, in these very words: 'His Imperial Majesty reserves to himself the right of giving to this state, which enjoys a distinct administration, such *interior extension* as he shall think proper;' and this it was which, for a moment, gained over the heart of old Kosciusko to the policy of Alexander.

The King of Prussia, if he left a brilliant part, and the formation of great projects to the Tzar, did not act differently from him. He held the same language to the Poles of Posen. 'You, likewise,' he said to them, 'have a country, and I esteem you because you have known how to defend her. You will be my subjects; but you will not, for that reason, be obliged to deny your own nationality. Your religion is to be respected, and your personal rights and properties are to pass under the guardianship of laws which, for the future, will be enacted by yourselves. Your language in all public affairs will be employed along with the German tongue. You will fill up all the offices of the Grand Duchy of Posen; and my Lieutenant, born among you, will reside with you.'

The formula of the oath imposed upon officials was peculiarly significant. It was conceived in these terms: 'I acknowledge his Majesty the King of Prussia as the only legitimate sovereign of this country; and *I acknowledge that part of Poland which, in consequence of the Treaty of Vienna, has fallen to the lot of the royal House of Prussia, to be my country,* the which I am ready to defend against all persons whatsoever, and under all circumstances, at the price of my own blood.' Such an interpretation long continued to be in use, since, in 1841, King Frederic William IV. engaged 'to respect in the Poles that love which every heroic nation cherishes, for its language, its customs, and its historic past.'

As to the Emperor of Austria, he, in 1815, did nothing. With his cold temper, the Emperor Francis laughed a little at the restlessness, and the liberal proclivities of Alexander of Russia. He was, however, uneasy about them, and ended by saying, 'I am not false enough for that,' which, of course, did not change the *meaning* of the arrangements of 1815. In recalling all these facts, it must not be supposed that I entertain the eccentric idea of making the last of the rights of Poland rest in the work of the Congress of Vienna; but still these treaties, such as they were, brought about a certain order of things. If it was not independence which they secured, at least they gave us a number of guarantees — the preservation of nationality even in partition, the autonomy of our institutions, and of our interests. Our name, our religion, and our language were all, under the sanction of Europe, saved from total shipwreck and loss.

But has experience shown us that this is the plan which has been followed now for nearly half a century? The truth is that, in accepting the situation created by the Treaty of Vienna (an order of events which had its conditions, its obligations, and its limits), Russia,

Prussia, and Austria have shaped their practice after the spirit which presided at the *first* partition — that is, after the idea of an assimilation so complete as to be equivalent to conquest. From these treaties of 1815, they have, to say the truth, reaped the benefit of having got a European sanction for the dismemberment of Poland; but they have troubled themselves very little about the guarantees which were designed to serve as a sad and impotent compensation for the partition; and each of these three powers has carried on its work after the fashion which has best suited itself, its politics, and its nature.

Not that the change was made suddenly, or openly visible. It has been developed by degrees, especially in the kingdom of Poland. Veiled at first, during the lifetime of Alexander, by constitutional forms, it was hastened, and no longer concealed, under the Emperor Nicholas, whose policy may be described in one word, the *denationalisation* of Poland. To accomplish this was the dream, the intense, unbounded, ardent passion of a prince who was perhaps a great Russian, driven by continental revolutions to play an exceptional part, but who left dangerous traces upon European policy, and bequeathed a weight of formidable difficulties to his successor. Yet it must not be said that the Revolution of 1831 placed Poland at the mercy of this Tzar, or that it released him from all his obligations, and gave him all the rights of a conqueror; for, in the first place, that revolution was nothing more than a reprisal — a desperate attempt at self-defence; and, what is more, against any such policy there rise at once all the stipulations of the Treaty of Vienna, and even all the words of the Emperor Alexander —'Your restoration is defined by solemn treaties. . . . I have obliged Europe to guarantee your existence by treaties. . . .' The Emperor Nicholas was, possibly, the fittest judge to determine what extent of liberalism he could put into the institutions of the kingdom of Poland; but he was not the only judge of what was, so to say, the European essence of these institutions — of that which concerned their spirit, according to treaty — of the preservation of the nationality of Poland. Diplomacy had placed that matter out of his power, by putting it beyond his reach. Now, this very nationality, placed under the guarantees of all Europe, became, unfortunately, a particular foe of Nicholas; and he persecuted it with all the inflexible vigour of his character, in our religion and our language, in the autonomy of our interests and institutions, in the independence of our hearths, in public instruction, in our manners, and in our very dress. This originated the system which, in 1831, substituted a new *statut organique* for the Constitution of 1815, and which, we must say, has been followed far too long, and followed, also, in all the bitterness of a spirit irritated by the resistance which it has met with.

The organic statute of 1831 made no secret of it; it was an absolute and definitive incorporation of the Kingdom into the Russian Empire. Thenceforward the ceremony of the coronation of the king of Poland at Warsaw was also abolished. The separate army disappeared, and military recruiting for Russia spread over the kingdom. The magistracy ceased to be unremovable, and Russian functionaries replaced Poles in the administration; while the constitutional chambers gave place to provincial assemblies, which have, moreover, never even been convoked. Thus a policy was disclosed, of which the only aim seems to have been to dissolve all the ties of national life in the kingdom, as well as in the ancient provinces. The high schools, the university, the library, the museum, and the mint of Warsaw vanished, or were transferred to St. Petersburg. Education was reduced to technical studies; Latin was banished at last; and the children in every parish, to whatever class of society they might belong, were obliged to attend the government schools, and to learn Russian, under pain of corporal punishment on the children, and of a fine in the case of the parents. One day, 5,000 families of the lesser nobility of Poland were ordered to be transported to the crown lands, or to the Caucasian border; and in the order of execution it was added, that, 'if the Polish gentry have no mind to be transplanted, you are authorised to oblige them, and to use force;' while another day the Council of

Administration at Warsaw adjudicated quietly on the transport of the *sons of noble Poles* to St. Petersburg, at the price of 120 roubles (paper money). I do not speak here of other orphan children carried off to Minsk, or of the multitudes of Poles of all ages removed to Siberia. Where persons are not safe, religion is also infringed. Sometimes it is attacked through the police, sometimes it suffers by the expropriation of Catholic Churches, by persecution, by the forced conversion of the United Greek to the Orthodox Church. The national costume is the next subject of interference; there is a law against wearing the national colours, against using blue, crimson, or white, though green and red are not wholly forbidden to the women, and we are permitted to put on white shirts. The Russian costume of a brown hue being much the most economical wear, the government undertakes to open clothing shops in all towns and villages! The reward of one rouble is offered to those who display the greatest alacrity in donning the Russian dress, and those who oppose themselves are flogged. In short, a vast attempt is made to efface everything that has the stamp of our country, or that can recall her existence. This hapless nationality in the midst of the empire must be made to disappear, and it must be made subordinate to the intentions and the interests of Russia.

The design of bringing about a forced assimilation, and of making the Polish give way to the Russian element, is often shown in the most futile administrative details, in the simplest questions of trade, and other material interests. Having once entered on this system, Russia is condemned to fear everything, and to watch every event. Not very long ago, Prussia drew up a set of complicated rules with regard to the importation of cattle into its territories, and established such a quarantine as might preserve its herds from those epizootic disorders which ravaged the southern parts of Russia. Who suffered from these difficulties? Of course, the kingdom of Poland (a country essentially agricultural, but possessing in its cattle one element of wealth) could not but suffer. It was then timidly requested that, in order to have the restrictions, made for the sake of Prussia, removed, and in order to leave the trade between Germany and Poland free, such precautionary measures as had heretofore been in force at the Prussian frontier of the kingdom should also be put in practice on the marches of the Russian provinces in which the contagion obtained. But nothing of the sort was done; and for this reason, that the sanitary *cordon* thus demanded must have been upon the old Polish boundary, and it would, oddly enough, have described the line of those frontiers which existed in 1792, and which the treaties of 1815 had laid down as the frame within which the commercial life of the different provinces of Poland was to exist. Russia was represented at Warsaw by a terrible man, a Director of the Interior, M. Muchanof, who could not bear to see Poland imaged even under the shape of a law of transit.

Another fact ought to be noticed. During the last years, a great question, from which the Russian Empire has much to fear, has been in agitation, I mean the emancipation of the peasantry; a problem of which the Emperor Alexander II. has attempted the solution. My business is not with the discussion of the subject in itself, but only to remark, that there is a great difference in regard to it between Russia and the kingdom of Poland. In the kingdom all the principles of the French civil code remain in full vigour. There is equality of persons in the eye of the law; but the constitution of property is a different thing. Thus, our peasants still pay, it is true, a feudal fine, or *corvée*, on the fields which they cultivate; but this fine is not a sign of personal servitude. The labouring man has his civil individuality. Thus, in the different countries his condition differs essentially; and yet when the question arose the other day, Polish proprietors were forbidden to do otherwise than follow the programme traced by the Russian government solely with a view to Russia.

My object in referring to this, is to point out in what a confusion of interests Polish autonomy now perishes by force; and yet that autonomy was placed under the sanction of the whole of Europe. In truth, must not Russian policy have passed all limits, if quite recently a permission to teach Polish in schools for *one hour* in the day (as if it was English or Turkish) came to be considered as a sort of reparation, almost as a liberal measure?

I do not say that a similar policy, under like conditions, or with similar measures, has been followed in Prussian Poland. There, at least, so much of liberalism prevails that the right of complaining is left. Our griefs are not lost in the silence of a boundless oppression. Polish deputies have to this day a place in the parliament of Berlin, where, inch by inch, they defend the privileges of their country. But are the two systems, after all, so very unlike each other? The latter is less violent in one way, but its object is at bottom the same; for Prussia, like Russia, labours to denationalise Poland. M. de Flotwell, a man who governed the Grand Duchy (Posen) for many years, explained his views when he said, that she did so, by insensibly stifling Polish manners, inclinations, and tendencies, and by introducing the German element in their place. The work of infiltering the German element is carried on in a thousand ways; by bureaucracy, by education, by the compulsory substitution of the German for the Polish tongue; by the transfer of land, with the connivance of the state, which sometimes buys up Polish estates, and sells them to Germans at a loss. There is not a single Polish notary in Posen. Justice is administered in German, and he who appears before the public tribunals is often examined, accused, nay even defended, in a language which he does not understand. It is the same with public instruction: it has hitherto been found impossible to establish a Polish high school (Lyceum), and where a working-man's college has been opened, the classes are taught and the course is in German. Even in private institutions it is forbidden to teach the history of Poland, and for this conclusive reason, 'that this history not being taught in the public schools, ought not any more to be taught in private ones!' The Prussian government, it must be said, makes no secret of its intentions; for it has promulgated in the parliament of Berlin, that 'the province of Posen is neither more nor less than a simple province of Prussia.'

We now come to Austria. As to that power, need I recall with what sinister dexterity she one day succeeded in putting hatred into the hearts of the peasants of Galicia, and in driving them upon the Polish nobility? And is it not a strange irony of fortune which has made Austria the guardian of the tombs of two heroes of Poland? The one is the grave of Sobieski, who sleeps in a church now abandoned and in ruins at Cracow; the other is that of Kosciusko. When Kosciusko died, the students of Cracow obtained leave to erect a humble monument to his memory on a height, at a little distance from the town. The Austrians came, they did not certainly do away with the tomb, but they covered it round with the works of a citadel, and placed by it an Austrian sentry! Finally, there came a day — a day which has not been forgotten, when the three powers were found united in the definite suppression of Cracow, that town, 'free, independent, and neutral to all perpetuity,' and all this with the sanction of Europe, which could do nothing but enter one protest more.

What result is evident from this assemblage of facts, from this eloquent demonstration of the lack of efficacy in European guarantees? This — that in reality the stipulations of Vienna have been set aside by the very powers in whose behalf they were made, by those who have, except these treaties, no other titles for the possession of Poland.

But the stipulations have disappeared under a series of violations, which have been systematically carried out, but which, while they enervate or nullify the guarantees that protected our nationality, also nullify the title of these governments, and give back their rights to nationalities, whose energy has been increased by their conflicts, or by the necessity of self-defence.

Further, it may be thought that these treaties created insoluble difficulties, attempted to make things live together which were utterly irreconcilable, viz., the contradictory rights and interests of the conquerors and the conquered. It may be so; but this only goes to prove that the Treaties of 1815 sowed the seeds of war and of disorder by the Vistula as by the Po; and the disturbances of half a century have grown up out of them, by the Po as by the Vistula.

Here we see what is most truly characteristic in these Polish matters. Here is no natural and peaceful developement of an order of things half constituted by the ruling power of public right. It is a history full of dramatic mysteries, of ardent protests, of which one-half only is known to the world, the other half being lost in dungeons, in subterranean vaults, in mines, in Siberia, in the Ourals. Above all, since 1831, it is the history of a dark and ceaseless conflict between a power which, in order to remain mistress, is obliged at every turn to exceed its rights, and a people which struggles, conspires and rebels, and to whom the permanent contact of a hard and foreign rule with a suffering nationality is a continual punishment — a people which passes its time in believing in hope even against hope, whom oppression raises more than it tames, and which even when conquered has the ingenuity to feed on its own sufferings, and to relish them with a dark and bitter delight.

Let any man represent to himself what that country is like, where to have read such and such a book by a Polish poet has sent thousands of young people to Siberia — a country where in the universities and schools the students, even the children, secretly practised beating each other with rods, in order to accustom themselves to tortures, and to be ready to bear every trial without flinching! This familiarity with pain, this sort of defiance to a hidden warfare, is one of the traits of the contemporary genius of Poland; and it is the theme of a song commonly sung in Poland to a slow and plaintive melody; an ironical and bloody lesson for the use of Polish mothers! 'Our Saviour, when still a child at Nazareth, played with the cross, the future instrument of his death; and thou, alas! oh, Polish mother, oughtest to amuse thy child with the instruments of his future play. Early, then, tie his hands with chains, fasten them to the infamous tumbril, that he may not grow pale at the executioner's axe, that he may not blush at the sight of the noose; for he will never go, as did the knights of old, to plant the cross triumphant at Jerusalem; nor yet, like the soldiers of later times, to till the fields of liberty, and to water them with his blood. He who will provoke your child will be a secret spy; he who will contend with him will be a perjured judge. His field of battle will be a dungeon underground; his sentence will be pronounced in some implacable cave. When conquered, no monument awaits him but the empty gallows tree; and for glory he shall have the stifled sobs of women, and the midnight whispers of his brother men!'

Thus has Poland existed for nearly thirty years, struggling and conspiring, trying both to interest

Europe in her misfortunes, and to accomplish within herself the great work of internal revolution — having to bear the back blow of every event, and of all those catastrophes which have crossed her efforts. In reality, perhaps Poland has suffered by three occurrences within the last fifteen years (occurrences which have had a conspicuous part in her fate) more than by any persecutions carried on against her. These events were believed to have proved fatal to her, but they have nevertheless been but as a new trial, a mysterious and a bitter prelude to a more serious manifestation of her powerful vitality. The first of these events was the massacre in Galicia in 1846 — the most terrible and bloody deception of all Polish patriots! The revolution of 1831, when it died out before the arms of Russia, had at least left this lesson, that for the future, any and every attempt at national enfranchisement must form part of such an internal transformation as should unite all classes, and interest the masses throughout the country in one common work for the emancipation of the peasantry, and for making them definitely holders of property. As to the means of doing this, the two parties, namely, the constitutional or aristocratic, and the democratic, differed. At bottom they had the same end in view, and the project was cherished more especially by the democratic propaganda, of which emigrants formed the central body. But all of a sudden, Austria, taking a part in the movement, turned the current of emancipative ideas against Poland, and by unloosing against the nobility the fury of the Galician peasantry, had taught the other dominant governments in Posen, and in the kingdom (Warsaw), how to establish their own reign most securely, by inflaming the minds of men, and by setting class against class. Thus ended the labours of the democratic conspiracy of the year 1846; and the work had to be recommenced, for this bloody act, brought about with most sinister shrewdness, had at least for the time being disconcerted every attempt in Poland, since action had lost its fulcrum in the masses who had been thus fatally led astray.

The French Revolution of February, 1848, was another of those events which, by deceiving Poland, have helped to weigh her down. It was the hour at which a great explosion was expected, for, in a French revolution, how could we do otherwise than see a movement affecting the world? How could we help thinking that all nations would free themselves from old claims, and that Europe would be transformed by democracy? But what, on the contrary, was the result? Everybody knows that this ill-starred revolution availed none of the nationalities. Neither could it have been of help to any, since it obliged France to concentrate her own forces, in order to save herself from dissolution. But the Polish cause had the misfortune of being united with those European commotions which were so much to be dreaded; and, what was worse, that cause served as the banner of the agitators of May 15th, 1848, who menaced everybody, and everything. This was its crime. Having become importunate and teasing, like some unpleasant recollection, its popularity was immediately lost; and, what was still more curious, it was Nicholas who became popular—that Emperor suddenly being transformed into the high priest of order and civilisation.

Then came the war in the East, and, at the prospect of inevitable complications in Europe, as at the sight of that strange combination — viz. a liberal alliance between France and England against Russia—the hopes of the Poles once more awoke. Had the Emperor Nicholas lived, his obstinacy might have occasioned such European complications as might have again given a place to Poland; but his death facilitated peace. The name of Poland cannot be spoken; and, inasmuch as the Revolution of February, 1848, deceived the democratic party among us, so did the war in the Crimea dissipate the illusions of these moderate politicians of the diplomatic party who reckoned upon Europe.

It is, then, after this series of mistakes and of hopes deceived, that Poland has retreated more and more into herself, and that she sits mutely waiting, having seen how conspiracies, European revolutions, and regular interventions, have all alike failed her. Poland feels that she has become unpopular; that, as a Pole expressed it, 'she is a bore,' and she avoids being spoken of. No doubt, she could not help feeling with secret bitterness, that liberal Europe takes interest in Italian nationality, in Hungarian nationality, in Moldo-Wallachian nationality, and forgets a little that there was a Polish nationality. But Poland is silent, and she endures this punishment of silence and indifference, which is more difficult to accept than war, more hard to bear than any persecutions; for it has to be borne by a people which has spent its life in seeking for a country, and which has filled the history of to-day with its heroism, its protests, and its distress. No one can imagine what an amount of suffering is inflicted on Polish hearts by the moral isolation in which we are left, and that, too, in the middle of the agitation occasioned by the revival of other nationalities. 'I see what it is,' said a Polish peasant; 'they will end in giving the Tsigans a king, but no one will ever think of giving one to us.' Poland had at one time so completely disappeared, that she was supposed to be dead; she was thought to be either resigned to her fate or conquered by suffering; and Europe was ready to go to sleep, as over an accomplished fact, thinking that now there was one question less in the world.

But Europe was wrong. These long years of silence and of loneliness, far from being the dark and unnoted end of the nation, were, on the contrary, but as the beginning of a new state, which late events have disclosed; of a new order of things formed by degrees, having its elements, its character, its personifications, and which, at a given moment, has turned out to be the unexpected manifestation of an energetic nationality, rallying to the cry of Dombrowski's legion, 'No, Poland is not dead!'

It was the era of conspiracies and of democratic propagandism which, up to 1846, furnished heroic men of strange intrepidity, such as Konarski, Zaleski, and Dombrowski; and, of this period of strife, the campaigns of 1846, in Galicia and Posen, were the bloody and mournful close. Ever since that time, and especially throughout the last years, we have had a work of practical renovation, which has used all means, which has been inoffensive in appearance, but not the less persistent because it was unobserved, and which has been accomplished, owing, in part, to that very silence of which I have already spoken. They who laboured felt deeply what danger lay in making their operations heard. 'Speak of us as little as may be,' wrote one of the leading men in Poland; 'speak, if you will, of our miseries, of our agonised state, but do not speak of our vitality, or of those signs of life which you remark in us, for that would be to kill us.' To this work, Prince Léon Sapieka greatly contributed in Galicia, as did Dr. Marcinkowski in Posen, up to the time of his death; while, in the kingdom, none gave themselves to it more than did Count Andrew Zamoyski.

Of what is that movement composed, which, thus suddenly disclosed, has again brought Polish nationality face to face with Russian power?

Doubtless, it has its source in many elements. All have a share in it; for there meet religious zeal heightened by persecution, the labours of mind, and the efforts made to raise the morals of the people. There is industrial enterprise, and there also are agricultural improvements; but what is most characteristic in the movement is chiefly this, that it has been born in some sort spontaneously from the soil, and upon the soil itself, independent of the action of emigration, or of the propagandism of parties. It has been the work of those who were unwilling either to conspire or to give in, and who, among the ruins of their native country, and after her violent struggles were ended, have sought to bring together elements for a new solution of the Polish question. It certainly was impossible for these patriots to throw themselves into politics. They would have been instantly arrested, if they had done so. Their only thought then was, how best, morally and physically, to remodel the country, and how most to steer clear of politics in doing so. They began by establishing Temperance societies; and even this ground required wary walking, because they ran against the Russian authorities, who protect drunkenness, in order to protect the inland revenues, and who issued circulars against these societies, declaring them to be contrary to law. One

Governor-General of Lithuania, M. Nazimof, showed his erudition by citing the marriage in Cana of Galilee, as a proof that the Gospel was not averse to the use of spirituous liquors.

Another institution has played a great part in the present movement: I mean the Agricultural Society of Warsaw. It had a very humble beginning. About 1842 an association had been formed for the publication of a small newspaper, called 'Annals of Agriculture,' from which all political questions and allusions had been strictly banished, which did not relate either to the situation of Poland, to its government, its foreign relations, or indeed to things that concerned it. But this was the germ from which grew, during the first part of the reign of Alexander II., in those first moments of liberality and good will, a more serious institution, the Agricultural Society itself, founded with the exclusive object of making physical improvements, having correspondents in all the provinces, and being authorised to hold two sittings yearly at Warsaw. However limited this institution may have originally been in its object, still it formed a bond of union, and it has ended by drawing together 4,000 landowners of the kingdom.

So slowly did the work proceed — creating on one day an Agricultural Society, on another day starting the navigation of the Vistula — sometimes forming banks, at another establishing a Temperance League —

recalling the country to a sense of its own interests, and drawing men together by making them co-operate in the same undertakings. Now, let us observe what were the effects of a labour so patient, so modest, so often crossed, and yet so efficacious. Instead of conspiracies, we learnt the habit of acting in legal ways, and we acquired a sense of the power which there is in regular, persistent, and pacific action. Such questions as the emancipation of the peasants, and others which have divided the public mind, and kept up divisions even among emigrants — such questions, mischievous while only a strife of theories, have now found their natural solution in practice; for the Agricultural Society has taken the initiative in this matter, and proposed a system by which the peasant is made an owner, and by which, through an ingenious combination of credit given, an indemnity is secured to the actual possessor; and this indemnity the peasant pays up in successive and limited annuities, without having to give more than he had formerly done. This may be called the Polish solution of the difficulty, as opposed to the Russian one. Finally, and what is most important, this secret regeneration of the country has done what we have just seen. No longer are parties embittered against each other, after a common defeat, nor do they dispute over a distant victory; but we have a compact mass — a nation welded together by one thought — where there is no distinction of classes, and of which the union has been cemented by the bloodshed of the 27th of February, 1861 — the day on which Russia made the first attempt to put it all down. Those intelligent Russian bullets did more than they were aware of; for they helped to cement the alliance by striking, as they did, victims of every rank, of every condition, of all religions, almost of every age.

One man, as I have said, personifies in himself all that is most serious and practical in this movement, and he has left upon it the stamp of his own character. This is Count Andrew Zamoyski, whom the people speaking his language simply call 'Monsieur André.' He is not the only one; but he has been, from the very first, one of the most active promoters of all that could awaken the land. By birth he is connected with one of the oldest Polish families — with the family of that grand-constable, John Zamoyski, of the sixteenth century, who laboured to constitute a body of lesser nobles, in the face of our aristocratic oligarchy, and who was one of the greatest of Polish captains. The family is one which has long been eclipsed, and which only reappears at certain epochs. There was another Zamoyski, who was Chancellor in 1772, but who laid down his office because he would not set his seal to the first division; and of this Zamoyski, Count Andrew is the grandson, as he is also the brother of the general who, at one time, was to have headed a Polish legion, at the time of the Crimean war. Count Andrew naturally found himself mixed up with the revolution of 1831. He was first Minister of the Interior at Warsaw, and then was sent on a mission to Vienna, to M. de Metternich, who, it was said, was, at the time of the last battle, inclined for an intervention. When that revolution was, at last, quelled by the Russians, he would not leave the country. He remained in obscurity, cherishing no deceptive hopes, but soon seeking how best to raise her, after her great defeat. No very great career offered itself to him; but he turned to material interests and pursuits, and he brought to the work an activity not the less singular, because it was narrowed by conditions which were strait and uncertain. He established breeding-stables (studs), helped to introduce steam-navigation on the Vistula, which was a tie with Galicia, and laboured to organise the '*Crédit foncier*.' He it was who started the little paper, 'Annals of Agriculture,' who afterwards became the principal promoter of the Agricultural Society, and who, up to the present time, has continued to be its President.

Count Zamoyski is characterised in all that he has done by his practical sense, by the clearness of his views, and by a moderation in action, which is joined to great natural dignity. The situation of Count Andrew is, moreover, a sufficiently singular one; for, by his moderation, he excites the suspicions of the more hot-headed among the Poles, who expect nothing except from revolutions, and, by his activity, he makes himself suspected by the Russians. The curious and difficult problem, how to live between these two, is the one which he has to solve. He has to be master over himself, and he cannot suffer himself to be led away by useless rashness; while he must not, on the other hand, sink the dignity and the name of a Pole. His secrets are hid in his actions. He never revealed them to anyone; and, to speak truly, is it perfectly certain that he had any secrets? He simply put in practice the old word 'laboremus;' and though constantly obliged to have dealings with the Government, he never yielded his ground; and he kept up an obstinate struggle against the venality of the Russian officials, to which he would not submit upon any terms. More than once he has had to go through some very thorny trials; but he has always acquitted himself well. On the day of the foundation of the Agricultural Society, a dinner took place, at which, of course, the Director of the Interior, M. Muchanof, was present. At last, the toast in use at all Polish dinners, 'Let us love each other,' was given by him. All eyes were immediately turned upon Count Zamoyski, who, calmly and simply, and with scarcely a perceptible smile, replied, 'Yes: but at home!' There was nothing more to be said. The spirit of this policy, if policy it can be called, is to do all that it is possible to do, to go as far as may be, and to measure one's steps according to the necessities of the day. It breathes no agitation; but it is to be an activity according to the laws, taking advantage of everything, making use of everything, and communicating life unawares to the country — this is precisely what has appeared in the late events, and this remains the character of the new crisis.

Are men aware of what it is that gives to this movement the weight of a true national manifestation? It is that it has nothing in it which is either artificial or evanescent. It is the work of the few, and also the work of all. Like all deep movements, it is at once simple and complex, it is sincere as is the passion of a whole nation; and far from resolving itself into a mere series of efforts for physical order, which have suddenly issued in a political question, it has a moral side, which agrees wonderfully with what I have said of its characteristics of practical and lawful action. One thing in these occurrences at Warsaw, interspersed, as they are, with scenes of bloodshed, is very striking, and that is, the passive attitude of a people, which appears unarmed and offers no resistance — which persists, and, though dispersed, constantly reassembles — which offers itself as a defenceless victim, and which refuses the arms which are left within its reach. And under such an attitude, there must be something more than mere obedience to a watchword or to an order. No conspirator could have been clever enough to have imagined it. It is the sign of a thorough revolution in the minds and in the souls of men, a revolution to which the mind of one poet was no stranger — I mean Krasinski, whose works have appealed to all Polish imaginations, and which will be imprinted on all hearts, even of the lowest orders of the people. He is that *anonymous* poet from whom we formerly had a few poems, all full of deep meaning, all marked by gloomy and ardent mysticism. Sigismund Krasinski is dead now; but he had endured the bitterest trials of spirit, both as a patriot and as a son. He was born in 1812, and was held at the font of baptism by Napoleon, for his father was that Vincent Krasinski (a descendant of one of the chiefs of the Confederation of Bar) who, at the end of the empire, replaced Prince Poniatowski in the command of the Polish army, and who subsequently played a part in the Chambers of the kingdom of Poland, after the Restoration. Unhappily, General Krasinski irritated public feeling by the vote he gave in the Senate, in regard to the conspiracy of 1828; and his son Sigismund received, in the public square, such a marked and cutting insult from his school-fellows, that he was obliged to leave the country. He travelled, and went to Rome. When the revolution of the 29th of November, 1830, broke out, he set out immediately for Poland; but, at Berlin, he had to stop. His father had been taken, at Warsaw, by the insurgents, and had only saved himself by promising devotion to the national cause; and now he had fled to

St. Petersburg. Sigismund despaired; he never could bring himself to remain in his own land, and the rest of his life, spent among strangers, was devoted entirely to the composition of his poems, which he published without ever acknowledging their authorship. Through him, Polish patriotism found a fresh voice.

When Mickiewicz addressed the revolutionary and warrior youth of Poland, he said, 'Strong through union, wise through self-denial, forwards! my young friends!' Krasinski said, in a song now as popular as once were Mickiewicz's words, 'No man can build with mud, and highest wisdom still is highest virtue.' These are the watchwords of two different epochs.

The ruling inspiration of the whole of the poetry of Krasinski is the abjuration of all hatred and of all vengeance — that force alone will not enable us to contend successfully against force, but that the weapons of our warfare must be superior powers of soul — that, in order to conquer one's enemy, it is not enough that we have the right on our side, unless that right rests upon strong and pure moral sentiments; that the most powerful levers are love, and the virtues of self-sacrifice and of heroic patience. One of the heroes of his 'Infernal Comedy' is Pancrace, the type of that brutal strength which yields and quails in helplessness before a superior power. The same inspiration reigns in his Greek poem 'Iridion,' where the Christian hero is a passive martyr, with a horror of vengeance, who triumphs over

Rome, and confounds the patriotism of Iridion, a man who had no thoughts beyond revenge, and who makes shipwreck in spite of the justice of his complaints and of his cause. This is also the thought embodied in 'Aurora,' in the 'Psalms of the Future.' In all these songs the Polish soul thrills with mystic ardour, glows with enthusiasm, and with inexhaustible youth. 'Lord!' says Krasinski, in one Psalm, 'what we crave is not hope, since she descends upon us like rain upon flowers. It is not the death of our foes, since that death is written in the clouds of to-morrow. It is not arms, since they are placed in our hands by Thee. It is not help, for Thou hast opened a free path before us; but we implore, put a pure spirit in our inmost hearts. O Holy Spirit! who dost teach us that our great strength doth lie in sacrifice, grant that we by love may lead the nations to the ends we seek!' But in a fragment of his 'Aurora,' Krasinski has still better described this part of heroic expiation:—'Is it then required that we should be murderers with murderers, and criminals with criminals? Must we lie, hate, slay likewise, and blaspheme? The world cries: At this price you may have power and liberty; without it, nothing! but nay, my soul! nay; not with such arms as these. The weight of sacrifice alone can in its turn crush down the weight which crushes us. In the world's story, sacrifice is lionlike and unconquered still; but crime is as the chaff which the wind in passing sweeps away.

'No! my country; yours is rather the patience which doth show, how stone by stone the building can be reared: yours rather the will inflexible, which, abiding humbly, prepares for future victory. Rather yours is calmness amid the storms, and harmony amid discordant cries: rather yours, eternal loveliness amid abhorrent shapes: rather yours to heap on cowards and Pharisees that mournful silence which doth overwhelm. Be yours the strength which lifteth up the weak; and yours the hope of those who cease to hope. For thy strife against this world's hell, be thine the peace and strength of love, against which hell itself cannot prevail. . . . . !

'The nations are all sought by God: all in Thy Grace, O Jesus, are concerned! to each from high a calling Thou hast given; in each a sense profound from Thee doth live, and weaves the woof of all their destinies; but some among the nations Thou hast chosen to defend the cause of Heavenly Beauty, and to give to the world an example, while they bear, through the long day, a heavy cross, and walk the world's paths red with blood. These by their sublime strife shall at last, O Lord, give to man a feeling higher and more divine, a holier charity, and a larger brotherhood, in exchange for that sharp sword which men have plunged into their breast. Such is this Polish land of thine, O Jesu Christ! Our love of man has caused our death, and men have seen the corpse of Poland carried to the tomb; but when the third day comes, the light shall shine, and shine through all the ages yet to be. Think you, that he who loves, in dying, disappears for evermore? Yes, to our fleshly eyes; but the whole world, through the soul's eyes, beholds him still. He who in love expires, leaves in his hour of martyrdom his soul to all his brethren. He abides in the sanctuary of human hearts, and every day, every hour, he lives, though buried; grows, though in the tomb!'

This thought of the power of sacrifice, and of passive heroism, has filtered through our youth, and permeated even the masses; and this it is which is visible in the Poland of to-day, for the inspiration of the poet has become the feeling of the people. One other cause, and it is a strange and curious one, has also helped, during the last few years, to spread and to popularise these ideas, by suddenly throwing a new element into Polish society. When the Emperor Alexander II. ascended the throne, he signalised his accession by an amnesty, which, however incomplete, opened the gates of their fatherland to a multitude of exiles. Some came from the West, the others (and these the most numerous) came from Siberia. Those who had lived in France, or in England, naturally returned to their country embittered by thirty years of sufferings, accustomed to a Western atmosphere, nourished with all sorts of revolutionary ideas; in short, half strangers in their mind and manners. But with that tribe of exiles, called in Poland 'Siberians,' it was not so. They returned hardened and strengthened by habits of secret and solitary suffering. Calm and resigned, they were mystics to a certain extent, but their mysticism was of that grave and gentle kind, which has nothing fierce or hateful in its nature. It is a remarkable thing that, among these exiles returned from Siberia, the country has for the last years found its best men, the most apt for journalism, for professorships, for the administration of private and national establishments, such as the Agricultural Society. There are writers of talent who could not, it is true, sign their works with their names; but their names were not, therefore, the less well known. One brought back from Siberia a translation of 'Faust,' and is one of our most eminent critics; another has translated Shakespeare. A newspaper in Warsaw published a series of sketches of Caucasus, and of Asia, which were the work of 'Siberians,' and in which there was an indefinable mixture of freshness and resignation.

These men spread over the country, and had a singular effect upon it. Thence the serious and religious tinge of striking originality, in all the popular demonstrations which have since happened, and in all those manifestations which are so thoroughly free from the revolutionary phraseology of the West. Theirs is, on the contrary, a nervous and sober speech, and except in its religious accent it has nothing exaggerated in it. The influence of the Siberians is peculiarly visible in that strange address by the artizans of Warsaw: 'Death is alike for all. Without sparing our persons, it is necessary that we should go to the slaughter, and show to the world what it is we wish. This is why we have walked in processions, and sung of the constitution, and we will do so again whenever it shall be necessary; if there are to be victims, it will be seen that that is according to the will of God, if more is required we are ready to draw lots for the one who is to be sacrificed—ready even to give our throats to the knife, or to expire under the knout, as did those three victims whom the waters threw up near Zakroczym, and which wrapped in straw were flung from the castle into the Vistula. Only if then there is no pity for our country, it will be ill! . . . .' Should one not say that this is the same obstinate idea of sacrifice, which has passed through the imagination of Krasinski, and through the action of the 'Siberians,' into the popular mind?

And now that all these elements are reunited, now that this union of practical efforts extends over all interests, and this lawful impulse has been communicated by Count Andrew Zamoyski, and instinctively accepted by a whole population, now that a moral and religious sense has been propagated in all minds, at once inflaming and satisfying them, and a national sentiment has spontaneously reappeared in all hearts, the movement is one, which, though imperceptible at first, and existing silently for many years, has been facilitated by the change of reign at a given moment, and it has ended in that brief but eloquent dialogue which took place recently between the Lieutenant-Governor, Prince Gortchakof, and the crowd assembled in one of the squares of Warsaw. 'What do you want?' 'We want our country!'

Evidently nothing has been accidental or unforeseen except the hour at which the explosion took place. For the space of one year already successive manifestations had revealed a sort of secret understanding in the populace. First there was a funeral service celebrated all over the country and at fixed epochs, in memory of the most eminent Polish poets, Mickiewicz, Krasinski, and Slowacki. Then came the interview which re-united at Warsaw the three Sovereigns of the north, and which piqued the popular sense. It was in truth an odd idea which assembled at Warsaw, for a conference in which it was suspected that designs hurtful to Italy were to be discussed, the three masters of Poland. Their reception from the populace was more than cold; and what is most curious is that, impressed by this disagreeable circumstance, they tried to ascribe to each other the blame of the annoyance which they had received. The Russian papers avowed that it was the Emperor of Austria who had earned this cold reception for the Emperor Alexander, while the press of Vienna proved no less clearly that this demonstration had been aimed at the Emperor of Russia.

Some months later a more serious manifestation followed. It was a commemorative service for the dead killed at that battle of Grochow, in which in 1831 the Polish army contended during three days with the Russian troops; and on that day it was (February 25th) that a new Poland appeared, personified by a populace which walked with tapers in its hands, reciting as with one voice this religious and national hymn: 'Holy Lord God! God Almighty, God Immortal, have mercy upon us! From plague and pestilence, from fire and sword, O Lord, deliver us! Be pleased to give us back our native land! Holy Virgin Mary, Queen of Poland, pray for us!' Then the crisis declared itself, and agitation spread, as the concessions of Russia alternated with scenes of blood; and thus it continued till April 8th, the day in which violent measures for repressing the movement finally prevailed. It is not what followed these events that I now have to describe. Everything in them bore the mark of those influences which I have pointed out. This movement, as has been seen, began with a religious service, and when it came to a crisis, what was the step taken by those who had some power over the people, and who felt the importance of the moment? A popular delegation, authorised by the Lieutenant-Governor, took the command of the town; a voluntary constabulary was organised for the prevention of all disorders, and the Agricultural Society itself interfered as a moderator, and a guardian of the peace. The addresses presented to the Emperor contained nothing but what was according to law, since they hardly even exacted all that had been assured to Poland by the treaty of 1815. And what was the attitude of the populace itself? It showed its *life*, if the expression may be permitted, by abstaining from all conflicts. It assembled to give vent to its wishes and to its complaints, but it presented itself unarmed and passive; even after it was dispersed by force, women, children, and old men crowded round a Madonna with weeping and with prayers. Strange insight into the nature of a movement, of which the tactics have been to resist, but not to take up arms! What constitutes its originality is the alliance already mentioned of practical sense with a feeling which is moral, religious, and even mystic — an alliance of which the secret is in the conscience of a people, and which accords marvellously well with all the instincts of the Polish nation, and indeed of the Slavonic race in general, which appeals to political minds because its tendencies are towards moderation and good sense, and at the same time offers the charm of a certain poetic mysticism to the young and to the mass of the lower orders. It is, then, the originality of this movement which also constitutes its strength, for it reveals sources of vitality ever new, in a race which has found in misfortune nothing but a generous incentive.

It is this same originality which in like manner has placed Russia in a position of singular difficulty, when opposed to a popular awakening of this sort; for this is no simple internal strife, but by considerations of humanity and of right it forms part of a crisis peculiar to the times, and of an order of things of European interest and extent.

It is said that after the first bloody scenes at Warsaw in this month of February, the Emperor Alexander II. being told that some of the people had fallen victims, asked immediately what loss their army had sustained, and what quantity of arms had been taken from the insurgents? He was told in reply that there was no loss in the army, and that it had not been possible to seize the arms of a populace who had none, and would not have any. The Emperor, it is said, was greatly surprised; and this astonishment at the beginning explains the vacillations of Russia, and the hesitation which is to be observed in her conduct. She seemed at first to fluctuate between all sorts of policies.

She gave up some of her officials, who were the most pointed at by public animadversion, and, if I may use the expression, only seemed to repress the movement by mistake. She made some concessions; she drew the programme of a new organisation; she promised a variety of reforms; she accepted the popular delegation as an auxiliary — accepted even the help of the Agricultural Society itself. But presently both delegation and Society were dissolved. Agitation was allowed to increase by her indecision, till the scenes of April 8th mark the fresh starting-point of a repressive policy. *Physically*, no doubt, Russia can repress and disperse the manifestations of Warsaw, and she can prevent the population wearing mourning for its dead; but when that is accomplished, I ask whether, *morally*, the question will be one whit less living or less important — whether it will be less *oppressive* — for the politics of Russia?

Truly, Russia finds herself to-day in a strange and a serious dilemma. She must make her choice. She may begin over again in Poland her policy of the last thirty years; and she may even push that system to extremity. It may be the interest of Prussia and of Austria to keep the Tzar to this plan; because they are always uneasy at the reappearance in the Kingdom of a centre of attraction for the parts of Poland which they possess. This is their interest (and it is odd enough that it should be so, because the strength of Prussia lies only in ideas of nationality and of liberalism); but is this the true interest of Russia at this juncture of the world's affairs? Russia has only to revert to her own counsels and to her own traditions to find in them incentives to a more equitable policy. The Emperor Alexander II. has only to open his mind to those ideas which are most intimately connected with the constitution of the kingdom of Poland, and with the epoch at which the Emperor Alexander I. founded it, saying to the Poles, 'You will preserve your language; you will have your laws, your army. Your restoration is defined by the most solemn treaties.'

If the world of to-day appeared such as it did thirty years ago, it might be possible that any physical victory should have the sad power of deadening in an unhappy nation its undying feelings, of at least discouraging it, and of adjourning to another day the solution of a question so often agitated. But to-day, against the continuance of an oppressive policy, are ranged the general sense of Europe, the principles of right, the interests of Russia in her other combinations and alliances, the irremediable decadence of the treaties of 1815, forgotten by the governments themselves even before they were abrogated by the peoples which returned, as it were, to life; and, finally, this movement on the part of united Poland—a movement which can but be accelerated, or kept up, by the new Diets in Galicia, by the incessant way in which the deputies of Posen remind the parliament of their country, and by the attitude of moral resistance assumed by the population of Warsaw. Be it what it may, there is certainly something moving, and morally important, in this determination of a people to *live*, and to preserve in itself the inviolable inheritance of its patriotic faith.

In the legends of the Saints it is related that, one day, in the age of martyrdom, some Christians had been assembled upon the ice of a frozen river, and that they were there abandoned, alone and naked, to all the severities of the air, having also no food to eat. Offers were made to them from the shore of clothes, and of delicious viands, if they would abjure their religion. Some of them yielded to the temptation, and, when they touched the banks, perished. The others, immovable under trial, invoked the Divine mercy, and were miraculously saved; for there fell from heaven upon them both food and clothing. In this behold a touching picture of a nation which suffers, but which will not allow itself to be tempted, and which sends up to heaven such a cry of faith as shall melt the rigour of its adverse fortune.

A YEAR OF AGITATION IN POLAND.

A YEAR OF AGITATION IN POLAND.

(April 1861–2.)

FOR some years past we have witnessed one of the most affecting and instructive sights—the breaking up, if we may say so, of an order of events, where the confused and dispersed elements join again, as from some mysterious and invincible unity in themselves. That which once appeared impossible becomes a startling reality, and perspectives suddenly open themselves such as our generation would hardly have allowed itself even to think of.

We have seen public right itself, or that which, at least, bears its name, giving way, and leaving a passage for those national and popular causes which agitate the world, and which are the harbingers of a new way of thinking. It is vain now to attempt to divide those national causes which appeal so strongly to public opinion — vain now to grant everything to one and deny everything to another — to limit justice to opportunity or to fitness of time or place. Policy may have its seasons, its measures, and its predilections, but at bottom *right* must exist everywhere, or it exists nowhere; and, from its one source, it must apply to all those peoples who aspire to the purest and the most legitimate of conquests—the conquest of themselves—as also to all those movements which, arising at one and the same time, form parts of a general situation, intimately and profoundly characterised by one universal work of transformation.

We must guard against mistakes. What we behold is no vulgar crisis, which may end in an ordinary peace: it is a warfare between two orders of things, between two principles; and it was proclaimed the other day, in a French Assembly, to be the new right—*the right of peoples*—and, when opposed to this, old political combinations are reduced to act laboriously and uneasily on the defensive. It is the question which agitates the modern world: the problem which, in the East as in the West, in the North as in the South, shows itself under a thousand different and startling shapes.

Certainly one of the most curious of these episodes—one of the most moving of these contemporary spectacles—is that dramatic *tête-à-tête* which, for the space of a year, has been carried on in Northern Europe between those two very unequal powers, Russia and Poland; where the one is embarrassed by its strength and its political traditions, and where the other makes an impregnable buckler of its rights, and of its very weakness. Nothing has been wanting to the play. Unforeseen events, passionate originality in demonstrations, tragic scenes—all have been supplied, together with those mysterious fatalities which so often make a perfect drama out of the affairs of men. This drama is laid in the heart of a country: it has its colours and its catastrophes; and across its stage there passes, like some chorus of old, a whole nation, which sends up to heaven its supplications and complaint. For a whole year has the spectacle been seen of a moral movement, perfectly new in its character, confronting a policy which is astonished to find itself so weak that, while possessed of so many means of physical power, it resorts to all expedients of apparent concession and of inefficacious repression, and uses both measures alike without conviction. After a year all seems again to have settled into silence. Outward manifestations certainly have ceased, but still the demonstration has been made. That which had been supposed to be dead was found to be still full of life. That assimilation of Polish provinces, which Russia believed to be accomplished, was found to be not even begun; and Europe suddenly saw that Polish question arise which brings in its train such prodigious difficulties, and in which are involved at once the fate of a nation, the policy of a great empire, and the balance of power in the West. By some vague instinct, Europe felt that she had not yet got rid of that problem which is, doubtless, so strangely complicated by the multiplicity of rules and of *régimes* spread over Poland; which changes its shapes according to the chances of dismemberments and of treaties; which is not the same in Posen as in Cracovia, at Warsaw as at Wilna, in the Kingdom, in Lithuania, or in the Ukraine; but to which one national sentiment, identical and vital in all the parts, has communicated an indissoluble unity. This character truly belongs to a question at once so energetic, so simple, and so complex, which sums up in itself the strifes of to-day, which is too often believed to have been stifled under the weight of impossibilities, and which comes to light again at a time when any palpitations of oppressed patriotism was least to be expected. I wish to set forth this question in its most recent explosion, in its elements, and in its progress, as well as in its relation to all that is in motion or in preparation in Europe, and even in the very heart of Russia.

An event which dates back to no very remote period is the source of many results which belong to the present day. I mean the Crimean war, which doubtless did nothing directly or ostensibly for Poland, but was very near (nearer than perhaps is supposed) doing a great deal for her. At the time when that great strife ended, the name of Poland, as we are now aware, ought to have been heard in the Congress of Paris, along with that of Italy. France and England were agreed, and the day was fixed, but the dexterity of the Russian plenipotentiaries, and of Count Orlof in particular, eluded this inconvenient call. They made it the interest of the West to be silent, and they promised far more than ever was asked of them, on condition that Europe would leave the Tzar at liberty to make none but spontaneous concessions to the Poles. This is no longer a secret; for Lord Clarendon said one day in Parliament, in reply to Lord Lyndhurst (that old champion of liberal causes), 'We had serious reasons for believing that the Emperor of Russia was, with regard to Poland, generous and kind. We were obliged to admit that the Emperor was not only disposed to publish a general amnesty, but even to give back to the Poles some of their national institutions; and while they received guarantees for the exercise of their religion, public education in Poland was also to be established on a more liberal and national footing. We also believed that we were warranted to hope that Russia was about to renounce for ever the severe system which she had hitherto pursued; and, moved by these convictions, we ceased for the future any discussion of the question.' Count Orlof gave promises, the Congress of Paris kept silence, and scarcely one month had passed before the Emperor Alexander II., while promulgating an amnesty which was nothing more than a cruel deception (according to Lord Clarendon's own expression), addressed, at the same time, two allocutions to the Polish nobility at Warsaw, wherein he harshly said, 'I expect that the order established by my father is to be maintained: so, gentlemen, above all, we will, if you please, have no dreams — no dreams! The happiness of the Polish people depends on its entire fusion with the people of my empire; what my father did, was well done, and I will maintain it: my reign shall be the continuation of his. In preserving to Poland her rights, and her interests, such as my father granted her, I have the unalterable wish to do good, and to favour the prosperity of the country. It rests with you to make this last possible for me, and you alone will be responsible if my intentions fail, on account of your chimerical resistance.' When one of the Marshals of the nobility seemed about to reply, the Emperor turned and said, 'Have you understood me? It is pleasanter for me to reward than to punish; but know this, once for all, gentlemen, that when it is necessary I shall know how to keep down, and to punish, and it will be seen that I punish severely.' This happened in the month of May 1856, immediately after the Congress of Paris.

It is not without reason that I recall to-day a vain attempt at negotiation broken off by an illusory promise. It determines the events which have since arisen, in the same way that the debate at the Congress of Paris has governed events in Italy; it also in some sort puts on the recent crisis in Poland a mark of European sympathy, and proves an intelligent wish, while it shows further how Russia had conducted herself up to the time that this crisis arrived. 'What my father did, he did well!' an expression which was perhaps highly filial on the part of the Emperor Alexander II., but which was certainly an imprudent and impolitic dictum. What was really that *order* established by Nicholas which he promised to maintain?

I do not refer now to the guarantees by which the treaties of Vienna had striven to surround a nationality which they abandoned; I do not speak of the constitution of 1815, the work of the Emperor Alexander I., but of the *statut* granted by the Emperor Nicholas himself in 1832 — a *statut* which was as a punishment, the penalty of a defeat sustained by Poland; and what had become of that? It was M. Tymowski, a Russian Minister of State, who last year, at the commencement of the affair, told us what *had* become of it. In a private report he stated that this *statut* had never been either abrogated, or put into execution. Of all the new authorities which it created, councils for towns, councils for palatinates and provincial assemblies, 'with the right of deliberating on questions of general interest in the kingdom,' not one has ever existed. There ought also to have been a Council of State, but that probably was held to be either too revolutionary a measure, or too visible a sign of autonomy. So in 1841 this Council of State was quietly replaced by two new departments of the directing Senate of St. Petersburg, which were called the ninth and tenth departments, and were transplanted to Warsaw. 'In a word,' added M. Tymowski, 'it may be said that since 1831 the kingdom of Poland has been given up entirely to bureaucracy, and that without any regard to the *statut* of 1831, it has also remained under the exclusive influence of officials, without the participation of any of its inhabitants, who are in this manner rendered incapable of sharing in the Government.'

It would, indeed, be useless to tell how bureaucracy and officials have for the last thirty years swayed the Government of Poland: and I shall content myself with reminding my readers and the public, that one day the Emperor Nicholas did 'with his own hand and with a quiet mind' (adds his minister) order the *transplantation* to the Caucasus of forty-five thousand families, all 'formerly Polish gentry, but bearing henceforward the name of freemen and burghers,' as it is phrased in this strange Government language. We have often heard that a painful yoke is laid by their rulers on the people of Lombardy, of the pontifical States, or of the old kingdom of the two Sicilies: nor is this said without reason; but we must also remember that there is a country where, in the daylight of this present century, it has been possible to *transplant* forty-five thousand families guilty of no other crime than of being suspected of patriotism, and of 'exciting the suspicion of the Government.'

From this specimen we may understand how unintentionally cruel and how mournfully deceptive were those words of Alexander II. — 'All that my father did, he did well' — words which were also, at least, an unfortunate answer to that expression of European sympathy which had been checked at the threshold of this Congress of Paris in 1856. It has been the mistake of all Russian policy for the last thirty years, to believe that an absence of all law means *order*, and to suppose that the omnipotence of force is at once illimitable and undefined. No doubt for the moment such policy succeeds. It can command silence, it can veil difficulties, and adjourn the discussion of them to another day. But it brings affairs at last into that impossible situation, of which illegality is the essence, and where we find a new nation, independent of all organisation and of all hierarchies, rising in spite of a monstrous system of repression — a nation which, as M. Tymowski expresses it, 'is undistrainable and yet ingenious in making arms for itself out of everything, even out of its own contempt of death.' Poland, though beyond the bounds of the law, has a profound sense of law, and this M. Tymowski again acknowledges. Having no public representation she has arranged one for herself, for she had that Agricultural Society, which at a given day proved itself to be a sort of national representation. No regular outlet was provided for the utterance of her wishes, instincts, or wants, but she has thrown herself into a passionate worship of her traditions, her popular festivals, and religious rites. Indeed, the time has come in which she has occupied herself for a year in reviewing her anniversaries and her recollections. She could not, certainly, dream of engaging in an armed strife, but she retired into herself; she appealed to moral power, and opened her soul to the strangest of all sentiments — that of voluntary sacrifice — till a whole nation adopted that terrible argument in Descartes' fashion, 'we die, *ergo*, we live;' and is it not a new and a surprising piece of reasoning, if we understand it aright? By all this Russia is placed in an extraordinary dilemma; this unexpected resurrection brings all her errors before her. She is obliged to punish a sedition which is not illegal, to make war upon peaceful manifestations, on religious services and hymns, on mourning apparel and inoffensive emblems; she has nothing to oppose to them but force, and feels therefore all the powerlessness of force itself. The same causes have impressed this movement: for though European events may have hastened it, though the accession of Alexander II. and the internal disorders of Russia may have favoured it, it is not less the result of a past of thirty years, not less the effect of a policy of which the whole fatality has not yet perhaps been exhausted.

The movement is extremely characteristic in this respect — that it is born in the heart of the country, and that it is independent alike of complicity with her emigrant children, or of any impulse from without.

Immediately after the Congress of Paris, the Emperor Alexander held this language to the Polish nobility—'No dreams, gentlemen! no dreams!' and from that moment did the national sentiment of Poland begin gradually to expand, till it broke out in February 1861. Several symptoms indicated the unexpected awakening that was to follow. When the sovereigns met at Warsaw, in 1860, the Emperor Alexander, before returning to St. Petersburg, wished to show himself to the five German princes who accompanied him in all the brilliancy of Polish popularity. He was to be in Wilna. Now in Lithuania, the first manifestation for the enfranchisement of the serfs had taken place, and the Emperor had returned thanks for it to the Lithuanian nobility. These circumstances all seemed auspicious, and the Governor of Lithuania was ordered to get up a ball. It was, as far as its externals went, simply a ball; but no one knows what an official ball is to the Poles, where the splendour of the fête covers so many hurts, so many thousands of secret wounds. In his 'Aieux,' Mickiewicz has introduced an official ball into that circle of Hell in which he paints all the sufferings of the Poles. General Nazimof made the most heroic exertions, and spared no persuasions among the Lithuanian nobility; but nevertheless he completely failed. The ladies declined the invitations; the gentry said that, though willing to pay the expenses of this Russian festivity, they should not appear at it; and there was nothing left for the Emperor but to refuse to go to the ball upon which General Nazimof had lavished so much useless zeal; and he hardly made any stay in Wilna.

At Warsaw, where the three crowned heads held a meeting which seemed to personify all the disasters of the land, things looked even worse. It must be said that, to choose Warsaw as a place of meeting between these three masters of Poland — the Emperor of Russia, the Emperor of Austria, and the King of Prussia — and to choose it, too, just when all Europe was ringing with the enfranchisement of Italy, was to throw a challenge to our unhappy nation; nor was it long before popular feeling took up a challenge which was the second it had received from Alexander — his first having been that address to the nobility of Warsaw which he made after the Congress of Paris.

After this, demonstrations increased.

One religious service followed the other, in memory of the patriot-poets, Mickiewicz, Krasinski, and Slovaçki; and on November 29th, 1860, that song was heard, for the first time, which for a year has been the impassioned watchword of the multitude, which has echoes in cathedrals, and which has gone up from the humblest country churches — that 'Boze cos Polske'—'Give us our country! Oh, Lord! give us our liberty!' In a short time, the whole face of affairs had changed, and an electric thrill ran through the country. Perhaps it ought to be called a revolution; it certainly was a moral revolution, and it revealed that which had hardly as yet been suspected — the existence of a nation, unimpaired by suffering and by trial. To be a revolution, it had a strange beginning. There was no violence, no bloody intentions, no insurrections; but there were psalms, and prayers, and manifestations, at once enthusiastic and regulated; and there was an outburst, as energetic as it was unexpected, of that irresistible force which is called the soul of a nation.

Everything converges to that month of February 1861; and then it was that this Polish insurrection really assumed the character of a passionate drama, full of startling originality. The 25th was the anniversary of that formidable battle of Grochow, in which the Poles, in 1831, disputed for the mastery with Russia during three whole days. Since the 21st, the Agricultural Society, founded by Count Andrew Zamoyski, and so rapidly popularised throughout the country, had held a session to deliberate on the definitive accession of the peasantry to property. From other quarters, the Polish students — who had come from Kiev, from Moscow, and from Dorpat, as to a secret rendezvous — might be heard agitating, and demanding a national university. To ask for a more liberal education, to effect the union of all classes by the abolition of the last vestiges of serfdom, and to commemorate mournful and patriotic anniversaries —

these were the subjects which preoccupied all minds. No doubt other thoughts mingled with them. The idea of presenting an address to the Emperor asking for a constitution began to be ventilated; and, oddly enough, it was warmly advocated by a man who was soon to play a part in these events — the Marquis Wielopolski. He became excessively excited, and went to Count Zamoyski to beg him to take the initiative in this manifestation; but Count Andrew refused. He was the firm and vigilant guide of his society, and he would not consent to alter its nature. Moreover, it was repugnant to him to place, as the Marquis proposed to do, the claims of his country under the auspices of the treaties of 1815.

What was Russia about all this time? Quite disconcerted, and more astonished than enlightened by what she saw happening under her eyes, she waited, and day by day the movement seemed to slip away from her. At that time she was represented in Warsaw by Prince Michael Gortchakof, the Lieutenant of the Tzar — a man who was a good soldier, and who had shown a great deal of vigour in the defence of Sebastopol. He had lived for many years at Warsaw, when head of the Staff to Prince Paskievitch; he knew Poland, and he liked living in it. To his soldierly nature extreme measures of repression were repugnant, and it troubled him to have recourse to them. But unfortunately, in the heart of the administration of which he was the ostensible chief, one man was, under shelter of the Prince's name, omnipotent — M. Muchanof, Minister of the Interior, of public instruction, and of religion. He was a Russian of the old school of Nicholas the Tzar — a vulgar instrument of that inflexible system which had no other object but the denationalisation of Poland. The dismissal of Count Skarbek, the Minister of Finance, had been effected by him, because the Count was an enlightened man, an author of celebrity, who had entertained the revolutionary notion of asking (as for a right) for a college at Warsaw. M. Muchanof was at war, in short, with everything that looked like an awakening or an act of individual life in the country —with Temperance Leagues, with the Agricultural Society, and with a taste for a more liberal style of education. The only exception he could make was in favour of the School of Arts. 'Let them paint, by all means,' he would say, 'and then they will not think.'

Between the gradually excited population of Poland and Russia, when thus represented and thus divided in her councils, a dialogue was to be commenced, which, stretching over a year, was to be furnished with such bloody interludes that the very Russian generals themselves seemed to grow weary, and to feel a secret aversion to the parts given them to act.

Nothing, at such a conjuncture, was wanted but one spark. The morning of February 25th dawned dark and misty. They were to go that day to pray for the slain of the battle of Grochow, and, from an early hour, the populace, impelled by one spontaneous passion, thronged the streets. An immense procession was soon formed; they marched without disorder, and with torches in their hands. Before them went a banner, with the white eagle. As they walked they sang the hymn, 'Swiety Boze'—'Holy Lord God Almighty, have pity upon us; be pleased to give us back our own country. Holy Virgin Mary, Queen of Poland, pray for us.' Up to this time, the Government had done nothing to stop the manifestation (it had not even been prevented), when suddenly Colonel Trepow, the head of the Police, appeared, and threw two squadrons of the armed police upon this dense crowd. The multitude fell on their knees, and continued their psalm, while being cut down by the troops. More than forty persons were wounded. At this moment the Agricultural Society happened to be sitting, and a violent emotion was produced there by the intelligence that an inoffensive mob had been massacred. Count Zamoyski, the President, mastering his own emotion, endeavoured to preserve calmness, and, putting an end to the sitting, he repaired to Prince Gortchakof, who seemed surprised, and certainly showed conciliatory intentions. The Russian officers were indignant at the tasks assigned to them, and one of them, General Liprandi, went so far as to say that, as long as he commanded the infantry, he would not permit them to be marched upon unarmed men. The truth is, that one more such victory as that of February 25th would have made everything look very doubtful for Russia. The work of thirty years vanished, before the apparition of a people ready to die undefended. The whole town was in inexpressible anxiety, and on the following day mourning was worn for the victims of the previous day.

But it must not be supposed that any signs of weakness entered into the popular emotion. On the contrary, a curious excitement filled all hearts; and, by the 27th, arrangements were made for a new funeral service, in honour of some patriots hung by the Russians, and of Count Zawisza in particular. In the Church of the Carmelites and its vicinity more than 30,000 persons assembled; and, when mass was said, this immense procession unrolled and marched to the palace of the Agricultural Society, which, for the last two days, had been besought to sign an address to the Emperor. This Count Zamoyski always resisted; and he certainly showed more intelligent heroism, above all, more patriotic foresight, by this resistance, than by yielding to any premature haste. He did not wish to compromise an institution which might again do effectual service to the national cause, and which was the only representative body of his nation. So, on the approach of the crowd, Count Andrew took the plan of closing a session which had been so strangely agitated.

But just round this point the whole affair centred, while, outside, squadrons of Cossacks drove the multitude before them at the point of their swords, and pursued them into the very churches. Hardly had the members of the Agricultural Society left their palace than a murderous fire was opened upon them; also a strange execution, for which the order had been given by General Zabolotsky, and in which there probably was no preconcerted design, since, in the Russian opposition of that day, every measure seemed disunited, and the work of chance. But the result of this attack was not the less fatal; ten persons were killed, and more than sixty were wounded.

A curious scene then took place. The exasperated crowd seized upon one of the corpses — one which was still warm — and they carried it to the house of Count Andrew Zamoyski. A feeling of reproach probably entered into this popular act. It meant, 'Why do you abandon us at the moment in which we are slain?' But this was a popular error. If Count Zamoyski, in his capacity of a public character, and when invested with a title which was almost official, had refused to compromise an institution which, in his eyes, represented the only lawful power in the country, not the less did there live in him a patriotism which could be both firm and manly. He received the body thus brought to him, and, in a voice of great emotion, he replied to the crowd, 'I thank you for the mark of esteem which you have given me. Bring in the corpse of this martyr, and I shall know how to honour it.' He had a *chapelle ardente* arranged in his house, and there, for two days, the body lay in state. By the incidents of his past life, by his name, by his active devotion to all his country's interests, by the attitude he preserved towards the Russians, so proud and so noble, and yet ever so moderate, Count Andrew proved himself to be the true chief, the wise and energetic guide of a movement, which found in his character its highest personification.

In this, the second day of bloodshed, which side had conquered? Russia certainly had not, for never, perhaps, did any power suffer such complete eclipse, while boasting of such apparent strength.

After the events of the 27th, Prince Gortchakof called his officers and chief functionaries together. The Archbishop soon appeared, complaining of the violation of the churches; and there came also several dignitaries of the town, who had held a meeting at the house of one of the principal bankers, M. Kronenberg. There was likewise Count Zamoyski himself, with two other delegates of the Agricultural Society, MM. Ostrowski and Poloçki, all holding discourses, of which the tenor was mournful and proud. Prince Gortchakof did not disguise from himself either the gravity of the situation, or the odium of the part assigned to the army. What is more, he absolutely denied having given the pitiless orders which had just been executed, and he let fall a curious expression as he did so. 'Do you,' he said, 'take me for an Austrian? I have given one order, and one only, and that is, that even on the production of an order signed by my own hand, the citadel is not to be given up to you.' What was most essential at this moment was to appease wrath, to calm men's minds, and to efface the late bloodshed. Prince Gortchakof showed himself ready for the most important transactions. He was ready to dismiss the head of the police, Colonel Trepow; ready for an enquiry into the conduct of General Zabolotsky; to withdraw the military to their barracks till the victims of the 27th had been buried; and also to create a Commission of Public Safety, under the auspices of Count Zamoyski, with the concurrence of a Russian much esteemed and honoured in Warsaw, Marquis Paulueri. He accepted the offer of the students to act as the police of the town; and by that evening an address to the Emperor was in general circulation. Thousands of signatures were rapidly affixed to this document, which was the energetic expression of the griefs and of the wishes of the Polish nation. 'Our nation,' it declared, 'which used to be governed by liberal institutions, has, for the last sixty years, endured the cruellest sufferings. Without any organ for sending up to your throne the expression of our pains and of our need, we are forcibly constrained to have no other utterances than the cries of those martyrs which are daily offered as a holocaust.

A country, once the centre of civilisation to its neighbours of the West, cannot, also, develope itself, either morally or physically, while its Church, its legislature, its public education, and its whole social organisation, do not bear the stamp of its national genius and of its historical traditions.' The signatures of the Archbishop and of the Grand Rabbi headed this address; and those Poles who were in Government offices, as well as the Marshals of the nobility, tendered their resignations, in order to join in the manifestation.

To tell the truth, the whole face of affairs had altered in a very short space of time. Two days had sufficed to show a nationality, fresh born and full of energy, pitted against a government which seemed struck with paralysis. Poland, that phantom which had not been allowed to appear at the Congress of Paris, and which the Emperor Alexander, during the interview of the sovereigns at Warsaw, had banished as an inopportune vision, was now suddenly alive, and become palpable to all. Henceforward, all distinctions of classes were to be effaced by one profound feeling of solidarity; and the very bullets of February 27th had cemented this union by striking, as they did, persons of all classes, of all religions, of all ages, and of every sex.

With what weapons did this reviving nation arm itself? Poland had no arms: she would not have any; or rather she had them but of one kind. She had a passive heroism which amounted to enthusiasm. She had a fanaticism of self-sacrifice, as might be seen in that address to the workpeople of Warsaw. The mark by which her sons recognised each other was mourning array; and from the first days of the month of March 1861, a proclamation throughout the whole country declared black to be the national colour. 'In all the parts of ancient Poland,' ran the notification, 'mourning will be put on, and worn for an indefinite time. . . . . For nearly a century our emblem has been the Crown of Thorns! That coronal adorned the coffins of our brethren, and you have all understood its meaning. It signifies patience under suffering, self-sacrifice, pardon, and deliverance. We invite every Pole, whatever be his creed, to spread these words in countries even the most remote.'

A population like this, when for a moment its own mistress, had a pride in avoiding riot and excess; and it even respected the Russian soldiers in Warsaw. It was the students who on March 2nd kept the peace during the funerals of those who had fallen victims on February 27th; and at these obsequies, where patriotism acted for the police, more than 100,000 persons were present. On the other side, it was quite the contrary: everything among the Russian authorities was in confusion, and they appeared to be the discomfited spectators of a movement which they could not check, and which was wholly incomprehensible to them. Prince Gortchakof himself was visibly affected by this extraordinary situation, and he was divided between astonishment and the strange recurrence of a soldier's instinct who feels himself to be powerless, because he seeks an adversary but cannot find him. Nothing can better pourtray both the character of this Polish movement and the embarrassment of the Russian power, than a conversation which took place between Prince Gortchakof and Count Zamoyski, on the 3rd of March, the day after the interment of the victims of the 27th of February. The Prince Lieutenant began by thanking the President of the Agricultural Society, with really good grace, for the order which, during the ceremony of the previous day, had been maintained in the town.

'The whole town obeys you,' he said. Then suddenly becoming animated, and having changed his train of thought, he continued, 'This cannot go on; and besides, I have now got troops, and I am not afraid of you.'

'We are ready to receive your bullets,' replied Count Andrew.

'No, no, we will fight!'

'We shall not fight; but you may murder us if you please.'

'If you want arms, I will give you some!'

'We will not use them.'

There, in truth, lay the secret of this movement, which was intangible from its moral nature, and which was terrible because it was vague. The address from Warsaw reached St. Petersburg; the Emperor Alexander read it out loud before several members of his family.

'But these Poles ask for nothing,' remarked one.

'That is just what is so serious about it,' replied the Emperor; and his retort was that of a sensible man.

If this perilous situation was not to continue, only one course could be pursued by Russia. She must arrange a termination, and reply to this passive revolution in Poland by sincere, efficient, and ready concessions. Russia did not do this, and she lost a month in delay. As to her sincerity, it was doubtful, to say the least of it. What was most obvious was her embarrassment; and by the confusion in which she moved, her policy allowed this embarrassment to be only too well perceived. At Warsaw, while Prince Gortchakof made some concessions, Count Zamoyski was challenged, but did not reply. A marvellous unity of wills kept order in the town, and the authorities waited for a solution of the difficulty to be sent from St. Petersburg. M. Muchanof, still master of the Ministry of the Interior, was inspired by the melancholy policy which Austria had followed in Galicia, and he did send out a clandestine circular, urging the peasants to rise upon their landlords. The Jews discovered this circular, and so much indignation was excited by it, that Prince Gortchakof was soon obliged to dismiss M. Muchanof from his office, and he left Warsaw amidst the yells and hisses of the populace. The affair, considered in all its bearings, is a strange mark of the persistent contradictions which distinguished Russian measures, and distinguished them at a time when to be sincere would have been to be judicious.

Even in St. Petersburg no one knew what to do. Time was gained, and then it was lost; and when the Emperor Alexander did, on the last day of March, resolve to send to Warsaw a plan for new reforms, the movement had by that time become too consistent; the minds of men were too strongly excited, and too much made up, to be contented with such timid and equivocal concessions as ill befitted the gravity of the case. For of what did the offered reforms consist? It is true, that they suppressed those two departments of the Senate which sat at Warsaw, and which were the signs of the complete assimilation of Poland with Russia. They promised the election of provincial councils, of district councils; they offered a new organisation of public instruction, with a creation of a Faculty of Rights, and with more respect for the Polish language. Finally, they summoned the Marquis Wiélopolski to the direction of public education; the Marquis being a Pole. This was always something, although it did not even entirely come up to the *statut* of Nicholas. And what at bottom was wanting, was a guarantee for the sincere adoption of a really liberal policy, which should be carried out by men truly devoted to their country, and animated by a national spirit. Unfortunately, to the suspicions of the Poles (suspicions which were only too well founded) Russia replied by a system of permanent contradictions, one which for the last year has shown itself to be never nearer to reaction than when there was a talk about concessions. Concessions so offered were for the edification of Europe, which looked on. The facts remain the same, or rather they become worse, and in appearing to yield to this all-powerful movement of public opinion, it was the object of the Russian Government to stain it, and to represent the movement as the work of a few incorrigibly factious persons. But they seemed to wish to treat with this reviving nationality, and on the 1st of April the plan of reform arrived from St. Petersburg was published; six days later, however, they dissolved, without any warning, that Agricultural Society in which the country beheld its image, which had never interfered except to make peace, which Prince Gortchakof had himself thanked, and which was now done away with, on the strange pretext 'that, under the present circumstances, and in consequence of the position which it had latterly assumed, it had ceased to answer its original purpose.' Of all those bodies of constables and delegates which had existed, and by means of which for a whole month peace had been maintained in the town, not one was allowed to remain. All, with a sort of impatience, were swept away, while proclamations were multiplied and troops were hastily advanced to Warsaw.

What was the result?

Public opinion resented as a provocation the dissolution of the Agricultural Society, and the minds of the people rose with indignation, not against the *reforms*, which might, perhaps, have been accepted, but against that double-faced policy in which they could see nothing but menaces; and peace thenceforward became more and more impossible between Russia and a people which, as M. Tymowski said in his secret report, was 'full of life and of obstinacy, and deeply penetrated by a sense of law. Everything,' he added, 'depended on the good faith observed with them.' On the 7th of April, 1861, an immense crowd went to the cemetery to pray for the slain of February. Later in the evening they marched to the square at the castle, which was occupied by troops, and there with loud cries demanded the repeal of the order by which the Agricultural Society had been dissolved. But this crowd was so far from threatening any violence, that the military did not continue to keep the ground, and they dispersed at last, promising to reassemble on the following evening. Accordingly, in the evening of the 8th, a still larger assemblage repeated the manifestation of the preceding day, in front of the castle. The Prince Lieutenant himself came down and mixed with the crowd in order to appease it. He asked them what they wanted; and the response was unanimous, being contained in these significant words, 'We want our country.'

For the rest, nothing in this excited concourse of men, women, and children betrayed any aggressive thoughts, or any intentions of strife. They were warned that they must disperse; but with dark passion they replied, 'You may kill us, but we will not move;' and before the troops drawn up in order of battle, they remained impassive, till suddenly a post-chaise happened to pass, and the postilion played on his horn the air of Dombrowski's legions: 'No, never shall Poland perish!' Immediately an enthusiastic cry burst from every breast, and as the populace fell on their knees, a movement was perceptible through the whole crowd. Did the troops believe that they were about to be attacked, or did they obey a command? Were they decided by the plain and conclusive reason, that a resolution to fire had been adopted the evening before, because a stop must be put to this state of affairs?

However it may have been, an instantaneous fire was opened. While some squadrons of cavalry received orders to charge, fifteen volleys from the infantry made many bloody openings in the mass of defenceless beings, who now found themselves hemmed in on every side. While being cut down, the crowd continued to kneel, and to pray. The women and the children were grouped together on their knees round an image of the Virgin, at the extreme end of the square, and there the people remained till late into the night; so late that the troops had been previously drawn off the ground. It is certain that more than fifty persons had perished, and that the number of the wounded was immense; but darkness has always been allowed to hang over the numbers who fell on that night. An eye witness wrote with emotion: 'Never shall I be able to make you understand this unparalleled contempt of death, which is so enthusiastic that it animates men, women, and children. Old soldiers, accustomed to being under fire, assure me that never, when so close, have the most solid troops preserved a heroism as calm and invincible as this crowd has displayed when furiously charged by cavalry and under fire.'

It was, indeed, a strange insurrection. The authorities in Warsaw had no difficulty in quelling it; but it rendered every future transaction more difficult, for it had placed between Russia and Poland a barrier of invincible suspicion. It was a misfortune for Russia, that, while gaining these melancholy victories, she added nothing to the security of her rule, and she certainly added nothing to her strength. Her difficulties were, however, greatly increased by them, and she remained weighed down by the weight of her own policy. It is true, indeed, that even after the 8th of April she maintained the reforms which she had already promulgated;

but the logic of her situation was, that she was at war with the most intangible thing in the world, with the soul of a nation. Russia could not lay her finger upon any conspiracy, but not the less did everything seem to threaten her, and she was constantly obliged to invent new plans for putting down she hardly knew what. At night no one was to go out without a lantern, and it was forbidden to be seen walking in certain localities. Against wearing mourning the rules were peculiarly stringent. Indeed, at one moment it was necessary to have permission from the police to wear black. Yet the genius of the police was at fault, and it was baffled by the provoking obstinacy in favour of universal mourning, and of the black dresses which the Polish ladies had adopted.

To do the Russian authorities justice, they did not feel their consciences at ease in the matter of this war. Even when using repressive measures they seemed to be agitated by a secret disquiet — a feeling which declared itself in a very striking manner during the last days of Prince Gortchakof, whom death overtook in the middle of this conflict, only two months after the scene of the 8th of April. It would seem almost as though the tragedies of Poland had something fatal in them to the Russian officials. Already, they tell us, that Prince Paskievitch, when on his death-bed, had been troubled by a sinister apparition; for everywhere before him rose a shade, that of the mother of Count

Zawisza, who had lain at his feet to implore pardon for her son, and who had implored it in vain. The last moments of Prince Gortchakof were disturbed in the same way. In Warsaw it was said, that ever after the bloody scenes of February and of April he had been vexed by sudden hallucinations, as well as by fits of gloomy irritation. A few days before his death, he went to the railway-station to meet his wife, Princess Gortchakof, who was to arrive from a journey. He saw one of the principal bankers of Warsaw, and, running up to him, he began: 'Oh, you there! so you play the patriot, do you? But I know how to crush you! I shall soon make an end of your d——d students! I will make dust of you!' During the last days of his life, he fancied that he constantly saw women in black, who followed him, or walked beside him. 'Oh, the women in black! oh, the women in black! send them away,' he would cry. If such were the sufferings of the Prince, there were to be others who, as we shall see, came to a yet more terrible end. The same secret trouble was betrayed by the words of General Souchozanett, the immediate successor of Prince Gortchakof, when, before leaving Warsaw, he said: 'You may accuse me of being an unsuccessful blunderer; but you cannot say that I am a cruel man, for I have never fired upon a single creature.' There was a strange fatality about this system, for it weighed upon those who carried it out, as well as upon those who were its victims; and such as it was, after the 8th of April, it stood complete, before the eyes of an angry and seething populace.

Throughout these events, one man made a great effort to procure a reconciliation. His figure is not the least original, or the least characteristic of those who meet in this drama, and I have already named him, for he is the Marquis Wiélopolski. Ever since the 1st of April, 1861, he had taken a preponderant place in the Councils of the Government, and, no doubt, his part is not yet played out. During February, as I have already said, the Marquis Wiélopolski resided in Warsaw; and he suggested that an address should be sent to the Emperor, wherein a constitution was to be demanded, but which should open with an act of submission, and with a testimony of their contrition; for it was to disallow, in some measure, the Revolution of 1830. Not having been able to make good this idea, he refused to sign the address that was sent to St. Petersburg, and held himself aloof from the movement. Very shortly after, the Emperor called him to the Direction of Public Education, and from that time he took a decisive part in all the measures that followed. Before long, and by the dismissal of the other directors, which was consequent upon the 8th of April, the Marquis Wiélopolski found himself alone in the Council, and associated with all its most rigorous proceedings. He is, perhaps, one of the most curious types of our times, for he is a proud, contemptuous, eloquent man, a scion of the family of the Gonzagas; and for this reason, perhaps, he exhibits, at times, traces of the old Italian policy. He is a great landed proprietor, and, by his different estates, is connected with all the provinces of Poland; and he is devoted to Russia, not by servility or interest, but by a passion of revenge which he nourishes against the West; and his system is the result of calculation, and of a line of policy which is powerful, although strange. In 1846, after the massacres in Galicia, the Marquis Wiélopolski wrote that 'Letter to Prince Metternich, by a Polish Gentleman,' which rang with such fiery eloquence, and which being, as it were, a new revelation, echoed throughout Europe. The author there advised Poland to embrace a resolution of heroic despair—to renounce, for the future, all help from the Western Powers, all deceitful and calculating sympathy, all cheap eloquence, all those guarantees which men have decorated with the pompous title of 'rights of peoples,' and then boldly to give herself to Russia. 'Go to the Tzar, and say to him: We come to you, as to the most generous of our foes; hitherto, we have belonged to you, as slaves, by right of conquest, and from terror; to-day, we come to you as free men, who have the courage to acknowledge that they have been conquered. . . . We do not stipulate with you about conditions — to yourself we leave it to judge when you may relax towards us the severity of your law. We make no reserve; but in our hearts, in letters of fire, you will read our silent prayer, this single petition, "Do not leave unpunished the crimes which strangers have committed; and in the blood of our brethren which has been shed, hear the Slave blood, which cries for vengeance" . . .'

In words like these, one can recognise a theorist, who is inflamed with panslavism, and whose revenge anticipates the day, when by this fusion, this sacrifice of the idea of national independence, this moral suicide, the Polish race may revive in the Empire, and again, through their intelligence, find an ascendency in the Council.

What the Marquis Wiélopolski had thought in 1846 he still thought in 1861; and he therefore kept himself apart from all attempts to warm up the thought of nationality, as also from all the practical labours which were to bring about a patient and invisible reorganisation of his country; and he never would become a member of the Agricultural Society.

The Marquis now entered on his official career distinguished by all the inflexible vigour of a character which was lofty and proud enough to brave unpopularity among his countrymen; and, while he consented to serve Russia, he did not the less preserve a haughty attitude towards her. In the month of February, while agitating for the adoption of his proposed address, he got a message from Prince Gortchakof, warning him to take care of what he was about; he proudly replied, 'Tell the Prince that my boxes are filled, and that I am quite ready to start for Siberia.' To his compatriots he would say, 'You are not at the height necessary for understanding me.' To the Russians he certainly appeared an enigma; for they could not comprehend this Polish gentleman, who, while a nobody in the ranks of the administration, suddenly became a minister, who refused all interposition, and who treated directly with the Emperor. What could such a man mean? What was the clue to his thoughts? But it can be believed how, between Poles and Russians, he occupied a solitary and difficult post; for the first had the greatest antipathy to his ideas, and the second looked upon him as a phenomenon rather more extraordinary than consolatory.

That it was possible to organise a lawful régime, the Marquis firmly believed. For the present he had no doubt of it, and he directed all his efforts to this end. But there is nothing that Russians understand so little as proceeding according to law; and, upon the death of Prince Gortchakof, this prepossession of the Marquis proved the origin of those quarrels with the new Lieutenant-General Souchozanett, in which the Polish gentleman was apt to have the better of the Russian, although he also was soon to be carried away by the current of a still more violent reaction.

This reaction was the system which Russia adopted,

and which she followed, without ever perceiving that, instead of calming and mastering the movement, every instance of repression so added to its energy and depth, that when, three months later, the wishes of the government seemed to incline to a more conciliatory method, the movement was then found to have gained head greatly.

Above all, it was found to have spread, and to have reached the provinces which formed the ancient Poland of 1772. Scenes similar to those of Warsaw were enacted at Wilna; and, by the application of a uniform plan of repression, Russia, by her own acts, set a seal upon that unity of the old Polish fatherland which it was her object to abolish.

One of her official proclamations spoke of Lithuania, as of a province which had always belonged to the Empire, and which had only been for a short time subjugated by Poland. Some French papers even lent themselves to help Russia at this juncture, and they undertook to represent to Lithuania, to the country of Miçkiewicz, of Kosciusko, and of the Czartorynski, that it was not in any way Polish, and ought to have nothing in common with Poland. And this it was which provoked one of the most curious scenes of the whole strange drama — a protestation on the part of Lithuania, under the form of a pilgrimage to Horoldo.

Horoldo is a little village beyond the river Bug, and there, more than four centuries ago, the union of

Lithuania with Poland was accomplished. Of this union the 10th of October was the anniversary. As early as the month of September, circulars were sent into all the parts of the ancient Polish realm, and delegates of the people were chosen in every place, even in Western Prussia. Everything was done that could be done to stop these strange travellers. Those who came from beyond the Bug were prevented from crossing the river, and those who came from Cracow were in the same way brought up at the passage of the Vistula. But the concourse of people was, notwithstanding these precautions, really immense; and the roads were lined with men on horseback, with foot passengers, with carriages of all sorts, heavy carts, tarantasses from Podolia, and phaetons from Léopol. On the eve of October 10, the houses, the villages, and the country seats round Horoldo, were filled with unknown guests, who were met everywhere with the readiest hospitalities. 'Enter, and welcome,' was said to all, while no one even asked their names.

On the following day, at six o'clock in the morning, an immense procession was formed, and when it reached the little village of Kopylowa (half a mile from Horoldo), the crowd fell into their ranks, and marched along in columns, singing as they went; for, though strangers to each other's names and faces, these men were all bound together by the one feeling which they had in common. Now arose a momentary doubt.

Were they to go on, and so risk meeting with a bloody reception? A cry rose, 'We came to pray at Horoldo, let us go to Horoldo!' and the procession continued its march, headed by an advanced guard of more than 200 priests and monks. But as they drew near to Horoldo, it became apparent that a large military force was drawn up in a half circle round the town. A feeling of inexpressible anxiety then prevailed. No one knew what was going to happen, but not the less they pressed steadily forward, because everything that could be called *arms* had already been thrown away. The violence of a commander might at once have turned the scene into a massacre; but, happily, General Chrustef, the Military Governor of Lublin, who was entrusted with the defence of Horoldo, was a humane and pacific man. At the head of his staff he advanced to meet the procession. He bowed deferentially to the clergy, and said, 'I have received strict and formal orders not to allow any manifestations to take place, and the choice of means has not been left to me, if any manifestation is attempted. Do not, therefore, oblige me to use forcible measures; for you would surely not wish to lay on your own consciences the responsibility of bloodshed.' A Canon then stepped out of the ranks, and said that the multitude had come from far, and that they could not be expected to retire without at least having heard mass. The General thought for a moment. His own anxiety was visible, and a terrible silence prevailed. At last, Chrustef addressed the priest: 'If you will pray, do it now, and here, in the fields before the town; my orders do not go so far as to forbid this.' Preparations began immediately, and a rustic altar was soon reared upon a rising ground. When all was ready, forty banners, representing all the provinces of ancient Poland, were unfurled, and above them all floated a great flag, with the united arms of Lithuania and of Poland.

The scene was a splendid one, and it was lit by a glorious sunshine. When mass had been said, a Basilican priest (of the United Greek Church) rose, and thus addressed the crowd: 'Behold to-day, assembled for the first time, the mutilated members of our beloved Poland! In our national history there is no better festival, and no memory more pure, than that which we have met to celebrate to-day. Look at that forest; count its trees; and for each tree that you count you may find upon the Polish soil the grave of a hero, of a martyr who has given himself for our liberty. Here, as everywhere in Poland, all are ready to sacrifice their lives; but the hour is not yet arrived. Let us pray, and, as we pray, not one of us will be found wanting when the summons comes. Let us not wish any evil to our enemies. See them to-day, how silent and motionless they stand! They look at us, and they now comprehend what we are, and what we may become. With one gesture they might crush us, they might knock us over, bleeding on the soil; but they are silent. They know that behind us there is a whole people, and that a nation cannot be slain.' Then, turning to the fluttering standard, the priest said, as he concluded, 'Stainless bird, white eagle! that wast wont to distribute crowns to others, and art so crownless to-day, float above thy brothers, and cry to the four quarters of the globe that thou art living still! Call together thy children, thine emigrants, and thy defenders of old, and point, still point the way! Thou must suffer, thou must suffer much; but one day thou shalt rise, rise higher than in the past, and spread thy wings over a people which, at last, is free.' After planting a wooden cross on the spot where mass had been said, the crowd dispersed, and they carried away with them the solemn memory of a scene which was passing strange.

But the real question had not ceased to live in Warsaw, the centre of Polish agitation; it had existed there before the manifestation of Horoldo, and from thence it had influenced that episode in the great movement, of which the spirit seemed to be as contagious as a passion. And here I must notice the diverse phases of Russian policy, and the fatality which seemed to attend upon its decisions. Let this be remarked, that in the last days of March, Russia showed herself ready for concessions, and promulgated some reforms. Then and there a reaction occurs which reaches its height on April 8th, and the reforms of March go for nothing, or, at least, are, like everything else for the time being, in abeyance. By the month of August, and after a period of repression and severity, which was also distinguished by a marked antagonism between Marquis Wiélopolski and General Souchozanett (the successor of Prince Gortchakof), the sky appears again to clear. To the kingdom of Poland, a new lieutenant is given, General Count Lambert, who starts for Warsaw on a conciliatory mission. He is to carry out new institutions, to call together 'enlightened and well-intentioned men,' and to 'find out the real wants of the country.' What was to be the result of these tactics, adopted again under an aggravated condition of affairs? Unfortunately in this as in every such attempt made in Poland by the Russian government, there was something unsound. Count Lambert, as far as his own qualifications went, doubtless did unite in himself all the conditions which were most favourable for a mission of peace. He was a gentleman of courteous and affable manners, of French origin, and by religion a Roman Catholic; his temper was candid and moderate, and he enjoyed the peculiar favour of the Tzar; but at the same time he had men placed under him, who were understood to represent the old Russian party; and these men were there to watch him, and keep him to the point if the occasion should require it. These were General Gerstenzweig, the Military Governor of Warsaw, Minister of the Interior, Krijanowski, the head of the staff, and the senator Platonof, a member of the Council of Administration. In spite of everything, Count Lambert, on his arrival at Warsaw, was received with favour, and looked upon as a plenipotentiary of peace; his first acts being indeed marked by a conciliatory spirit. With the heads of the national party and with the bishops the Count held conferences, and even received a confidential memorandum from M. Wyszinski, a Canon of note in Warsaw, whose paper pointed out the conditions under which peace might be possible; namely, conditions which meant a constitution for the kingdom, and an organisation founded upon the national autonomy of Lithuania and Ruthenia. Finally, Count Lambert bestirred himself to put into practice the new institutions which had been talked of, namely, elections in districts and provinces, and a reformed organisation of the Council of State.

It was important for the country and for the national party to know what steps it ought to take when these elections were impending; and when affairs under the new lieutenant had assumed a new aspect, several meetings took place. To reject everything and to hold their own hands, was as yet the opinion offered by those who formed the *advanced* party, and whose votes were for action. The *moderate* party, however, had more practical sense, and seeing the necessity of not rejecting any legal means, they combatted this idea of not participating in any way in the forthcoming elections. The moderate party carried the day, but one combination was devised as a rallying point for opinions of every shade. Two petitions were to be signed at the same time — the first, addressed to the Council of State, was to demand the complete emancipation of the Jews; the other, addressed to Count Lambert, was to claim a national representation, as being the only institution proper for seeking out and making known the wants of the country, as it was expressed in the imperial rescript. These two petitions, it was intended, should be signed by all the electors when they gave their votes; and thus at the end of September they came to the ballot. In spite of some attempts made by the most hot-headed partisans, great unanimity prevailed; the peasants in particular showed a vast amount of zeal, and the two petitions thus agreed upon were signed by the electors throughout all the districts of the country. One circumstance of this transaction is a curious one, and that is the secrecy with which the signatures were affixed. So well indeed was the secret kept, that of one of the addresses the text has never transpired. In all the elections the moderate party had a great advantage, and thus a new character was given to the movement, for, instead of mere agitation, it assumed the nature of a legal claim, and it was settled that all manifestations were to terminate in a religious fête, in honour of Kosciusko, on October 15th, while the addresses were to be sent up by a deputation on the 18th.

On the 17th, however, the city was suddenly declared to be in a state of siege. What had happened?

No fear of possible troubles and tumult on the 15th had driven the authorities to this step, but they had become aware of that new plan of action which I have just described as adopted by the national party.

Some of the bishops, taking the initiative, had sent a paper to Count Lambert, which he had refused to receive, while in another way the business about petitions signed at the elections had got wind, and had occasioned the greatest uneasiness, above all, in St. Petersburg.

This was, moreover, the very moment at which the disturbances among the students had broken out in Russia. Such a complication of symptoms in the political world terrified the government, and a state of siege was proclaimed; certainly, less with the view of interrupting the Kosciusko fête than of stifling the petitions which were to be presented four days later. Once more the face of affairs was altered; from having been a matter of politics and of legal claims, it went back to the old dramatic aspect, and the scenes of October 15th were a new tragedy. The era of reaction had recommenced, and this reaction swept everything before it.

Of the many heavy days which had succeeded each other, the morning of October 15th was perhaps the saddest that ever dawned. From an early hour the populace had crowded into the churches, to take part in the funeral services which invoked and hallowed the memory of Kosciusko. The troops, employed in the military occupation of the town, offered no hindrance to the faithful at the doors of the sacred edifices; and it was not till the churches were filled, that the army had orders to surround them. From some of the buildings escape would have been easy, and these were the last to be encircled. The cathedral of St. John and the church of the Bernardines had the honour of being really besieged; while at the same time hordes of Cossacks, spread all over Warsaw, committed every sort of excess, and spared neither the women nor the strangers within the gates. An Englishman (Mr. George Mitchell) was a sufferer and an eye-witness of this day's work, and he wrote, 'troops of infuriated Cossacks and Circassians swept the streets, and they cut down men and women without any distinction whatever. They entered into the dwellings, they maltreated the inhabitants, and they sacked the houses.'

When the order was given to surround the churches, it had most certainly not been anticipated that the crowd would embrace the strange resolution of refusing to quit them as long as the troops were on the ground, and that it would be necessary to drive them out. Thus, one rash and ill-considered resolution led, a little later, to the most disastrous consequences. During the whole day things continued on this wise; the crowd was in the churches, breathless, excited, hungry, but unalterable; and still the soldiers camped before the doors. At eight o'clock in the evening, a General appeared, and he offered pardon to the crowd, if they would surrender at the mercy of the Lieutenant of the Kingdom. The reply was, that the people knew what mercy meant, and that as long as the troops were not withdrawn they should not stir. Tapers were now lit round the catafalque which had been reared the night before for the late archbishop, and hymns were chanted from time to time.

At two o'clock in the morning a new envoy came to parley with the multitude, who answered as before, that they did not ask for pardon. Two long mortal hours now passed away, when at seven o'clock, that is to say, after a siege of seventeen hours, the soldiers were ordered to force their way into the churches and to drive out the occupants. More than two thousand persons were seized, and carried to the citadel. But this was not all; and here again appears that fatality which I have said attended upon the Russian officials. Count Lambert, it would appear, had in no way anticipated or intended either this invasion of the churches or these wholesale arrests. Both had been executed in obedience to the commands of General Gerstenzweig, the Chief of the state of siege, and thence arose an altercation between the two generals, which was tragical enough in its close. Count Lambert vehemently reproached Gerstenzweig for all the horrors of the day, and Gerstenzweig retorted with equal violence. What next? It seems a fact no longer to be doubted, that General Gerstenzweig then took a pistol, and blew out his brains, while Count Lambert quitted Warsaw without any warning.

The results of the scene which was played out on the 15th of October were soon felt. The administrator of the diocese ordered all the churches in Warsaw to be closed, and the leaders of the other religious bodies soon followed his example; for the same thing was done by the grand rabbi, and by the head of the Protestant Church. For the last year, every school in Poland had been locked, and the theatres were in a like case; and it was now the turn of the churches to be shut.

Thus and then did Russia inaugurate a new period of reaction, which has not yet come to an end (April 1862).

Of a drama which has lasted for a whole year, we behold the sad and eventful epilogue. And yet all that happened on the 15th of October, bad as it was, was simply a revision of all that had gone before — of all the punishments which, since February 1861, had been indiscriminately applied by martial law to all classes, all religions, and all professions. Let us see, whom do we find, among this crowd of men, punished, deported, or confined in prisons?

There is M. Szlenker, the Provost of the Merchants of Warsaw, himself the richest and the most honourable merchant of the kingdom.

There is M. Hiszpanski, the head of the Shoemakers' Guild (the grandson of that Kilinski who was so loved and influential in Warsaw), a member of the delegation formed in 1861, and elected, in September of that same year, a member of the Municipal Council.

Poles who, by reason of the amnesty, had returned from Siberia have since been sent back, 'by way of precaution'— so run the terms of their sentence; and of this number is M. Ehrenberg, the celebrated poet, and M. Krajewski, one of our most eminent critics, the most moderate and sensible of writers, the author of the translation of 'Faust.'

An immense number of students and artizans have been sent to the Caucasus and to Orenbourg. The Grand-Rabbi Meiselz, and the Rabbis Kramstuk and Jastrow have been expelled; and Otho, the Evangelical pastor, has been sentenced to deportation. The Chapter of Warsaw alone has lost ten of its members, among whom the most conspicuous were M. Stecki and the Canon Wyszinski, from whom General Lambert once asked for memoranda. Last and worst, have we not seen M. Bialobozeski, the very Administrator of the diocese of Warsaw, an old man of eighty years of age, condemned to death because, after the 15th of October, he ordered all the churches to be shut. By way of favour, his sentence was commuted to imprisonment in a fortress, where he languished, and where his character was aspersed by the publication of a retractation. If we can ever suppose it to have been made by the victim himself, it only renders his sentence of death more inexplicable than it had been before.

On seeing such a multitude of punishments, it is not unnatural for the reader to inquire, what are the crimes and the offences of which they are the reward? In the government publications, and in the sentences of the sufferers, he who runs may read, that they were awarded for prayers, hymns, processions, for doubtful gestures made when perusing official handbills, and for wearing national emblems and black clothes. Only (and this is perfectly true) they were so inflicted because under songs, prayers, and mournful apparel, there lay the soul of a people, of a whole nation, which has been saddened by excess of tyranny, which has been terribly tried, but which, even now, is not disheartened.

At this period of agitation in Europe, when new problems complicate her political life, the true importance of the events of the last year must be seen to lie in their suddenness, and in the fact that Poland is not discouraged. Judge of the last twelve months as we may, we cannot but allow that they have shown us a people which, though often stricken, is again on foot (though *how* this is so we cannot tell); that this nation has found within itself the secret of an indestructible life; and that, so far from being dead, she lives with a new and more abundant vitality.

The drama which has been enacted before us, coloured, though it may be, by the tender and excited imagination of her sons, and, at times, seeming more like a legend than a page of history, cannot be mistaken for the convulsions of a nationality that is dying, and which, in expiring, utters one last and piercing cry. It is the expression of a force which, during thirty years, has been purified, tempered, and trained afresh, and which now appears to prove itself at once passionate and calm.

What are the signs by which any true nationality is to be recognised? Must a nationality have genius, intelligence, and true imagination? Then Poland, during the last hundred years, has had a legion of poets, all singularly gifted and inspired, and she still possesses a flourishing and varied literature; for her language has remained, although she has not had the freedom of her schools. Is the love of the past and its traditions required? Then that feeling has been both evident and rampant for the last year. Must there be originality of life and manners? Polish manners have preserved all the savour of their nationality, and, most assuredly, have not been influenced by Russia. Is it by unity among all classes, and by social peace, that a nationality approves its integrity and its strength?

The present movement has demonstrated precisely that there is a unity, a fusion of all classes, and that this fusion is sealed by the abolition of the last traces of serfdom, by the definitive acquisition of property by the peasants—a measure which the landlords themselves favoured in a practical and liberal manner; for if, in this agitation, we have seen only its moving and dramatic externals, we must not forget that under all this passion lies a spirit of political sagacity, which is patent, and which has been enlightened by all the faults, and by all the history of the past. Lastly, is religion one of the signs of a truly deeply-living nationality? In this Polish awakening, religion has been prominent, showing itself in the hymns of a people which assembles and takes refuge in churches. I have no doubt but that, by some great democrats, Poland is suspected on account of her religious fidelity. Men of this stamp do not see that there is something in suffering which opens the sources of religious feeling, till they rise to passionate mysticism. Moreover, in a country like Poland, the Church is the only organised power—the only body which has its own laws and independence. Catholicism is truly one of the shapes of Polish nationality; only, into her catholicism a great sense of toleration is now admitted; and we have seen priests, bishops, rabbis and Protestant pastors, all joined in the same manifestations, and suffering under the same measures of repression. Thus, Polish Catholicism realises the phenomenon, unhappily so rare, of a profound and intimate alliance between religion and all the instincts of liberty and nationality. Thus, also, this union renders Polish agitation something very different from any of those ephemeral fevers of revolution which give way before sharp measures of suppression.

For the same reason, the Polish problem remains a threatening one to Russia; for it engages Russia in a conflict as ungrateful as it is impotent. It compromises her in the eyes of Europe; it occupies her politicians, and it lies a weight upon her own internal developement. I do not know what is to happen; no one, indeed, can tell. She may again be stern, or again she may relent in her rule; but the problem is the same, and, without any compensation to set it off, it becomes more and more serious in the empire of Tzars. Doubtless, when, a hundred years ago, Russia, realising the dream of Peter the Great, marched upon Poland, rent it, and carried off its spoils, she then violated all the principles of justice; but she had a reason for it. She wished to draw towards the West, and, through her western possessions, to enter among European affairs. But everything has changed since then. Does Russia now require Poland to give her a place in the world, and among European powers? Russia now approaches the western world, less by her presence at Warsaw, than by that multiplicity of communications, that mixture of interests and ideas, and by those iron lines which, bringing all countries together, have made distances disappear. And what happens now?

This: that in order to maintain a supremacy, which is always precarious, and always contested (because lawful wishes have not been responded to), Russia is obliged to compromise her whole policy. At every turn, in each combination or alliance, she is tied and bound, because evermore between her and those who might be her allies, there rises the phantom of Poland. But not only is her external policy hampered and entangled, but her internal rule is affected by the necessity for incessant tyranny. The great Lord Chatham once said, 'If the English government subjects America to a despotic rule, so surely will England herself be obliged to submit to it.' And herein exactly lies the bond which connects Polish agitation with those liberal aspirations which at the present time appear in Russia. It is no longer a secret that throughout all classes of Russian society sentiments of sympathy with Poland are being rapidly propagated, and that Russians begin to foresee, without disturbing themselves, that a separation of the two countries is really possible. A newspaper, which is published secretly in St. Petersburg, the *Welicorus*, expressed this very distinctly not long ago. 'In order to maintain our rule in Poland, we are obliged to keep there a supplementary force of 200,000 men, and annually to disburse 40,000,000 of our money over and above those revenues which we draw from Poland. Now, our finances will never be better as long as we squander our resources in this way. . . . We must let Poland go, in order to save ourselves from destruction. . . . We can no longer conquer Poland, as in the time of Paskievitch, because there are now no internal discords in Poland; and in spite of the efforts of our government to sow division between the two classes, her patriots have consented to deprive themselves of a part of their own estates, and have settled them on the peasants. . . . For us Russians, it is a question whether we are to wait till we are ignominiously expelled from Poland, which, self-emancipated, will be our enemy, or whether we will be wise enough voluntarily to renounce a ruinous ascendency, and thus make the Poles faithful friends of Russia.' Such is in very truth the question now in agitation; and Europe looks on attentively.

And as regards Europe herself, we must say, that this question of the relations of Russia with Poland, after the terrible drama of last year, is by no means an indifferent matter. The western world is at present passing through one of those crises, during which everything is experienced, where everything is renewed, and everything alters in appearance. That which forty years ago was called the order of Europe no longer exists; nor have the peoples alone violated it. The governments themselves have so far lent a hand to the work, that, piece by piece, the fabric has fallen away.

The public order of 1815 is on the eve of disappearing, and what may be the new order which shall be brought forth by the labours of to-day assuredly no one can tell; but simply because we live at a time in which everything is recast, and re-elaborated, it is our first and best interest to watch the elements of this vast and universal movement, and carefully to consider every serious manifestation of the conscience of the nations. We must notice what dies and what lives. Russia, it has been said, 'has a certain fear of the opinions of Europe.' This opinion, most surely, has nothing in it hostile to Russia. On the contrary, Europe cannot but feel an interest in such labours as the emancipation of the serfs, of which the initiative was taken by the Emperor Alexander II., as also in that liberal work which is at present, day by day, evidently pursued in the heart of the Russian nation; but not the less, at the same time, is the eye of Europe upon that black spot at Warsaw. She sees and weighs both faults and misfortunes, and she says to herself, that, if faults have consequences, which follow them inevitably, there is not the less a fixed limit to a people's misfortunes, and to a nation's pangs.

CPSIA information can be obtained
at www.ICGtesting.com
Printed in the USA
LVHW100520120522
718524LV00004B/163

9 783375 002824